In the distance, the sound o
convoy of police vehicles v
would soon follow. They'd camp out on my front lawn,
demanding to know my connection to this latest murder. Because
they'd long ago decided that Westfield's own Miss Marple/Jessica
Fletcher/Nancy Drew was always somehow connected to every
murder, not only on our street or within our town or county but
throughout the entire tri-state region. Or so it seemed.

Worst of all, the moment the press connected me to the
murder, I'd receive a blistering call from my mother, berating me
for sticking my nose where it didn't belong and risking life and
limb.

Not this time, though. I'd never even spoken to the man. He
and his wife had only moved in three days ago. I hadn't discovered
the body. I hadn't called the police. And yet, somehow, I knew I'd
get sucked in. Because I always do. It was only a matter of time.

Acclaim for the Anastasia Pollack Crafting Mysteries

Assault with a Deadly Glue Gun

"Crafty cozies don't get any better than this hilarious confection...Anastasia is as deadpan droll as Tina Fey's Liz Lemon, and readers can't help cheering as she copes with caring for a host of colorful characters." – *Publishers Weekly* (starred review)

"Winston has hit a homerun with this hilarious, laugh-until-your-sides-hurt tale." – *Booklist* (starred review)

"A comic tour de force...Lovers of funny mysteries, outrageous puns, self-deprecating humor, and light romance will all find something here." – *ForeWord Magazine* (Book-of-the-Year nominee)

"North Jersey's more mature answer to Stephanie Plum. Funny, gutsy, and determined, Anastasia has a bright future in the planned series." – *Kirkus Reviews*

"...a delightful romp through the halls of who-done-it." – *The Star-Ledger*

"Make way for Lois Winston's promising new series...I'll be eagerly awaiting the next installment in this thoroughly delightful series." – *Mystery Scene Magazine*

"...once you read the first few pages of Lois Winston's first-in-series whodunit, you're hooked for the duration..." – *Bookpage*

"Fans of Stephanie Plum will love Lois Winston's cast of quirky, laughable, and loveable characters...clever and thoroughly entertaining—a must read!" – Brenda Novak, *New York Times* bestselling author

"What a treat—I can't stop laughing! Witty, wise, and delightfully clever, Anastasia is going to be your new best friend. Her mysterious adventures are irresistible—you'll be glued to the page!" – Hank Phillippi Ryan, Agatha, Anthony, and Macavity award-winning author

"You think you've got trouble? Say hello to Anastasia Pollack, who also happens to be queen of the one-liners. Funny, funny, funny—this is a series you don't want to miss!" – Kasey Michaels, *USA Today* bestselling author

Death by Killer Mop Doll
"Anastasia is a crafting Stephanie Plum, surrounded by characters sure to bring chuckles as she careens through the narrative, crossing paths with the detectives assigned to the case and snooping around to solve it." – *Booklist*

"In Winston's droll second cozy featuring crafts magazine editor Anastasia Pollack...readers who relish the offbeat will be rewarded." – *Publishers Weekly*

"...a *30 Rock* vibe...Winston turns out another lighthearted amateur sleuth investigation. Laden with one-liners, Anastasia's second outing points to another successful series in the works." – *Library Journal*

"Winston...plays for plenty of laughs...while letting Anastasia shine as a risk-taking investigator who doesn't always know when to quit." – *Alfred Hitchcock Mystery Magazine*

Revenge of the Crafty Corpse
"Winston peppers the twisty and slightly edgy plot with humor and plenty of craft patterns. Fans of craft mysteries will like this, of course, but so will those who enjoy the smart and snarky humor of Janet Evanovich...." – *Booklist*

"Winston's entertaining third cozy plunges Anastasia into a surprisingly fraught stew of jealousy, greed, and sex...and a Sopranos-worthy lineup of eccentric character..." – *Publishers Weekly*

"A fun addition to a series that keeps getting stronger." – *Romantic Times Magazine*

"Chuckles begin on page one and the steady humor sustains a comedic crafts cozy." – *Library Journal*

"You'll be both surprised and entertained by this terrific mystery." – *Suspense Magazine*

"The book has what a mystery should...It moves along at a good pace...Like all good sleuths, Anastasia pieces together what others don't." – *The Star-Ledger*

Decoupage Can Be Deadly
"*Decoupage Can Be Deadly* is the fourth in the Anastasia Pollock Crafting Mysteries. And the best one yet." – *Suspense Magazine*

"What a great cozy mystery series...Every single character in these books is awesomely quirky and downright hilarious. This series is a true laugh out loud read!" – Books Are Life–Vita Libri

"This adventure grabs you immediately delivering a fast-paced and action-filled drama that doesn't let up from the first page to the surprising conclusion." – Dru's Book Musings

A Stitch to Die For
"If you're a reader who enjoys a well-plotted mystery and loves to laugh, don't miss this one!" – *Suspense Magazine*

Scrapbook of Murder
"This is one of the best books in this delightfully entertaining

whodunit and I hope there are more stories in the future." – Dru's Book Musings

"...a perfect example of what mysteries are all about—deft plotting, believable characters, well-written dialogue, and a satisfying, logical ending. I loved it!" – *Suspense Magazine*

"I read an amazing book recently, y'all — *Scrapbook of Murder* by Lois Winston, #6 in the Anastasia Pollack Crafting Mysteries. All six novels and three novellas in the series are Five Star reads." – Jane Reads

"...a quick read, with humour, a good mystery and very interesting characters!" – Verietats

Drop Dead Ornaments
"I always forget how much I love this series until I read the next one and I fall in love all over again..." – Dru's Book Musings

"I love protagonist Anastasia Pollack. She's witty and funny, and she can be sarcastic at times...A great whodunit, with riotous twists and turns, *Drop Dead Ornaments* was a fast, exciting read that really kept me on my toes." – Lisa Ks Book Reviews

"...such a fantastic book...I adore Anastasia! She's clever, likable, fun to read about, and easy to root for." – Jane Reads

"I love this series! Not only is Anastasia a 'crime magnet,' she is hilarious and snarky, a delight to read about and a dedicated friend." – Mallory Heart's Cozies

"It is always a nice surprise when something I am reading has a tie in to actual news or events that are happening in the present moment. I don't want to spoil a major plot secret, but the timing could not have been better...Be prepared for a dysfunctional cast of quirky characters." – Laura's Interests

"*Drop Dead Ornaments* is an enjoyable...roller-coaster ride, with secrets and clues tugging the reader this way and that." – Here's How It Happened

"...a light-hearted cozy mystery with lots of energy and definitely lots of action and interaction between characters." – Curling Up By the Fire

Handmade Ho-Ho Homicide

"Merry *Crises*! Lois Winston has brought back Anastasia's delightful first-person narrative of family, friends, dysfunction, and murder, and made it again very entertaining!" – *Kings River Life Magazine*

"Once again, the author knows how to tell a story that immediately grabbed my attention and I couldn't put this book down until the last page was read.... This was one of the best books in this delightfully lovable series." – Dru's Book Musings

"The story had me on the edge of my seat the entire time." – 5 Stars, Baroness Book Trove

"Christmas, cozy mystery, craft, how can I not love this book? Humor, twists and turns, adorable characters make this story truly engaging from the first to the last page." – LibriAmoriMiei

"Take a murder mystery, add some light-hearted humor and weird characters, sprinkle some snow and what you get is *Handmade Ho-Ho Homicide*—a perfect Christmas Cozy read." –5 stars, The Book Decoder

A Sew Deadly Cruise

"*A Sew Deadly Cruise* is absolutely delightful, and I was sorry when it was over. I devoured every word!" – *Suspense* Magazine

"Winston's witty first-person narrative and banter keeps me a fan. Loved it!" –*Kings River Life Magazine*

"The author knows how to tell a story with great aplomb...this was one fantastic whodunit that left me craving for more thrilling adventures." – Dru's Book Musings

"Overall a fun read that cozy fans are sure to enjoy." – Books a Plenty Book Reviews

"Winston has a gift for writing complicated cozy mysteries while entertaining and educating." – Here's How it Happened

Stitch, Bake, Die!

"Lois Winston has crafted another clever tale...with a backdrop of cross stitching, buttercream, bribery, sabotage, rumors, and murder...vivid descriptions, witty banter, and clever details leading to an exciting and shocking conclusion...a page-turner experience to delight cozy fans." – *Kings River Life Magazine*

"...a crème de la crème of a cozy read." – Brianne's Book Reviews

"...a well-plotted mystery that takes the term 'crafty old lady' to new heights." – Mysteries with Character

"...fast-paced with wacky characters, a fun resort setting, and a puzzling mystery to solve." – Nancy J. Cohen, author of the Bad Hair Day Mysteries

"Lots of action, a bevy of quirky characters, and a treasure trove of secrets add up to another fine read from Lois Winston." – mystery author Maggie Toussaint/Valona Jones

Guilty as Framed

"Engaging and clever!" – *Kings River Life Magazine*

"This is another great entry in the Anastasia Pollack series." – Dru's Book Musings

"Winston not only combines (New) Jersey, well-crafted characters, and tight plotting, but she adds her own interpretation and possible solution to a factual museum art crime." – Debra H. Goldstein, author of the Sarah Blair Mysteries

"Author Lois Winston deftly frames the fast-moving investigation...with a dollop of mother-in-law hijinks, mama drama, home renovation, and doggie intervention." – mystery author Maggie Toussaint/Valona Jones

"Reading a book in this series is like visiting an old friend." – Nancy J. Cohen, author of the Bad Hair Day Mysteries

A Crafty Collage of Crime
"Rich in descriptions of the countryside, and alive with characters you'd recognize if you saw or overheard them, this book held my interest throughout and gave me more than one chuckle. It's a delightful read." – *Kings River Life Magazine*

"Winston imbues her story with current references, an appealing setting, layered plotting, and an unsinkable sleuth. Well done!" – Muddy Rose Reviews

"*A Crafty Collage of Crime* is yet another terrific cozy mystery featuring reluctant amateur sleuth Anastasia Pollack." – Lynn Slaughter, author of *Miss Cue*

"*A Crafty Collage of Crime* was a cute, fun, and entertaining read with independent, engaging, and delightful characters, and the mystery was outstanding, too!" – 5-stars, Novels Alive

"If some days it seems the world is too much with you, I suggest you read *A Crafty Collage of Crime*. You'll probably want to go back and read the rest of the series. Anastasia is irresistible." – Judy Alter, award-winning author

Sorry, Knot Sorry

"If you like your mysteries with a healthy dose of humor, Winston delivers... A delightful read whether you're at the beach or in your favorite recliner with a glass of wine." – Kings River Life Magazine

"A humorous quick reading release from the real world." – Debra H. Goldstein, author of the Sarah Blair Mysteries

"A twisty-turny plot spiked with red herrings and a double shot of moxie." – award-winning author Maggie Toussaint

Lois Winston serves up another fast-paced cozy mystery that will have you chuckling through to the end. Add to your beach reads basket for a fun escape!—Nancy J. Cohen, author of the Bad Hair Day Mysteries

"5 out of 5 stars. Another great read!" Kathleen Kendler, Cozy Review Crew

Books by Lois Winston

Anastasia Pollack Crafting Mystery series
Assault with a Deadly Glue Gun
Death by Killer Mop Doll
Revenge of the Crafty Corpse
Decoupage Can Be Deadly
A Stitch to Die For
Scrapbook of Murder
Drop Dead Ornaments
Handmade Ho-Ho Homicide
A Sew Deadly Cruise
Stitch, Bake, Die!
Guilty as Framed
A Crafty Collage of Crime
Sorry, Knot Sorry
Seams Like the Perfect Crime

Anastasia Pollack Crafting Mini-Mysteries
Crewel Intentions
Mosaic Mayhem
Patchwork Peril
Crafty Crimes (all 3 novellas in one volume)

Empty Nest Mystery Series
Definitely Dead
Literally Dead

Romance, Romantic Suspense, Chick Lit
Love, Lies and a Double Shot of Deception
Lost in Manhattan
Someone to Watch Over Me
Talk Gertie to Me
Four Uncles and a Wedding
Hooking Mr. Right
Finding Hope

Novellas and Novelettes
Elementary, My Dear Gertie
Moms in Black, A Mom Squad Caper
Once Upon a Romance
Finding Mr. Right

Children's Chapter Book
The Magic Paintbrush

Nonfiction
Top Ten Reasons Your Novel is Rejected
House Unauthorized
Bake, Love, Write
We'd Rather Be Writing

Seams Like
the Perfect Crime

LOIS WINSTON

Cover design by L. Winston

ISBN: 978-1-940795-78-2

DEDICATION

In memory of Camille Minichino, brilliant scientist, amazing mystery author, and wonderful friend. I will always cherish the time we spent together in New York and California.

ACKNOWLEDGMENTS

To my newsletter subscribers who enthusiastically gave a thumbs-up when I told them about the real-life Stoop Sitters and asked if they thought I should include them in my next book. And a special shoutout to Emily Cheang Catan whose suggestions I incorporated in crafting the fictitious Stoop Sitters.

In writing this book, I relied on the expertise of many professionals who willingly educate clueless authors and keep us from making dumb mistakes. Special thanks to Crimescenewriter members Dr. D.P. Lyle, Bob Mueller, Christine Husom, Margaret Mizushima, Amanda Marbais, Cindy Goyette, Patrick Hanford, Cynthia Rice, and Alicia Rene Kennedy for answering my medical questions on everything from broken hips to drugs.

To Crimescenewriter member Alan Brenham for answering my questions about inheritances.

To Crimescenewriter members Wesley Harris, Wally Lind, and J.J. Robinson for continuing to expand my knowledge of police and FBI procedures with each book I write.

To deputy coroner Chris Herndon for educating me on autopsy procedures.

To Shelley Noble, best of friends and Broadway companion, for providing me with an escape back to New Jersey whenever I need it, along with offering a sympathetic ear at all times.

And as always, my undying appreciation to Donnell Ann Bell and Irene Peterson for their superb editorial skills as well as their continuing friendship.

ONE

Mama birds boot their little tweeters out of the nest as soon as they learn to fly, hanging around only long enough to make sure the wee ones learn to fend for themselves. However, as I stood on the sidewalk, watching my oldest son walk off into the next chapter of his life, my eyes filled with tears. A sense of abandonment washed over me, as if the cosmos had flipped the script, and I was the one forced from the protective nest.

I choked back a hiccupping shudder. Zack looped an arm over my shoulders and drew me into a side hug. He planted a kiss on my temple and said, "He'll be fine."

The rational side of my brain agreed, not that it seemed to matter. Besides, I wasn't the only person currently battling emotional upheaval.

"What about him?" I whispered, nodding toward the third adult making up our parental threesome. Shane Lambert appeared even more distraught than I was. I had Zack, who had bonded with Alex and Nick, becoming their de facto dad from nearly the moment the three had met.

As a single parent, Shane had no one besides his daughter Sophie, no significant other to offer a hug and remind him that his child was now an adult and that he'd done an excellent job of raising her. That she'd be okay. More than okay. Thanks to him.

Of course, Zack had given the same speech to me countless times during the last few weeks. At times like this, though, even the most rational parent can become an irrational basket case.

Zack followed my gaze. "You will both be fine," he said, his free hand patting Shane on the back. "And so will Alex and Sophie."

With my son Alex and his girlfriend Sophie Lambert attending the same college, we had rented a super-sized SUV to transport the bolting offspring and their multitude of boxes to Cambridge, Massachusetts. The kids were now moved into their rooms, but whether unable or unwilling to let go of that last apron string, Shane and I had made one excuse after another to delay our departure as long as possible.

Zack had humored us, but the kids, antsy to get on with their new adventure, had finally given us one last hug before they headed to the dorm with not so much as a backward glance. Like it or not, the time had come to make the return trip to New Jersey. Reluctantly, I hoisted myself into the SUV.

"I suppose this officially makes me an empty nester," said Shane from the back seat as Zack pulled away from the curb.

Zack chuckled. "Feel free to borrow Lucille any time the house gets too quiet."

"Thanks, but I'll pass. That woman scares me." He reached across the seat and gave my shoulder a pat. "Your wife has the patience of a saint."

"I think I'm more like a glutton for punishment," I muttered.

My name is Anastasia Pollack, and Lucille Pollack is the gift that keeps on giving—in the worst possible ways. When Karl Marx Pollack, my first husband, dropped dead in a Las Vegas casino nearly two years ago, he'd bequeathed me his communist mother as a permanent houseguest, debt greater than the GNP of Uzbekistan, and a bookie demanding fifty-thousand dollars. The jury is still out on which of the three was the most horrific shock.

Through moonlighting, side gigs, and more than a little serendipity (albeit, often involving corpses and killers), the bookie is now a permanent resident of a government facility, and my Uzbekistan-sized debt is now closer to the GNP of Djibouti.

However, I'm still stuck with Lucille, 'til death do us part. My only hope being that she predeceases me. Hopefully, from natural causes, but with Lucille, that isn't necessarily a given. The woman excels at rubbing people the wrong way, and I feared someday someone might rub her out. Especially since we live in New Jersey, a state known for a certain element of the population adept at rubbing out those they deem in need of permanent elimination.

Zack glanced at me before responding to Shane. "My wife has a heart of gold, but if the roles were reversed, I've no doubt Lucille would have kicked Anastasia and the boys to the curb the moment Karl died."

I couldn't disagree with his assessment. Lucille had loathed me from the moment Karl introduced us, but that doesn't keep her from continuing to take advantage of nearly free room and board at my expense.

Zack did his best to cheer us up throughout the trip home and a short dinner stop in Connecticut, but for most of the journey, we drove in silence to an accompaniment of a classical jazz playlist. I spent much of the drive with Shane's empty nest comment rattling around in my brain. In two short years, Nick would also take flight. This mama bird was suddenly having a tough time confronting the circle of life.

~*~

After dropping Shane at his house, Zack cut through downtown Westfield toward home. As we turned onto our street, I groaned at the sight of a police car, its lights flashing, parked in front of our house.

I wasn't worried about Nick. He'd texted earlier to say he was going to the movies with friends and would be home by ten o'clock. It wasn't quite eight-thirty. I knew he'd still be sitting in a darkened theater watching the latest edition to the Marvel Universe.

After Karl's demise, my life took multiple unwelcome and often chaotic turns, some involving a propensity for finding dead bodies. All others involved my mother-in-law. Since I hadn't stumbled across any murder victims so far today, by process of elimination, a visit from the police meant only one thing. And that begged the question, what had Lucille done now?

Harriet Kleinhample, my mother-in-law's mini-me, had blocked the entrance to our driveway with her circa nineteen-sixties VW minibus. When Zack parked behind the patrol car, I noticed two of Westfield's finest standing at the front door. In the waning light, I recognized both officers.

Officer Harley pounded on the door and loudly demanded Lucille open it. Officer Fogarty, Harley's junior partner, had turned his head at the sound of our car doors closing. After waving us over, he tapped Harley on the shoulder. Harley turned, took one look at us, and ceased his pounding and shouting. As we approached, he said, "Boy, am I glad to see you."

I frowned at my front door. Not knowing what to expect on the other side, I wanted details before we entered. "What's she done now?"

"Possibly nothing," admitted Harley. "An avocado green VW minibus was spotted in the vicinity of a jewelry store smash and grab earlier today. Not many of those vehicles on the road these days, especially around here. We put two and two together and—"

"Surely, you don't think—"

Harley dismissed my question before I finished asking it. "No, we're looking for a gang of five or six individuals, late teens or early twenties. Possibly both men and women. Looks like it might be the same gang that struck in Summit and several other nearby towns the last few weeks."

"We only want to ask your mother-in-law and Mrs. Kleinhample if they saw anything," said Fogarty. "To help in identifying the suspects, but they refuse to answer the door."

Nothing new there. The only people Lucille hated more than me were members of law enforcement. The feeling was mutual. I've no doubt every one of Westfield's finest would relish locking her up and jettisoning the key fifty miles offshore into the murky depths of the Atlantic Ocean.

Zack moved to the door and inserted his key but stepped back to allow the officers to precede us inside. "Police," shouted Officer Harley as he and Fogarty entered.

Before we could follow, Fogarty yelled, "Look out!"

With his left arm, he shoved his partner to the side while his right hand grabbed hold of the hooked end of Lucille's cane. Both women let loose a string of insults as Harriet fought Fogarty for possession of the cane. However, she was no match for someone half her age, more than a head taller, and with the physique of someone who spends hours working out each week.

Fogarty yanked the cane from Harriet's grip, but she lost her footing and tripped over Lucille's feet as my mother-in-law came to her aid. Both women hit the hardwood floor in a tangled mess of limbs, Lucille smacking her head and Harriet landing on her hip.

Between moans, Lucille ranted about police brutality, excessive force, and lawsuits, slapping Harley's hand away when he tried to help her up. Meanwhile, Harriet screamed in pain the moment she attempted to move and immediately passed out.

Harley cursed under his breath and radioed for an ambulance.

Fogarty stood paralyzed, staring down at both women. "I was only trying to keep her from attacking us," he mumbled.

"No one's blaming you," Zack assured him.

"You were defending us from an assault," I added. "You hadn't drawn your gun. No shots were fired. My mother-in-law and Harriet are entirely responsible for what happened. At least Harriet's weapon of choice was Lucille's cane and not a carving knife."

Fogarty scrubbed at his jaw. "Doesn't mean I won't face possible suspension while the incident is under review."

"You have witnesses," said Zack.

"Not to mention those two have a long list of priors," I added.

Hearing that, my mother-in-law hurled a litany of rambling, semi-coherent insults at me.

The ambulance arrived minutes later. After assessing the situation, the EMTs announced that Lucille showed signs of a concussion and Harriet may have fractured her leg, hip, or both. Once the two women were strapped to gurneys, the EMTs transported them into the ambulance. Zack and I followed the ambulance to the hospital.

On the way, I texted Nick with an update. Of course, Nick being Nick, he texted back: *Grandmother Lucille lost her wheels? We're stuck with her 24/7? For how long?*

I scowled at the scowling emoji he'd added to the end of his text. Our only respite from my mother-in-law occurred when she was off fomenting Marxist uprisings and insurgency with Harriet and the eleven other Daughters of the October Revolution.

A revoked driver's license hadn't stopped Harriet Kleinhample from continuing as the group's chauffeur, but I'd think a broken hip or leg would put her out of commission for some time, although I had no experience with either.

"What do you know about recovery from broken hips?" I asked Zack.

"Nada. Ask Siri."

I pulled out my phone and posed the question, specifically narrowing the search down to driving. Instead of speaking to me, Siri responded with a series of website links. As Zack continued to drive, I tumbled down the Internet rabbit hole, finding answers that ranged from as few as five days to upwards of several months. A caveat suggested full recovery might take as long as a year. "Not helpful," I huffed, relaying the various answers to Zack.

He reached over and squeezed my thigh. "Harriet is one feisty old bat. She'll haul herself up behind the wheel of that antique hunk of junk the day she's released from the hospital."

"One can only hope." Even though I viewed Harriet as a menace on the road, so far, she'd miraculously steered clear of *most* pedestrians and other vehicles.

However, she'd taken out more than one curbside tree on my

street and probably countless others elsewhere. She'd also unwittingly rid the world of an assassin when she recently plowed into a parked car.

For selfish reasons, I stood firmly in Nick's camp and wished Harriet a speedy recovery. Otherwise, I feared a convoy of Ubers depositing the Daughters of the October Revolution at our house each day with me arriving home every night to find they'd cleaned out my fridge and pantry and trashed my house. Bad enough when it occurred once or twice a week.

If it happened daily, could I throw myself on the mercy of the court and plead justifiable homicide after I killed them all?

~*~

We spent the next several hours in the hospital waiting room as various healthcare professionals poked, prodded, and tested my mother-in-law. Lucille was finally admitted at nearly two in the morning with a confirmed concussion. Given her advanced age and her previous stroke, the attending doctor advised admitting her for observation. Luckily, Lucille was too doped up on pain meds to object.

"What about Mrs. Kleinhample?" I asked. "I'm assuming you can't divulge any medical information to us, but I believe my mother-in-law may have been her health care proxy. Is there someone else you were able to contact?"

The doctor nodded. "I can tell you we've admitted her. She listed a daughter as a secondary proxy, but she's not answering her phone." He checked his watch. "Given the hour, most likely she's sound asleep and will contact us first thing in the morning."

"Is Mrs. Kleinhample still unconscious?"

Maybe even divulging that much violated HIPAA laws because he responded with only a cryptic, "She's resting comfortably."

With no further reason for us to remain at the hospital, Zack and I dragged ourselves home. Mr. Sandman was waiting, and we both conked out the moment our heads hit the pillows.

~*~

Sometime later, a discordant racket of metallic clanking, thudding, thumping, bellowing, and shouting, accompanied by the roar of an engine, startled me awake. Either I was dreaming, or I'd somehow been transported to midtown Manhattan during 4am trash pickup.

I pried one sleep-deprived eye open and stared at the alarm clock. My body might feel like I'd only recently fallen asleep, but the digital display registering through my one bleary eye claimed I'd slept five hours. Every cell in my body screamed that someone had messed with the space/time continuum. Although I was in my own bed and not somewhere in Manhattan, I refused to believe it was seven-thirty.

I groaned, rolled over, and pulled the quilt over my head, but it did little to drown out the noise. "What is that racket?"

Getting no response, I swept my arm across the sheets in search of Zack, only to find his side of the bed empty. My other senses had awakened, though, and the aroma of coffee—not to mention my full bladder—forced me from the bed.

Two minutes later, I dragged myself into the kitchen. At the table, Nick sat wolfing down pancakes, scrambled eggs, and sausage while Leonard camped out at Nick's feet, impatiently waiting for any scraps that might fall from Nick's fork. Around a mouthful of food, my son managed a mumbled greeting.

Zack stood at the stove. After taking one look at me, he stopped flipping pancakes and poured me a large mug of coffee.

He added a generous amount of half and half before handing me the much-needed infusion of caffeine along with a quick lip peck.

I stared at him with eyes still refusing to focus completely. "How can you look so wide awake after so little sleep?"

Nick answered for him. "Spy training, Mom."

Zack frowned and shook his head. "It's way too early in the morning for conspiracy theories."

From his perch atop the refrigerator, Ralph flapped his wings and squawked, "*O heinous, strong and bold conspiracy.*" *Richard the Second.* Act Five, Scene Three."

In my opinion, it was also way too early for editorial commentary from our resident Shakespearean scholar. However, Zack was more of a pushover than I when it came to the African Grey I'd inherited from Great-aunt Penelope Periwinkle. He rewarded Ralph with a sunflower seed.

I had never quite figured out if my sons delighted in teasing me or if my suspicions about my husband were correct. From nearly the moment I'd met Zack, I suspected his career as an award-winning photojournalist was a cover for his true calling as a member of one of the alphabet agencies. Of course, he categorically denied my suspicions, claiming I had a wild imagination. But don't all spies deny that they're spies?

Zack turned his attention back to the stove, filled two plates, and brought them to the table. All the while, I continued hearing the noise that had awakened me. "What's going on outside?" I asked, taking a seat.

"Our new neighbors are moving in," said Zack.

Both our bedroom and the kitchen were situated at the back of the house, yet the decibel level sounded more like the noise emanated from our backyard, not the front. "I've never come across such loud movers, much less ones that begin work this early."

"That's far from the weirdest thing going on across the street," said Nick.

"Meaning?"

"Mom, you've got to see this for yourself."

I raised one weary eyebrow, silently conveying that nothing short of an alien invasion would get my rear in gear at the moment.

Nick persisted. "Trust me, Mom. You're going to want to see this with your own eyes."

I glanced at Zack. "Is it really worth the effort?"

He shrugged. "A picture's worth a thousand words."

Reluctantly, I hauled myself out of my chair, grabbed my coffee mug, and headed for the living room with Zack and Nick following. Nick pulled the cord to open the blinds.

I stared gape-mouthed at the odd sight across the street.

TWO

A moving van had parked in the driveway of the McMansion that now stood on the former site of Betty Bentworth's old bungalow. Assorted furniture and cartons half-filled the interior of the van and sprawled along the driveway as four burley men hauled items through the garage and into the house.

No one had bothered to turn off the van's ignition. While the men worked, the vehicle's tailpipe loudly continued to belch polluting diesel fumes and black smoke onto the street. I already smelled the stench beginning to seep inside our house. "I suppose it would be bad Karma to hope they run out of gas and the engine seizes," I said.

"If they haven't turned it off by the time we finish breakfast and dress, I'll say something to them," said Zack.

"With or without your gun?" asked Nick, which garnered a Mom Look from me and a chuckle from Zack.

I turned my attention back to the driveway. The movers were hauling what appeared to be battered, secondhand furnishings, circa mid-last century, into a newbuild that had probably sold for a million dollars, judging from recent real estate sales in Westfield.

However, a stranger scene was taking place to the right of the driveway. A barefoot man dressed only in a pair of garish Hawaiian print Bermuda shorts, his enormous naked gut hanging over the waistband, walked back and forth, pushing a noisy, beat-up gas lawnmower over the tiny plot of land that constituted the front yard. "What in the world is that man doing?"

"He was at it when I walked Leonard an hour ago," said Nick, "and he's still at it. I could have mowed every lawn on the block in that time."

"But there's no grass to cut," I said.

The McMansion had been built on a lot meant for a small bungalow, leaving only a postage stamp-sized front yard. From lack of watering, the sod installed prior to the house going on the market had since withered and died, leaving a carpet of matted brown death in place of the Kentucky bluegrass.

Although scores of people had shown up for the open house four months ago, the home had failed to sell until recently. Apparently, people get squeamish about living on a property where the former owner lost her life to a hitman. It didn't seem to matter that Betty's home had been razed and a new one built in its place.

"Maybe he's not the new owner," I said. "Just someone hired to do yardwork."

Nick offered me one of his classic teenage eye rolls, adding, "Rumor has it, there's a bridge for sale in Brooklyn, Mom."

Zack chose a slightly more diplomatic response to my hopeful comment. He looped his arm around my waist and said, "Come on, Pollyanna. Our breakfast is getting cold."

~*~

Once it had become obvious that Zack and I wouldn't arrive home from the hospital until the wee hours of the morning, I had emailed Human Resources to let them know I planned to work from home Friday. Now that we weren't under the thumb of Trimedia, our former corporate overlords, the *American Woman* magazine staff no longer had to abide by their draconian rules.

Not wanting to worry her, I also shot off a text to my BFF and workmate, food editor Cloris McWerther. Cloris was one of the few people at work who knew the full extent of my reluctant amateur sleuth involvement in recent murders. I didn't want to send her into a panic when I failed to show up this morning.

After showering and dressing, Zack headed across the street to speak with the polluting movers while I made my way to the apartment we used as an office above our detached garage. The noise hadn't abated, and as I traversed the short distance, the reverberating sounds bombarded my ears, but by the time I'd climbed the staircase on the side of the garage, I knew Zack had succeeded. At least with the movers. The lawnmower noise continued.

A minute later, Zack entered the apartment. "Semi-success. The crew chief apologized." Zack shook his head. "At first, he didn't know what I was talking about. Claimed he didn't realize the engine was running all this time."

"Unless he's deaf, I'm not buying it."

"That makes two of us, but at least he took care of it."

"Is the dirt mower the new homeowner?"

Zack shrugged. "Not sure. The crew chief said a woman inside the house is directing the movers. I sent the mower a friendly wave, but he refused to make eye contact. Just ignored me and continued mowing."

"Maybe he suffers from obsessive-compulsive disorder."

"Or something."

I could deal with lawnmowers. After all, it was summer. As annoying as the constant engine droning was, someone in the neighborhood was always using a power mower, trimmer, leaf blower, or weedwhacker. These, along with cicadas, crickets, and the roving ice cream truck, were the instruments that provided the soundtrack of summer in the suburbs. I'd learned to tune them out most of the time.

Still, although a few of the more macho neighborhood men liked to show off their six-pack abs while doing yardwork, none of them were dumb enough to wield power tools while shoeless. What was the guy across the street thinking?

However, that was his problem. We currently had a more pressing matter. "What do we do about Harriet's minibus? Our cars are trapped in the driveway, and we need to return the rental today."

"Harley texted me a few minutes ago," said Zack. "The police are sending a tow truck to move the VW to the impound lot."

"Harriet will blow a gasket, but it won't stop her for long. Given how often she needs to replace her wheels, I suspect she does business with a no-questions-asked, cash-only used-car salesman who specializes in 60s-era VW minibuses."

"Probably a *communist* no-questions-asked, cash-only used-car salesman."

"True." I thought for a moment. "Maybe his brother is their lawyer. Shyster and Shyster. We specialize in rust bucket VW minibuses and ironclad alibis for dedicated commies. Terms negotiable."

Zack barked out a laugh. "You're wasting your talents, sweetheart."

I squinted at him. "As a crafts editor?"

"And a reluctant amateur sleuth."

"And what should I be doing instead?"

"Standup comedy."

"Don't laugh. Truth is often stranger than fiction. Look at the guy across the street."

~*~

By the time we left the office and returned to the house for lunch, Nick had headed out for his shift at Trader Joe's. Harriet's VW had been towed, and the movers had finished. Either the half-naked man or his lawnmower had run out of gas, the mower sitting silent and abandoned in the middle of the dead yard.

As Zack and I crossed the living room, I stopped short in front of the bay window. Mower Man had parked himself with a six-pack of beer at the top of the McMansion's front steps, an area too small to be called a porch by any stretch of the imagination. It reminded me of a brownstone stoop and stood out as a serious architectural design flaw of the quasi-Craftsman mini-McMansion.

I watched mesmerized as he guzzled the contents of one can, tossed it aside, and grabbed another. The front door opened, and a woman joined him. She settled next to him and helped herself to a beer. They never uttered a word to each other, just sat, sipped, and stared blankly across the street.

The two looked enough alike to be twins, or at least brother and sister. Both had ruddy complexions and dishwater brown frizzy hair in dire need of a barber and beautician.

She wore a neon yellow ruffled halter top that barely contained her breasts. Massive love handles spilled out between the halter and a pair of bright pink capris. Like Mower Man, she was also barefoot.

I reluctantly accessed my neighborly gene and asked, "Should we go across the street to introduce ourselves and welcome them to the neighborhood?"

"You sound like you'd rather get a root canal."

"You know me so well."

"Let's wait. There's still a chance they're not the new owners. Besides, I'm hungry."

~*~

Later that afternoon, Zack and I left the house to return the rental. Mr. and Mrs. Stoop Sitter still occupied their stoop. The only difference being that Mr. Stoop Sitter now lay stretched out across the concrete landing, his bare, hairy beer belly pointed toward the sky, while Mrs. Stoop Sitter puffed on a cigarette and continued to stare blankly across the street. Half an hour later, we returned to find them in the same positions.

My curiosity had gotten the better of me. I was supposed to be working on the first book in our new *American Woman* series on crafts, decorating, and recipes through the decades. Along with republishing the original features from our archives, each book would include updated versions. We were starting with the 1960s, a decade that had seen a resurgence in the handmade and homemade, thanks in part to the hippies and the Flower Power movement, as well as the inception of our magazine.

However, I found it difficult to concentrate on crazy quilts when my mind kept returning to the Stoop Sitters. I decided to take a detour down the Google rabbit hole to see what I could find out about them.

With next to no information to go on, other than the address of the McMansion, my efforts turned up zilch. After a frustrating hour, I closed my laptop. "I'm walking around the corner," I told Zack. "I want to speak with Robyn about something."

Buried in a project of his own, Zack barely acknowledged me. Without looking up, he offered a slight head nod and an almost inaudible, "uh-huh."

I had been in a book club with Robyn Konopka before fate and a certain deceitful Dead Louse of a Spouse had turned my life upside-down. Her husband was the contractor who'd recently renovated my circa 1950s rancher, the reno a wedding present from Zack. However, because I was instrumental in discovering the identity of the man who'd tried to kill him, Jesse Konopka had refused to take a penny for labor costs.

Robyn greeted me with a huge smile and invited me in for coffee. While the coffee brewed, I explained the reason for my visit. "I'm interested in finding out who bought the house across the street from us. I thought you might know how to access such information."

She raised an eyebrow. "You're not involved in another murder investigation, are you?"

"No, it's more curiosity than anything." I told her about the Stoop Sitters, their odd behavior, and the furniture that looked like Salvation Army rejects, which the movers had hauled into the McMansion.

"Now you've got me curious," she said. "And I know just the place to look."

"I thought you might."

After Robyn poured two mugs of coffee, I followed her into the Konopka home office where she handled the business end of her husband's home construction and renovation company.

Robyn sat herself in front of a laptop connected to a large external monitor and proceeded to access a Union County website that hadn't popped up in my trip down the rabbit hole. "What's the house number?"

Seconds after I gave it to her, she'd brought up the record. "The house sold three weeks ago for 1.25 million."

My eyes bugged out. "Seriously?" Not believing my ears, I leaned over her shoulder and stared at the extremely large number on the monitor.

Sure enough. My ears hadn't deceived me. "Unbelievable."

Due to the lot size, the McMansion was more of a mini-me version, compared to others that had popped up around town since the onset of the tear-down craze. Along with the miniscule front yard, the house only had a one-car garage, not the requisite three-car of most McMansions. And the backyard was only slightly larger than the front yard, containing neither an enormous patio with outdoor kitchen nor an inground swimming pool, two other must-haves for true McMansion status. "How can that be? The house took forever to sell."

"But it did, although at less than the original 1.4 million asking price."

I whistled under my breath.

Robyn tapped a few more keys. "You can thank our short train commute into Manhattan. We're all sitting on prime real estate." She pointed to the screen. "This is the current estimated value of your house."

I gulped. My home was worth nearly four times what Karl and I had paid for it twenty-two years ago. "I had no idea."

"Crazy, isn't it? And this figure doesn't include the added value from the recent renovations."

Mindboggling was more like it. The estimated value of my home exceeded my remaining debt by several hundred thousand dollars. Someone had surely been looking out for my kids and me after Karl took out that home equity line of credit behind my back. He'd only had a chance to borrow a few thousand dollars against it before he dropped dead at a roulette table in Las Vegas.

Given all I'd dealt with at the time, I wasn't even aware of the extent of the credit line, only the amount owed. I shuddered to think how much worse off I'd be had he lived to gamble away the entire amount.

But I was here for a different reason. I shook my head to rid thoughts of the deceitful dead louse. "Does it say who purchased the house?"

Robyn clicked back to the previous window and scrolled down. "Forester Family Trust. Paid in cash. Maybe they won the lottery. Want me to keep surfing?"

"Thanks, but I don't want to take up anymore of your time. I'm supposed to be working from home today, and I've accomplished nada so far."

I'd try to satisfy my curiosity later. A little digging should unearth information on the Foresters if they'd won the lottery. As Shane Lambert had discovered, even winning big in a state that allows for anonymity, was no guarantee your identity would remain a secret.

As I started to round the corner onto my block, I stopped short, hearing the unmistakable verbal brawling of a catfight. Not between cats, though. This fight involved two women.

Our street contained only seven houses on each side, all on small plots of land, the entire block less than the length of a football field. The two women were not only close enough for me to get a good look at them, but given the decibel level of their shouting match, I heard every word.

Mrs. Stoop Sitter and another woman stood across the street on the sidewalk in front of her house. Mr. Stoop Sitter had abandoned his concrete bed and was nowhere in sight. In a high-pitched voice, Mrs. Stoop Sitter shrieked at the other woman, "Get off my property!"

Before either woman noticed me, I ducked into the shadows behind an overgrown rhododendron bush and peered out through the branches and foliage. The second woman was a full-figured, big-haired, over-bleached blonde wearing a glittery, low-cut emerald-green Spandex top and matching Spandex hotpants. She placed one hand on her hip and waved the index finger of her other hand in Mrs. Stoop Sitter's face. In a shrill singsong tone, she taunted, "News flash, Gloria. You don't own the sidewalk. I can stand here all day, and there's nothing you can do about it."

"Get out of my face, you skank." Mrs. Stoop Sitter, aka Gloria, then attempted to swat Ms. Spandex's hand but the other woman quickly withdrew it, leaving Gloria swatting at air. "I know what you're up to," she continued, "and you won't get away with it."

Ms. Spandex cackled. "Oh, yeah? You gonna make me? I'd like to see you try."

Gloria clenched her fists and reared back with her right arm, ready to strike.

"Oh, I'm so scared!" feigned Ms. Spandex. She planted her fists on her hips, took a step closer to Gloria, and raised her chin. "Go ahead and hit me. I'll have you locked up faster than you can throw that weak punch."

Gloria had enough sense not to allow the other woman to

provoke her. She lowered her arm and sneered, "I've got a news flash for you, Tonya. If he walks out on me, he gets nothing. Did you know that? I'm guessing he failed to mention it while you were spreading your legs for him."

Tonya laughed. "Guess again, Gloria. New Jersey is a community property state. He'll get half of everything."

Gloria smirked. "You guess again, Tonya. You don't know the first thing about anything. Inheritances are considered separate property, even in a community property state." She paused before adding, "But just to make doubly sure that drunken bum could never get his hands on anything, my father tied it all up in a family trust."

Hmm...scratch a Stoop Sitter lottery win. Maybe Gloria's father was the one who'd struck it rich on Powerball or MegaMillions.

Gloria continued taunting her nemesis. "You planning to support him on what you make punching a register at Walmart? You can't even afford to pay his weekly beer bill."

Tonya's jaw dropped, but she quickly recovered and called Gloria's bluff, "You're lying."

"Am I?" Gloria turned her back on the woman and stomped up the path toward the steps that led to her front door. Tonya stared at her departing back. When Gloria reached the landing, she turned and threw one last parting shot. "We'll see who gets the last laugh when I kick his cheating ass to the curb." Then she walked into the house and slammed the door so hard, the sound reverberated down the street.

When Tonya began strutting down the sidewalk in my direction, I quickly darted behind the corner house and cut through my neighbors' backyards until I reached my own property.

I found Zack channel-surfing on the couch. "Done working for the day?"

He clicked off the TV. "Taking a break. Did you enjoy your visit with Robyn?"

"I did. It was quite educational. As was what happened afterwards. Want some gossip?"

He patted the cushion beside him, and I took a seat. After I told him what I'd learned and overheard, I said, "Those two women should try out for the next season of *Jersey Housewives*. I vote for steering clear of the Stoop Sitters. We have enough drama of our own with Lucille and her group of octogenarian commies. I don't want us getting sucked into whatever is going on across the street."

Zack had studied me intently as I unspooled my tale, his knit brows unable to mask his worry. After I finished, he exhaled what I took as a sigh of relief, leaned over, and kissed me. "Agreed."

Of course, I should have known by now that the gods always have a way of getting the last laugh.

THREE

Bright and early the next morning, Mr. Stoop Sitter returned to mowing his dead grass. When the motor consumed its last drop of fuel, he abandoned it where it had died, trudged up the front steps and into the house, returning moments later with a six-pack of Budweiser, breakfast of champion dipsomaniacs.

This time, Gloria Stoop Sitter didn't join him. I watched transfixed as Mr. Stoop Sitter took his seat on the landing and began guzzling. He consumed all six cans of beer in record time, crushing each empty on his forehead before tossing it off to the side of the landing. Then he stretched supine onto the concrete. His hairy naked belly rose and fell rhythmically as he succumbed to what I assumed was an alcoholic stupor.

Zack joined me at the window and handed me a cup of coffee. "Turning into a voyeur?"

I took a sip of coffee before answering. "It's like watching a train wreck. I feel sorry for his wife, but for the life of me, I can't imagine what she sees in him. Let alone, why Tonya or any other woman would want anything to do with him."

"From what you told me yesterday, Tonya was probably after his money."

"Money that's not his, according to his wife."

"Which means Tonya won't be back."

And that would be a very good thing. We'd had enough drama on our street, including five murders in less than two years, the most recent only weeks ago. If the universe were playing fair, that should be enough for one small Westfield block of fourteen families.

I was about to mention this to Zack when my phone rang. The display read Overlook Hospital. After answering, I placed the call on speaker for Zack to hear.

"Mrs. Pollack?"

"Yes." I saw no point confusing the issue by explaining I was now Mrs. Barnes.

"This is Dr. Pavlochek. I'm calling about your mother-in-law. We'd like to keep her a few more days to run some additional tests, but she's refusing to cooperate and is demanding we release her immediately."

Dr. Pavlochek had treated Lucille after she suffered a minor stroke a little more than a year ago. The man had the patience of a saint when it came to my mother-in-law. And probably many other elderly patients he'd treated over the years.

"You have my permission to strap her to the bed, Doctor, if that's what you're asking."

He chuckled. "Restraining a patient is illegal. We'll just have to hope she cooperates."

"I hold her medical power of attorney, and I'm authorizing you to perform whatever tests you deem necessary. But what do you suspect?"

He hesitated for a moment. "Have you noticed increasingly erratic behavior?"

"Yes, but nothing different from what I've observed in her friends." I told him about the Stand Up for Your Right to Frown campaign that the Daughters of the October Revolution had mounted last month.

He tried to choke back a chuckle and failed miserably. "That's a new one on me."

"I've chalked it up to increasing age and their communist leanings."

"Was the campaign your mother-in-law's idea?"

"I believe another member suggested it, but as their fearless leader, when she agreed, they all jumped onboard."

"I see."

I asked the question I feared most. "Are you suggesting she may have dementia?"

"It's one possibility, but there are other reasons for behavioral changes in the elderly. For one, she may have had another minor stroke. Drug interactions are another possibility." He rattled off the medications listed on Lucille's chart. "Do you know if anything has been added recently?"

"Not unless she's frequenting the black market."

"Are you suggesting she may be taking illicit drugs?"

"Frankly, Doctor, nothing would surprise me. We've had to lock up the alcohol after I caught her washing down her meds with Merlot. I've suspected she occasionally overmedicates, but I haven't caught her in the act."

"You don't dole out her pills?"

"I've tried, but she wields a mean cane, and she's not averse to using it." I filled him in on what precipitated her current hospitalization. "I've learned to choose my battles with her."

"I see." A huge sigh—one I interpreted as either frustration, resignation, or a combination of both—came through the speaker. "Thank you, Mrs. Pollack. This is all very helpful. I'll be in touch when I have the test results."

I thanked the doctor, ended the call, and turned to Zack. "What do you think?"

He shook his head. "We may have some hard decisions ahead of us."

"I know. If it is the beginnings of dementia, we can no longer leave her alone in the house."

"Let's wait until we get the test results." He took both my hands in his. "I don't want you worrying about the cost. Whatever insurance doesn't pay for, I'll cover."

I shook my head. "This isn't your problem."

"I'm making it my problem. We're married now. What's yours is mine, and what's mine is yours. For better or worse, remember? Lucille is top of the list in the Worse column."

This brought tears to my eyes. I tried to blink them away but failed miserably. "What did I ever do to deserve you?"

Zack grinned. "I don't know, but whatever it was, I'm glad you did it."

That released the floodgates. A torrent of tears streamed down my cheeks.

~*~

The three Hs—hazy, hot, and humid—define August in New Jersey, but every so often, the weather gods decide to grace us with a perfect day for outdoor events. Today was one such day, and it coincided with the annual Westfield summer street fair.

Nick and some of his friends had decided to get a jump on their junior year volunteer project by assisting with setup and other jobs as needed throughout the day. He'd left the house shortly after breakfast.

A few hours later, Zack and I decided to walk into town to check out the various booths and food trucks. We brought Leonard with us. Unlike all-muscle, no-fat Zack, both the French bulldog and I needed to walk off excess baggage.

Along with the normal booths handing out pamphlets for everything from gutter and window replacement, insurance, and chiropractic services, there were crafters selling handmade soaps, jewelry, pottery, fabric crafts, and specialty food products for both humans and their four-legged friends. Every religious denomination had a booth, as well as a few of the local dentists and day care services.

The local historical society featured a woman churning butter and another spinning cotton. A man dressed as a Revolutionary War soldier cleaned a musket. Another hawked historical pamphlets and small bags of crystalized maple, candied fruits, and sugar-coated nuts, sweets common to the era. On either side of the booth, reenactors, some dressed as members of the Continental Army and others as Redcoats, passed out flyers of upcoming battle reenactments throughout the state.

After checking out all the booths, we made our way to the food truck area and chose a lunch of Asian tacos and cupcakes. So much for walking off excess baggage, but how could I possibly pass up a cupcake truck? Besides, this was no ordinary cupcake truck. It was the mobile extension of my favorite cupcakery in Princeton.

Purchases in hand, we headed toward Mindowaskin Park and settled onto a shaded park bench along the perimeter of the pond.

Zack pulled three water bottles and a bowl from his backpack. He poured water into the bowl and placed it on the ground for Leonard. As we ate our lunch, Leonard slaked his thirst while eyeing the ducks, geese, and swans gliding across the calm pond.

Across the pond, a dozen patriots and Redcoats commenced a choreographed skirmish. The shouting drew a small crowd of onlookers and pulled Leonard's attention from the waterfowl. When one of the patriots landed the first punch, smack in the middle of a Redcoat's face, we realized we weren't watching part of the day's entertainment.

"Ouch! I don't think that's supposed to be in the script."

"Doubtful," said Zack.

The Redcoat responded by jabbing the butt end of his musket into the patriot's shoulder, knocking him to the ground. He then tossed his musket aside, jumped on top of the downed man, and began pummeling him with his fists. The patriot fought back, the two men rolling around, alternating top dog position and beating the crap out of each other.

Instead of breaking up the fight, the other reenactors jumped in. Within seconds, a full-fledged melee had broken out between the two groups. Many of the onlookers started filming with their phones. Zack pulled out his to call the police.

After he'd reported the fight, I said, "I suppose they never got the message that we've been allies for more than two hundred years. You think they're all drunk?"

"Don't you?"

"I suppose." Who in their right or sober mind would start a turf war directly across the street from the police station? Within seconds of Zack ending his call, half a dozen of Westfield's finest had streamed out of the building and dashed across the street.

Several mounted police galloped in from the direction of the street fair. Others arrived on foot.

From across the pond, Zack and I watched the police handcuff all the participants. As they marched them into headquarters, I channeled Gilbert and Sullivan, *"My object all sublime, I shall achieve in time. To let the punishment fit the crime. The punishment fit the crime."*

Zack raised an eyebrow. "Meaning?"

"Under the circumstances, instead of locking them up for disorderly conduct, maybe the police should consider a colonial alternative."

"Tar and feathers?"

"I was thinking something a bit less messy. Stocks or pillories.

"I think those alternatives fall under cruel and unusual punishment these days."

"Probably. Still, it might prove more of a deterrent against future brawls than a few hours of drying out in a cell and paying a fine."

"Social media is the modern-day equivalent and much more effective. Videos and memes are popping up all over the Internet, many naming the perpetrators." He passed me his phone. "Check it out."

I squinted at the screen, but since the enactors hailed from throughout the state, I didn't expect to recognize anyone. Besides, they all wore wigs, and their tri-corner hats cast shadows on their faces. Even those who'd lost their hats in the fight, were too obscured by other brawlers.

However, someone watching the fracas across the pond did know the names of all the men and had already posted them with a video of the knock-down scrum. Although I didn't know them personally, I recognized the names of three local men—a school board member, a bank president, and a local realtor.

"Yikes!" Such embarrassment would live on the Internet and follow those guys around forever.

I handed the phone back to Zack. I had no sympathy for grown men behaving badly. Been there, done that. Although, clueless as I was at the time, my confrontation with the truth of Karl's misdeeds hadn't occurred until after his death. I'd reserve my compassion for the wives and children of these colonial Neanderthals.

With our lunch eaten, and the impromptu show ended, Zack grabbed Leonard's leash, and the three of us meandered our way back through downtown Westfield to head home. Along the way, we stopped at the farmer's market to pick up a few items for the week. We arrived home to find no sign of Mr. Stoop Sitter mowing his patch of dirt, guzzling beer on his stoop, or taking a concrete nap.

Unfortunately, our peace and quiet was short-lived. The doorbell rang the moment we'd finished stashing away our food purchases. Zack checked the app on his phone. "Ira and his kids."

"How many times have I asked him to call before dropping in on us?"

"Too many. I think he's onto you."

"How do you mean?"

"On the rare occasions when he does call first, you always tell him it's not a good time."

"Because it never is. And it's not now."

"My point, exactly. By the way, there's a woman I don't recognize with him."

"A woman?" I studied the image on his screen. Equally curious,

Ralph swooped down from his perch atop the refrigerator and settled onto Zack's shoulder. The woman bore an eerie resemblance to Ira's second wife, minus the aristocratic haughtiness Cynthia had worn like a badge of honor. Her features were also softer, her blonde hair more natural, and she didn't give the impression of someone who subsisted entirely on lettuce leaves and sparkling water. She also appeared closer in age to Ira. "I've never seen her before. Dare I hope Ira's dating?"

"Only one way to find out." Zack pocketed his phone and headed toward the front door.

Ira Pollack, Karl's previously unknown half-brother, showed up on my doorstep the summer after Karl's death. At first, I thought he might be trying to scam me, given his brother's duplicity. Maybe deceit was genetic. However, I soon learned if there were a deceit gene, Ira hadn't inherited it, which was one of his few good traits.

Besides, I didn't need a DNA test to determine the biological link. Ira was the spitting image of Karl, albeit a younger, thinner, less-bald version. He wanted nothing from me and my sons other than acceptance as a member of the family. Unfortunately, his family included three extremely spoiled brats who had their now twice-widowed father wrapped around their pinky fingers.

Generous to a fault, Ira lives by the motto that money solves everything. However, his tactics hadn't worked during his short-lived disastrous second marriage after the death of his first wife, nor when he tried to woo me away from Zack. And it only continues to exacerbate the questionable behavior of his adolescent son and twin daughters.

The coward in me wanted to pretend we weren't home, but for all I knew, Ira had seen us at the street fair or farmer's market and followed us home. After heaving a huge sigh, I reluctantly followed Zack to the front door.

"Surprise!" said Ira, his face beaming a huge grin, the moment Zack swung open the door.

Yes, a surprise, indeed. I forced a less-than-enthusiastic smile onto my own face and bit my tongue, not wanting to embarrass him in front of the woman. I'd leave that to Ira himself and his children.

Ira shooed his kids inside. All three had their eyes glued to their phones. Without glancing up, either twelve-year-old Melody or Harmony contorted her face into a sneer and asked, "How long do we have to stay?"

"There's never anything to do here," complained her sister. After more than a year, I still couldn't tell the twins apart.

Their ten-year-old brother Isaac stamped his foot. "You promised we were going for ice cream. Why are we here?"

"I wanted to introduce Rowena to your aunt Anastasia." Ira then reached for her hand and led her across the threshold.

I darted a sideways glance at Zack as he stepped behind our uninvited guests to close the door. His expression mirrored my thoughts.

"Why?" asked Melody. Or Harmony.

The other twin was more direct. Pulling her attention from her phone, she glared at her father. "You're not going to marry her, are you?"

Deep scarlet embarrassment raced up Ira's neck and spread into his scalp. All color drained from Rowena's face. I wasn't sure whether it was from the twin's comment, Ira's reaction, or that Rowena's darting gaze had landed on Ralph. She slipped her hand from Ira's grasp and stepped backwards until she nearly stumbled against the door.

"He won't hurt you," I assured her, but my words didn't appear to calm her.

"He's just a dumb bird," said Isaac.

I peered down at him. In my best former schoolteacher voice, I asked, "Exactly how many Shakespearean plays can you quote from memory, Issac?"

As he glared tight-lipped at me, Ralph leaned toward him, squawked once, then responded, "*And how quote you my folly? Two Gentlemen of Verona*, Act Two, Scene Four."

Rowena gasped.

Zack addressed Ira's kids, "Why don't the three of you go into the den? I'm sure you can find something to watch on TV."

As they raced down the hall, I reluctantly channeled Miss Manners. "May I offer you something to drink? Coffee? Iced tea?" I cocked my head and raised an eyebrow toward Rowena as she continued to eye Ralph. "A potent potable, perhaps? It's five o'clock somewhere."

She released a nervous chuckle. Turning to Ira, she asked, "How long before the natives get restless?"

His eyes darted in the direction of the den, then back to me. "They're testing you."

"Of course, they are."

"Don't worry," I said. "If they misbehave, Ralph will handle them."

Ira blanched, and his jaw dropped. "You wouldn't!"

Rowena turned to Ira. "Who's Ralph?"

He scrunched his nose. "The bird."

"Ralph is so much more than a bird," said Zack. He handed Ralph a sunflower seed as he ushered us toward the kitchen. "He's my wife's winged bodyguard."

"Not to mention my stiffest competition for my husband's affection," I added.

Zack headed to the apartment to grab some bottles of wine. Ralph resumed his sentry post atop the refrigerator. Rowena and Ira settled around the kitchen table. While I pulled some cheese from the fridge and crackers from the pantry, I offered Rowena the Cliff Notes synopsis of the history of Ralph.

Throughout, her attention darted between Ralph and me, but she gradually began to relax. Especially after Zack returned and she'd downed two glasses of wine.

With the kids camped out in the den, the atmosphere improved. My brain segued from conjuring up ways to get all of them to leave as soon as possible to curiosity about the woman seated in my kitchen. However, I didn't want to make Rowena uncomfortable by asking probing questions about her background. For all I knew, she and Ira had only recently begun dating, and she'd already decided the relationship had no future. After all, what woman in her right mind would want to become stepmother to Ira's kids?

Eventually, though, we learned Ira and Rowena had met at a singles mixer for parents without partners, that Rowena Milford taught French at Union High School and like Ira, had also lost a spouse to cancer several year ago. Her nineteen-year-old daughter attended Swarthmore College. Rowena's looks might remind me of Cynthia, but unlike Ira's last wife, she didn't give off a gold digger vibe. I doubted she was after Ira's money.

Two hours later, Isaac, Melody, and Harmony stomped into the kitchen. All three stood with arms crossed as Isaac said, "The movie's over, and we want ice cream."

Rowena rose. "We should leave, Ira."

Ira appeared reluctant to depart. Nothing new there. I often wondered if he looked on Zack and me to play bad cop in opposition to his overindulgent parenting. When Zack and I also rose, Ira had no choice but to follow.

At the front door, Zack and I exchanged our nice-to-have-met-you pleasantries with Rowena. Impatient to leave, Isaac swung open the door. The kids raced out of the house and into their car.

As Ira and Rowena turned to leave, a police car pulled up across the street. When the officer opened the rear driver's side door, I was shocked at the sight of Mr. Stoop Sitter stepping from the patrol car. Bruises covered his face and blood stained his Continental Army uniform.

One of Ira's kids leaned on the horn. Mr. Stoop Sitter stopped and turned. He glared at the car, then noticed the four of us staring at him. His face contorted in a snarl as he flipped us the bird.

Rowena gasped. At first, I thought it was due to his appearance and the obscene gesture, but then she stiffened and yelled across the street, "What have you done now, Barry?"

FOUR

Mr. Stoop Sitter, now Barry, didn't respond. As the patrol car pulled away from the curb, he turned his back on us. With an uneven gait, he hauled himself down the path, grabbed onto the railing, and hoisted himself up the steps onto the landing. After shoving open the door, he stepped inside, slamming the door behind him.

I turned to Rowena. "You know him?"

She made a face. "Unfortunately. He's my ex."

Ira's jaw dropped. "You told me you were widowed."

Rowena shook her head and heaved a huge sigh. "I am. Barry Sumner was an extremely brief youthful mistake I made during a teenage act of rebellion. We eloped. Less than a week into the marriage, I came to my senses and realized my mother and father were right about him. I ran home to my parents and apologized profusely for causing them such pain. They took the appropriate steps to have the marriage annulled. I went off to college and never saw him again. Until now."

She closed her eyes and hugged her chest. We all stared at her, waiting to hear more. Finally, she opened her eyes and spoke to Ira. "The guy was a total loser back then, and I was a complete idiot. I grew up and matured. Looks like he never did."

She then turned to Zack and me. "I find it hard to believe he can afford a house like that. Barry spent all his time and money on his motorcycle, video games, guns, and beer. Not necessarily in that order."

"His wife recently inherited a trust fund." I told her the little that I had learned from Robyn, then mentioned his bare-chested, shoeless mowing obsession. "When the mower runs out of gas, he heads to the stoop to guzzle a six-pack, then falls into a stupor, flat on his back on the landing."

She rolled her eyes. "The beer routine is classic Barry. The dirt mowing sounds bizarre, but it could be the result of a severe motorcycle accident he had several years ago. According to him, real men don't wear helmets."

"You've kept in contact with him?" asked Ira.

Rowena shuddered. "Heck, no. I read about the accident in the newspaper. He suffered serious head trauma and was in a coma for weeks. I'm no psychiatrist or psychologist, but maybe that accounts for the mowing obsession. As for what we just witnessed, he always had trouble controlling his temper. Looks like he still does."

Zack mentioned the brawl we'd witnessed earlier.

Ira nodded. "We heard the buzz as we left the street fair."

"Neither Zack nor I recognized him at the time," I said.

"We weren't close enough," added Zack, "but in hindsight, I think he's the guy who threw the first punch."

Rowena shrugged. "Not surprising. I'm just glad I wised up

before he knocked me up. Worst mistake of my life."

One of Ira's kids leaned on the horn again, this time not letting up. "You should go," I said.

Ira glanced toward his car, then back at us. Rowena tugged his arm. "Come on, Ira. We've taken up enough of Anastasia and Zack's time."

After they drove off, Zack and I reentered the house. "Well, that was interesting," I said.

"On several levels. Rowena seems nice, but I doubt she'll stick around."

I laughed. "Nothing like stating the obvious. Ira can't keep a housekeeper, much less a girlfriend. Not with his kids sabotaging him at every turn."

Tino Martinelli had made some headway toward straightening out Ira's kids during his brief tenure as their manny. However, even the former member of Special Forces had his limits. He eventually gave up and took a less stressful position working for Homeland Security. Which says volumes about living day to day with Isaac, Melody, and Harmony.

Zack and I spent the remainder of the afternoon tackling household chores that had piled up during the week. After Nick arrived home and cleaned up, the three of us went out to dinner.

Mr. Stoop Sitter, aka Barry Sumner, was back mowing his small patch of dirt when we left for the restaurant. However, although barefoot, he hadn't changed out of his torn Continental Army uniform.

We returned home from dinner to find our new neighbor once again supine on the concrete landing. This time, the remnants of several six-packs lay scattered around him.

~*~

Sunday morning, Nick took Leonard out for his morning walk while Zack and I prepared breakfast. Ralph kept an eye on our progress from atop the refrigerator. Moments later, Nick and Leonard reentered the house.

"That was quick," I said.

"Leonard started barking and pulled me across the street. That weird new guy was still flat on his back at the top of his steps. Like he hadn't moved since we came home from dinner last night." He paused for a moment, took a deep breath, then said, "I think he's dead, Mom."

Zack turned off the stove and held his arm out for Ralph. Once the bird alighted on his favorite human, Zack returned him to his cage. Ralph squawked his indignation, but Zack only said, "Sorry, pal."

Hopefully, Ralph wouldn't pick the lock, one of his many talents. To prevent parrot temptations, I covered the sausage with a heavy lid and placed the uncooked eggs in the refrigerator before Nick and I followed Zack.

Before opening the door, Zack turned to us and said, "Best if you two stay here. Let me check it out."

We remained inside the house but left the door open. Leonard's barking resumed as we watched Zack bound across the street. After climbing halfway up the steps of the McMansion, he stopped short, turned toward us, and shook his head. As he descended the steps, he pulled his phone from his pocket.

"The police are on their way," said Zack once he'd returned to the house.

"What about an ambulance?" I asked, continuing to focus on what little I could see of the still body across the street. "Are you sure he's dead? You didn't even check for a pulse."

"No need. Someone plunged a bayonet into his heart."

My brain reeled as my body gave off an involuntary shudder. Another murder on our block. How was that possible? This was Westfield, not Camden or Newark. But you'd never know it from the string of murders that had occurred during the past ten months. First Betty Bentworth and Carmen Cordova last October. John Doyle and Cormac Murphy in April. Jared Oberman a month ago. Now Barry Sumner. On the exact site of the razed house where the first murder on our street had taken place. All on one short block. How long before someone started bus tours to capitalize on the notoriety of the deadliest street in New Jersey?

I reached for my son. "You okay, Nick?"

He allowed me to draw him against my side. "Yeah, I think so, Mom." He cocked his head and forced a grin. "After all, as I've heard you say, not my first rodeo."

"Really, Nick?"

"Too soon for homicide humor?"

"Probably."

Nick was right, though. Barry Sumner was the second murder victim Leonard had sniffed out on our street, then dragged Nick toward the scene of the crime. Four months ago, the Dog Whisperer and his canine with a nose for murder came across Corman Murphy's body in a shallow grave behind our garage.

In the distance, the sound of sirens grew louder. Any moment a convoy of police vehicles would round the corner. The press would soon follow. They'd camp out on my front lawn, demanding to know my connection to this latest murder. Because they'd long ago decided that Westfield's own Miss Marple/Jessica Fletcher/Nancy Drew was always somehow connected to every murder, not only on our street or within our town or county but throughout the entire tri-state region. Or so it seemed.

Worst of all, the moment the press connected me to the murder, I'd receive a blistering call from my mother, berating me for sticking my nose where it didn't belong and risking life and limb.

Not this time, though. I'd never even spoken to the man. He and his wife had only moved in three days ago. I hadn't discovered the body. I hadn't called the police. And yet, somehow, I knew I'd get sucked in. Because I always do. It was only a matter of time.

And now my younger son was following in his mother's reluctant sleuthing footsteps. "You tell no one you discovered the body, Nick."

Zack and Nick stared at me. "I don't want the press hounding you," I explained. "They're relentless, and they won't care that you're only a teenager."

"Don't I need to talk to the cops?" asked Nick. "I found the body."

"Did you touch anything?"

Nick shook his head. "I know better than that, Mom. I stayed on the sidewalk. I guess Leonard smelled blood, but I couldn't see any, and I sure didn't see a bayonet sticking out of the guy's chest."

I placed my hand on his shoulder. "Zack will speak with Detective Spader. If the detective needs to hear from you, he knows where to find you."

"I can't even tell Alex and Sophie?"

I tightened my lips and shook my head. "No one."

Zack indicated his agreement with a nod. While he waited for the police to arrive, I grabbed Nick's hand, and pulled him and Leonard away from the front entrance, closing the door behind us.

"What now?" asked Nick.

"Take Leonard into the backyard before he has an accident."

With both Nick and Zack occupied for the moment, I directed my attention to our abandoned breakfast. Fat had congealed around the half-cooked sausages. I turned the burner on low to melt the fat, then raised the heat to finish browning the links. While the sausage cooked, I sliced a cantaloupe, placing a few pieces in Ralph's cage, a reward for staying put, and left the door open. The eggs sat ready for scrambling once Nick and Zack returned.

Even though I had no intention of getting sucked into the investigation of Barry Sumner's death, my brain had parked itself on the topic and was raising all sorts of questions. For one, where was Gloria, aka Mrs. Stoop Sitter? She apparently hadn't bailed her husband out of jail if he'd been charged or bothered to pick him up at the station if he hadn't been charged.

He didn't drive himself home. Even though he walked back and forth for hours as he mowed his dirt, he didn't strike me as the sort of man who would walk a mile into town in full Continental Army attire, especially in the middle of the summer. Those uniforms were made of heavy wool, not light cotton.

If he'd taken his car downtown, why hadn't he driven himself home? Was he so intoxicated even after cooling his heels in a cell that the police kept his keys?

If Gloria had gone out for the day, wouldn't she have noticed her husband lying on the stoop when she arrived home? Wouldn't she wake him before she went to bed?

Maybe she didn't notice him because she pulled into the garage, but then, wouldn't she have realized he wasn't in the house?

Or perhaps, after her altercation with Tonya yesterday, she no longer cared where he was or with whom. Hadn't she inferred she planned to divorce him?

If Mrs. Stoop Sitter was still sound asleep this morning and unaware of her husband's murder, she was in for a huge shock. Unless she'd killed him while he slept. After all, hell hath no fury like a woman scorned, no matter that the man in question was no one's idea of Prince Charming. But why kill someone she planned to divorce, especially if she wouldn't financially benefit from his death?

The sound of the front door opening pulled me from my mental gymnastics. Hearing two sets of feet striding across the hardwood floor, I knew Detective Sam Spader had accompanied Zack into the house. I was expecting the visit. I'd even added a few more eggs to the bowl.

As Zack and the detective entered the kitchen, I began to remove the sausage links from the frying pan and placed them on a paper towel-covered plate to absorb the excess fat. I then drained most of the remaining fat into an empty aluminum can before adding the egg mixture to the frying pan. "Breakfast in five minutes, gentlemen." I locked eyes with Spader, "I'm assuming you're staying?"

The detective had become a semi-regular at my table. I didn't mind. I'd even encouraged it. I suspected the meals he ate with us were often the only nutritionally balanced ones he consumed all day.

My relationship with Detective Samuel Spader had started out rocky last summer when he'd zeroed in on my mother-in-law as his prime suspect in the murder of her roommate during Lucille's brief stint in rehab after her stroke. A year later the relationship had segued from adversarial to a grudging appreciation and eventually moved on to full-out acceptance of my unique investigative talents. Last month, he'd even asked for my help on a case.

Spader's eyes drifted to the perfectly browned sausage, the bowl of cantaloupe, and the scrambled eggs nearing completion. "If you have enough. I didn't even have time to grab a cup of coffee this morning before I was called in on this case. It's supposed to be my day off."

"Still understaffed?" asked Zack, pouring cups of coffee for the three of us.

Spader accepted the mug Zack offered him and downed the contents before answering, "And likely to remain that way for the remainder of the fiscal year."

Nick returned from letting Leonard relieve himself. Seeing Spader, he added a fourth plate and utensils to the table. After carrying the sausage and bowl of melon to the table, he removed a carton of orange juice from the refrigerator while I transferred the eggs to a serving dish.

Zack grabbed the coffee pot and refilled Spader's cup. Having gotten over his snit, Ralph flew into the kitchen and perched onto his usual kitchen observation post.

After we'd settled around the table and served ourselves, Spader removed his notepad and a pen from the inner pocket of his suit jacket. He flipped the pad to a fresh page and placed it and the pen alongside his plate.

As he dug into his eggs, his eyes zeroed in on me and said, "I understand you know some interesting facts about your new neighbors. What can you tell me?"

While I ate, I related the odd behavior of Mr. and Mrs. Stoop

Sitter, AKA Barry Sumner and Gloria Forester, and what I'd learned about their finances from Robyn's online search. I ended with a recap of the altercation I'd observed between Gloria and Tonya.

Spader had performed an ambidextrous feat as I spoke, jotting notes with one hand while eating with the other. When I'd finished, he raised both of his shaggy salt and pepper eyebrows. "I wouldn't have pegged the deceased as a babe magnet."

"Some women will do anything for money," I suggested. "Besides, prior to the cat fight yesterday, Tonya had no idea Gloria controls every penny."

"Assuming Gloria wasn't lying," said Spader.

"There is that." Never having laid eyes on her before Thursday and little more since then, I couldn't vouch for her relationship with the truth.

Nick spoke around a mouthful of food. "Maybe this Tonya person killed the weird dude because he deceived her into thinking the money was his."

Spader pointed his fork at him. "You're thinking like a detective, young man. She'll certainly be receiving a visit from me." He directed his next question to me. "I don't suppose you know Tonya's last name."

I shook my head. "No clue. I'd never seen her before, but you should also speak with Rowena Milford. She'll be able to provide you with some background information about the victim, but it won't be anything current."

Spader jotted her name in his notepad. "Who's Rowena Milford?"

"Ira's new girlfriend," said Zack. "They were leaving here when a squad car pulled up and dropped off Barry yesterday afternoon.

She recognized him."

Spader showed heightened interest in this nugget of information. "How does she know him?"

"They were briefly married decades ago," I said, "but she was quick to point out she hadn't seen him in years."

"She called the marriage an act of teenage rebellion that ended shortly after it began," said Zack.

"And the worst mistake of her life," I added.

"Maybe she killed him," said Nick.

I tossed him a Mom Look. I didn't care for how excited he sounded. We didn't need another member of the family getting dragged into murder investigations.

Spader set his pen on the table and turned to Nick. "A crime needs a perpetrator capable of three things—method, opportunity, and motive. What are they in this case?"

Nick eagerly jumped into his first impromptu Criminology 101 lesson. "The method was the bayonet."

I interrupted. "Was the bayonet an antique or a reproduction?"

"A reproduction," said Spader. "Why?"

I shrugged. "I'd think you'd have had a greater chance of tracking down the owner of an antique."

"Yeah, too bad that's not the case. Reproductions of that model bayonet are available all over the Internet." He turned back to Nick. "What about opportunity?"

"The dude was passed out drunk. He never saw the attack coming."

"Most likely, given there were no signs of a struggle. And motive?"

Nick grew thoughtful. "She could've been nursing a grudge for years."

Ralph, who had intently followed the discussion, chose this moment to add his Shakespearean two cents. "*Braaack! I will feed fat the ancient grudge I bear him. Merchant of Venice.* Act One, Scene Three."

Spader shot a quick side-eye at Ralph and added a harrumph before waving his hand to prompt Nick to continue.

I, on the other hand, fought the urge to haul off and give Spader a swift kick in the shin under the table. Instead, I tried subliminal *don't encourage him* eye daggers, which he either ignored or failed to interpret.

Meanwhile, Nick had come up with a theory. "When she saw him, bad memories she'd repressed for years came flooding back. She snapped and decided to make him pay for whatever he'd done to her."

Repressed memories? Now that was impressive—in a somewhat scary way—coming from a kid who hadn't yet taken a course in psychology. Maybe I should pay more attention to all those Marvel Universe movies he watches to get a better handle on the full scope of his knowledge.

Spader had no such qualms. Then again, as far as I knew, he had no children. The detective never spoke about his personal life other than the few times he mentioned his health. Right now, he seemed to be relishing his Mr. Miyagi role. "Such as?" he asked.

"Maybe he got her pregnant, and her parents forced her to marry him."

I stared at my son while doing some mental calculations. "Rowena said she has a nineteen-year-old daughter." I turned to Zack. "That would make her only thirty-seven or possibly younger, depending on when she got pregnant. I thought she was

SEAMS LIKE THE PERFECT CRIME

closer in age to Ira. Wouldn't you agree?"

He nodded before turning to Spader. "The legal age to marry without parental consent is eighteen, isn't it?"

"It is now. Used to be sixteen."

"I suppose it's possible," I said, "but she made a point of stating she was lucky she hadn't gotten pregnant by him."

"Doesn't mean she didn't," said Spader. "Women have been known to lie about a child's parentage."

I rose to retrieve the coffee pot and topped off everyone's cups. "If you want my opinion—"

Spader barked out a laugh. "Let's have it."

"Rowena is a longshot. Given the murder weapon, I'd concentrate on the other reenactors from the street fair. I find it highly unlikely that either Rowena or Tonya would own a bayonet. There must be a reason Barry threw that first punch. Was it just because he took offense to something the other guy said, or was there longstanding animosity between the two of them?"

"We plan to interview all of them," said Spader.

"Were they charged?" asked Zack.

"With disorderly conduct. Then released. Meanwhile, when was the last time any of you saw the victim's wife?"

"Not since Friday," I said.

Nick and Zack agreed.

"Why?" asked Zack.

Spader's mouth tightened into a thin line. "Because she's missing."

FIVE

My mind raced back to my earlier theories. "She wasn't in the house?"

I knew that statistically, it's often the spouse who's the killer. Usually, though, the husband kills his wife. But sometimes wives do kill their husbands. Or hire someone to do their dirty work for them.

Spader shook his head. "No sign of her. We knocked and rang the bell. No one answered, but the door was unlocked. After announcing ourselves, we did a quick sweep to make sure she wasn't somewhere inside, lying injured or dead."

Not looking good for Mrs. Stoop Sitter. "Is her car missing?"

"No car in the garage, and we saw no signs of a purse, keys, or phone anywhere in view. Also, no evidence of a break-in or a struggle. We're not even sure of her name. Does she go by Sumner or Forester?"

I shrugged. "No clue. Both are relatively common surnames, aren't they?"

Spader concurred. "I had someone check the Motor Vehicle Commission database. It showed licenses for half a dozen middle-aged women named either Gloria Sumner or Forester but none living at the house across the street."

"Not unusual since they just moved in," said Zack. "Most people put off going to the MVC as long as possible."

Spader pulled a face. "Present company included. However, if they moved within the state, they only have a week to register a change of address. Sixty days if they moved from out of state."

"Based on Gloria's altercation with Tonya," said Zack, "my guess is they didn't move from out of state. From what Anastasia witnessed, those two women had history."

"Definitely," I said. "Barry's wife is probably one of the Glorias who turned up in the database. I'll bet not a single person in the history of the MVC has ever rushed to register a change of address within seven days of moving." I also wondered how often that law was enforced, but I kept that to myself.

"Makes sense," said Spader. "Which is why we need to track them all down to confirm."

In the three days since the Stoop Sitters had moved in, I hadn't noticed either of them arrive or leave in a vehicle other than Barry returning in the squad car yesterday. I mentioned this to Spader, then addressed Zack, "I don't even remember seeing a car parked in front of their house the day they moved in, do you?"

He whipped out his phone. "I don't, but I'll check the security cameras."

"Do they capture the front of the house across the street?" asked Spader.

"To some extent but spying on our neighbors wasn't my intent. I positioned them to capture the front of our property and the street."

"Send me whatever you've got from Thursday through this morning," said Spader. "Maybe we'll get lucky."

"Don't you need a subpoena?" asked Nick.

"Only when someone doesn't cooperate with a request," said Spader.

"Which I've just done," said Zack, handing Spader his phone. "A car dropped Barry and Gloria off early Thursday morning prior to the moving van showing up. A different car pulled up early yesterday morning to pick up Barry. A third car arrived for Gloria an hour later. No sign of Gloria returning home yesterday or earlier today."

"Which means she didn't kill her husband," said Nick.

"Not necessarily," said Spader.

"Huh?" Nick's confused expression suggested he thought the detective had misplaced his logic gene. "How could she have killed him if she wasn't home?"

"She may have returned at any point, cutting through neighbors' yards to enter the house through the back door. We'll check security cameras from nearby houses."

Nick's brow furrowed. "Because she wanted to sneak back into the house to kill him?"

"Possibly, but she may have had another reason," I said.

"Like?"

"I don't know, Nick. Maybe she was sneaking his birthday present into the house."

"Really, Mom?" The look he tossed me spoke volumes—all compliments of the sarcasm gene he'd inherited from me. "Maybe she killed him because she found out he planned to kill her to get his hands on all that money."

"That would certainly be a motive," mumbled Spader as he continued to study the videos, then added, "Kind of hard to live in the suburbs without wheels."

"Not with the availability of Uber and Lyft," said Zack. "Given the amount of drinking we noticed, maybe they've both had their licenses revoked."

"Westfield PD didn't find any evidence of recent prior arrests for the victim when he was booked Friday," said Spader. "There were a handful of misdemeanors from years ago, though. I'll have someone do a deeper dive."

His phone dinged with a text. After a quick glance, he said, "The crime scene unit is finishing up." He pushed his chair back and stood. "Thank you, once again, for both your hospitality and cooperation."

"Let us know if we can be of further help," said Zack.

As we crossed the living room to accompany Spader to the front door, I saw the first news van pull up to the curb. Another quickly followed. Then a third. A fourth. And a fifth. ABC, NBC, CBS, Fox, and CNN. I groaned. "Hail, hail, the gang's all here." Any moment our doorbell would start ringing. And ringing. And ringing.

I checked my phone. Sometime within the next ten minutes, my mother would receive a breaking news alert from one of the networks and learn of the latest murder on our street. I braced myself for the blistering lecture and guilt trip to come. I'm not sure which is worse. Either way, it all came down to each murder somehow being Karl's fault, even if he'd been dead a year and a half. And if not Karl, then Lucille. And by extension, mine for having married Dead Louse of a Spouse and not kicking Lucille out on her commie tush after he died.

Zack looped his arm around my shoulders and led me away from the window. "Any chance you can disperse the vultures?" he asked Spader.

I wasn't sure whether the look Spader gave me was one of understanding or sympathy. Maybe a combination of both. "The best I can do is tell them that you won't have any comment now or in the future. That they're wasting their time and better stay off your property if they don't want a citation for trespassing. I'll also make sure the uniformed officers know to enforce the no trespassing."

"That works," I said. "Thanks."

"My pleasure." He patted his stomach. "Consider it payment for saving me from a breakfast of mediocre donuts and cop shop coffee."

To avoid the press spotting us, Zack and I hung back as Spader exited and closed the door behind him. I returned to the living room and stood off to the side where I had a bird's eye view of the front yard but remained hidden from detection by anyone peering toward the windows.

Good to his word, I watched as Spader laid down the law to the mic-holding gaggle of reporters and the camera crews that blocked his path as he tried to make his way toward the street. Some argued with him, but he held his ground, and they eventually gave up theirs, moving off our lawn and onto the sidewalk.

Before crossing to the McMansion, Spader also spoke to a couple of Westfield's finest. When he gestured toward our lawn, both officers nodded. Message delivered, received, and understood.

I followed Zack toward the kitchen and entered to find Nick

had already placed the breakfast dishes on the counter and started to load the dishwasher. I had taken only a step toward the sink to help with the remaining cleanup when my phone rang.

A check of the screen confirmed my suspicion. At least one of the major TV networks had broken a speed record. "Good morning, Mama."

"What's so good about another murder on your street?"

"That I'm in no way connected to it?"

"Honesty, Anastasia. It happened mere feet from your front door. That's a connection."

"An extremely tenuous one. I never met the man. He moved in three days ago."

"Then why was that detective filmed leaving your house?"

"He joined us for breakfast."

Mama's voice grew shrill. "Do you think I was born yesterday? I don't appreciate your sarcasm."

"It wasn't sarcasm, Mama. Detective Spader often joins us for meals. You know that."

"Only when he's there on police business."

"Not always."

"I'm not stupid. Stop lying to me. I want to know what you've gotten yourself into this time."

Mama was shouting so loudly that I hadn't had to place the call on speaker for Zack and Nick to hear every word. Nick offered me an eye roll. As much as he loved his grandmother, she could try a saint's patience.

Zack took the phone from my hand. "Flora, your daughter is telling you the truth. If you want to hear what we know, which isn't much at this point, we'll tell you over dinner this evening. For now, you have nothing to worry about."

Maybe not the best choice of words. Mama immediately zeroed in on them, her voice climbing another two octaves. "*For now?* What does that mean?"

"It means you should stop looking at your news feeds and go about your day. We'll pick you up at six." Before she could argue further, he ended the call.

"There," he said, handing the phone back to me. "Problem solved."

I raised an eyebrow. "For now?"

"For now."

Zack had the right idea, though. Mama, a member of the Daughters of the American Revolution and a woman who claimed descent from Russian nobility, placed protocol and decorum high on her list of righteous virtues. Unlike my mother-in-law, she'd never make a scene in public. However, she felt no such compunction on the phone or in the privacy of our home. To avoid her ranting and raving, it was best to relate the tale of the Stoop Sitters inside a crowded restaurant filled with the chatter of other diners. Preferably a restaurant far from Westfield where we'd have little chance of running into anyone we knew.

For an added layer of protection, Zack decided to invite Shane Lambert to join us. Mama liked Shane. His inclusion would guarantee she'd behave in her most ladylike manner.

Zack caught Shane up on events since we'd dropped him at his home on Thursday and asked that Shane pick us up in front of Rosalie Schneider's home to avoid any reporters who might still be camped in front of our house late this afternoon.

That required a phone call to Rosalie to explain why we'd be traipsing through her property yet again. This wouldn't be the first time I did so to duck the press. The poor woman was beginning to think our town had turned into a war zone. I couldn't blame her.

Nick had the day off and made plans to spend the afternoon at the pool with friends, then settle in for pizza and a pre-season football game on TV. It must be a slow news day because none of the press had so far given up and departed. When he left shortly after lunch, he also ducked out the back door to cut through the azalea bushes into Rosalie's yard.

Zack and I eventually headed up to the office above the garage to spend the remainder of the afternoon catching up on work. We were both on deadline and running behind. A regular occurrence for me, unusual for him, but I was probably to blame, thanks to the previous dead body on our street last month.

Ralph and Leonard joined us with Ralph settling onto his parrot perch, and Leonard immediately falling asleep under the coffee table.

An hour later, Cloris called. She took a page from Spader's playbook and dispensed with any greeting. "What in the world is going on?"

"Not much."

"Really? Do you not know that someone else on your street was murdered?"

"It's kind of hard to ignore with all the press and police milling around outside."

"Spill!"

So I spilled.

After I'd finished, she said, "I think I once told you that when I grow up, I want to be you. I take it back."

I laughed. "In what context? You want my debt? My communist mother-in-law? All the dead bodies I trip over? Help yourself."

"I think it had something to do with having a husband like yours, but if he comes with all that baggage, forget it."

"I take it Gregg isn't within earshot?"

"Don't get me wrong. I love my husband, but he's a mere mortal. You're married to a god."

"I'll tell the god you said so. See you at work tomorrow."

Before she hung up, Cloris added, "Do your BFF a favor, please? Promise me you'll keep out of trouble until then. No more dead bodies today."

"I promise."

I ended the call and decided a glass of wine was in order. Like magic, one appeared in front of me. "From your god," said Zack, grinning ear to ear. "You should consider turning the volume down on your phone if you want some privacy. The people who call you lately are prone to shouting."

~*~

At six o'clock, we arrived at Mama's condo to find her waiting outside, arms crossed, the toe of one Ferragamo tapping her impatience. Finding us in a vehicle not our own, a look of confusion crossed her face. It immediately segued into displeasure before she recovered and formed a tight smile.

Zack jumped out of the front passenger seat and helped her step into the back of Shane's SUV. She skewered me with a look that spoke volumes. "I didn't realize Shane was joining us this evening."

Translation: She had planned to harangue me on the ride to the restaurant but now realized I'd outfoxed her.

Mama being Mama, though, without taking a beat, she resurrected her Miss Manners demeanor, reached across the seat to place her hand on Shane's shoulder, and asked, "How are you, Shane?"

"Getting used to an empty house, Flora."

Mama offered a dramatic sigh. "I remember what that's like."

I decided not to remind her that when I left for college, she had my father to console her. Now that Sophie was a freshman at Harvard, Shane was alone in the house without even a goldfish for a companion.

Instead, I tried for some small talk, a conversational talent I've never mastered. Mama wasn't buying it. Eventually, I gave up. Maybe this dinner wasn't such a great idea. In hindsight, I should have opted for Mama erupting into a ranting and raving tirade in the comfort of my own home. She'd get it out of her system, and I wouldn't have to deal with an evening of passive-aggressive manipulation from a woman who had perfected the art.

Zack had made reservations at a steakhouse in Bernardsville. Sixteen miles and more than a half hour from Westfield, the chances of running into anyone we knew were slim to none.

The moment the maître d seated us, Mama dropped her passive-aggressiveness and segued into full-fledged Flora demand mode. She speared me with a look that had once caused me to cower during my childhood and teen years. "Out with it, Anastasia."

I was no longer a child, or a teen, and I held my ground. Besides, this conversation required an extremely large and potent margarita. "Let's order first so we're not interrupted."

Mama huffed. "Fine." She grabbed her menu and buried her face in it.

Zack squeezed my thigh, leaned his head toward my ear, and whispered soft enough that Mama couldn't possibly hear him,

"Whatever you plan to order, better make it a double."

That would be a double margarita and a double helping of mile-high chocolate fudge cake. With whipped cream, chocolate chips, hot fudge sauce, and at least three maraschino cherries. Nothing less would get me through this evening.

Across the table, Shane offered me a look that either offered compassion or pity. I wasn't sure which.

At Mama's insistence, the waiter took both our drink and meal orders at the same time. Once he returned with our beverages and salads, Mama said, "I've waited long enough, Anastasia. I know when you're stalling. Tell me everything that happened, and you'd better not leave anything out."

I began by telling her about Mr. and Mrs. Stoop Sitter and their odd behavior. I moved on to what Robyn had discovered online, the fight between Gloria and Tonya, the melee at the street fair, and a bruised and bloodied Barry escorted home by the police. Her expression told me she didn't believe a word of what I'd said. "You're making this up."

"I wish I were, Mama, but if you don't believe me, ask Ira."

"What's Ira got to do with it?"

"He and his new girlfriend witnessed some of it," said Zack.

"And," I added, "it turns out his girlfriend was once briefly married to the guy."

Mama speared a cherry tomato and popped it into her mouth. She said nothing until she'd chewed and swallowed it because Mama would never do anything as uncouth as talk around a mouthful of food. "Let's say for argument's sake that I believe you, dear."

Which meant she still didn't. She stabbed a forkful of lettuce. "What does any of that have to do with someone being murdered across the street from you?"

"That's the guy who was murdered, Mama."

The fork froze halfway to her lips. "Oh." She said nothing for a moment, her face growing thoughtful. "Well, it's obvious his wife killed him. Why haven't the police arrested her?"

"So far they have no proof she killed him."

"Why not?"

"For one thing, she's missing."

Mama slammed her fork onto her salad plate, the sound loud enough for a few heads to turn our way. Her voice rose above the din of the other diners. "So once again, you have a killer on the loose in your neighborhood, and I suppose that detective has lured you into helping him again."

"Shh! Lower your voice, Mama. I'm not involved. I told you earlier, I've never even met the man or his wife."

Tears gathered at the corners of her eyes, and she sniffed them back. "When have you ever let that stop you, Anastasia?"

"Anastasia?"

I scanned the room, hoping another Anastasia was dining at the same restaurant and would respond. When we'd arrived, the table behind us had been empty. No longer. As I twisted to face behind me, I locked eyes with one of my newest coworkers.

SIX

What were the odds? Given my life? Even if we'd traveled as far as Philadelphia for dinner, I should have known we'd bump into someone I knew. Once again, the God of Irony had yanked my chain. I suppose I should feel grateful I wasn't confronted by one of the reporters from earlier in the day.

Not that running into Danica Magee was much better. Although a pleasant enough addition to our staff, the thirty-something young woman from the Midwest had apparently been raised by helicopter parents and was having difficulty adjusting to life in New Jersey.

From her reaction to learning I'd discovered several murder victims, including two at work, you'd think crime was nonexistent in Nebraska. Yet, as freaked out as she'd gotten over the workplace murders, she also wanted to know if anyone had ever spied any ghosts in the building. Because, strange as it sounded, Danica Magee believed in ghosts and yearned to come face to face with one. Go figure.

Danica was the editorial director of Creativity Books, which specialized in crafts, decorating, and culinary publications. The company had recently merged with us after Hugo Reynolds-Alsopp, our former owner, wrested back control of what was left of his magazine publishing company from the clutches of Trimedia. Both *American Woman* and Creativity Books now fell under the umbrella of Reynolds-Alsopp Media.

As part of the merger, Cloris and I, along with our decorating editor Jeanie Sims, were tasked with creating a series of books featuring updated versions of crafts, recipes, and décor from each decade since the launch of *American Woman* in the nineteen-sixties.

Danica rose, followed by the man sharing her table. Both traveled the short distance to our table. After I scraped my jaw off the floor, I took the hint and introduced them to Zack, my mother, and Shane.

Danica, in turn, introduced her dinner companion, a man who appeared old enough to be her father. It turned out he was. "Dad flew in to help me get settled in my new apartment."

She turned back to her father and said, "Anastasia is the coworker I told you about, the one who keeps finding dead bodies."

He eyed me with a mix of awe and trepidation, then asked, "But no ghosts?"

"None." The fascination must run in the family. "But I told Danica if I ever run into Casper, she'll be the first to know."

I had no idea how much of the conversation between my mother and me they'd overheard. I didn't want to know, but they continued to hover, as if hoping to hear more. Luckily, at that moment the waiter arrived with our main courses. Danica and her father took the hint and returned to their seats.

I leaned across the table and spoke slightly above a whisper. "Mama, I'd appreciate tabling the previous conversation. At this point, you now know as much as we do. There's nothing more to discuss."

Her lower lip trembled. "But—"

Zack cut her off. "You have nothing to worry about, Flora. We're not involved, and we won't be involved. That's the end of it."

She directed a steely-eyed glare at him. "You just make sure of that, Zachary. You keep my daughter safe, or you'll answer to me."

Issuing hollow threats served no purpose. What would Mama do? Cut Zack from her Christmas card list? However, I knew her anger stemmed from her fear of losing me. I reached across the table, clasped her hand, and gave it a comforting squeeze. "You know you can trust Zack, Mama."

She narrowed her eyes at him, then shifted to spear me with the same skeptical look. "Really? This coming from the woman who still believes her husband is a government spy, no matter how often he denies it? Where's your trust?"

Beside me, Zack huffed out a loud sign of frustration. Across the table Shane fought to stifle a chuckle. I withdrew my hand, grabbed my glass, and downed the remainder of my first margarita in one long guzzle. Afterward, I raised the empty glass and motioned to the waiter for another.

I then tried my best to salvage the evening. "Mama, Zack is not a spy. It's my way of teasing him. He knows that. And so should you." But my words sounded hollow, even to my own ears, because truthfully, I still had my doubts.

Zack leaned over and whispered in my ear. "Nice try." I knew sarcasm when I heard it. After all, I practically invented the verbal art.

The remainder of dinner passed in more silence than conversation. Most of the sounds issuing forth from our table came from utensils clicking against plates. When the waiter arrived to clear our dishes and present the dessert menus, I placed a double order for chocolate cake with hot fudge, chocolate chips, whip cream, and extra cherries to go. I had no intention of sharing it with anyone.

Since Danica and her father arrived after us, they were still eating their dinner when we rose to leave. To avoid further conversation about ghosts and dead bodies, I waved and offered her a cheery, "See you tomorrow," as I practically dashed past their table to the exit.

~*~

Monday morning, Cloris and I were in the break room, enjoying pineapple macadamia muffins and coffee. As I caught her up on the remainder of my weekend, Danica entered. I figured she wanted more details about the murder across the street, but she surprised me by asking, "Who was that good-looking guy with you last night?"

Caught off-guard, I stammered, "Uhm...my husband?"

She giggled. "Not him. The other one. The guy seated next to your mother. Dane? Lane?"

"Shane."

"Right. Is your mother dating him?"

Cloris and I exchanged double takes while I wrapped my mind around the unexpected direction of this conversation. I'd prepared myself for something quite different.

Shane's rugged, weathered good looks came from years of

working outdoor construction while putting himself through college. Although only in his mid-thirties, he looked much older. Pour a batter of half Hugh Laurie and half Daniel Craig into a cake pan, stick it in the oven, and you'd baked up Shane Lambert.

On the other hand, Mama looked a good ten to fifteen years younger than sixty-six. She often pretended that I was her younger sister. Always on the prowl for her next husband, she had even briefly batted her cougar eyelashes in Shane's direction when they first met. He quickly made it clear he wasn't interested in a reverse May/December relationship. I could see why Danica might think the two were dating.

"No, Mama and Shane aren't dating. He's a bit young for her." I studied Danica as my mind raced. On the one hand, Shane needed to meet someone. The guy was lonely. Now that Sophie was off to college, he should start thinking about himself. But did I want to fix him up with a coworker? What if it didn't work out?

Danica dropped into one of the seats around the table, grabbed a muffin, and began picking at it. "I know no one here other than coworkers," she said, "and workplace romances are never a good idea."

"What about online dating?" asked Cloris.

Danica pulled a face. "Been there, done that, won't do it again."

I got right to the heart of the situation and blurted out, "Are you asking me to fix you up with Shane?" Subtlety has never been one of my strong suits.

Danica shrugged and trapped me with what could only be described as puppy dog eyes. "I'm lonely. I miss my friends in Nebraska. It would be nice to go out to dinner or a movie with someone now and then, even if that someone is a bit older."

I headed to the counter to start a fresh pot of coffee. "Shane is much younger than he looks."

Her face perked up, her voice growing eager. "Really? How old is he?"

"Mid-thirties."

She once again attacked me with those wide puppy dog eyes of hers. Combined with her guileless freckle-face, Danica could be the poster child for any Midwestern County fair. She probably carved a mean butter cow. It suddenly hit me that she might be perfect for Shane. Still, I felt uncomfortable playing Yente the Matchmaker.

Luckily, Cloris stepped in with the perfect suggestion. As she grabbed the cream from the mini fridge, she said, "Weren't you planning to host a party now that the renovations on your house are complete?"

No, I'd never considered doing any such thing, but Cloris was a genius. Hosting a party with several dozen friends and coworkers provided an opportunity for nature to take its course without creating an awkward situation for any of us. If Danica and Shane hit it off, that was entirely up to them. And if nature didn't cooperate, so be it. No one could blame me.

I corralled my inner actress and said, "As a matter of fact, I had decided on sometime over Labor Day weekend."

Danica grinned from ear to ear. She jumped out of her seat and rocketed toward me, her arms extended, ready to embrace me in a huge bear hug. Luckily, before she got within arm's length, my phone rang. I held up one hand to ward off the hug. The other reached for my phone.

Danica is nice enough, and someday we may become close friends, but we'd known each other less than two months. I reserve workplace hugs for my BFF Cloris. After all, she'd previously saved my life. Literally. I'd only agreed to play quasi-matchmaker by hosting a party.

I waved good-bye to Danica and Cloris, stepped from the break room, and answered my phone. "Good morning, Detective. Making any progress?"

"As a matter of fact, I wanted to let you know you were right about one of those other Glorias listed in the MVC database being Barry's wife. They moved from Roselle Park. An older model Ford Mustang is registered in her name. No vehicle registered in the deceased's name. No current driver's license, either."

"That could be a result of the head trauma he sustained from the motorcycle accident."

"Looks that way. We've put out a BOLO on her. Hopefully, we'll have her brought in for questioning soon."

"Then what?"

"She either gives us permission to search the home for clues as to who killed her husband, or we get a search warrant."

"I don't think she killed him. What would be her motive?"

"Maybe Nick is right. She might've decided to kill him before he killed her."

"My gut tells me there's more to this killing than an unhappy marriage. Unlike murder, divorce doesn't run the risk of a prison sentence."

"And that's why we're leaving no stone unturned. You never know what kind of vermin will crawl out from underneath."

"Good to hear. By the way, are you off any time over Labor Day?"

"Why? You inviting me to a cookout?"

"Something like that. I've agreed to host a party."

"I'm on call Saturday and Monday. Supposed to be off Sunday, assuming you don't discover anymore dead bodies that day."

"Surely, I'm not the only county resident who's had the misfortune of stumbling upon a murder scene."

"True, but you hold the top spot."

"Gee, I always wanted to be number one at something. I just never thought it would be in the Dead Body Derby."

He barked out a huge laugh. "Gotta run. I'm sure I'll see you soon."

Hopefully, not due to another corpse.

I reentered the break room as the last drip of brew dropped into the carafe, refilled my mug, and headed to my cubicle. While my computer fired up, I called Zack. "Looks like we're hosting a Labor Day Party a week from Sunday."

"You don't sound thrilled at the prospect. Care to explain?"

I clued him in on how Danica blindsided me with her request and how Cloris stepped in to bail me out of a Yente the Matchmaker gig.

"Tell Cloris, since it was her idea, she's supplying the desserts."

"You don't mind?"

"Of course not. Should be fun."

"Assuming anyone wants to risk stepping onto our street."

"Let's hope Spader has the killer caught by then."

"If not, he can provide protection. I've already invited him." I went on to tell Zack of my phone call with the detective. "He's issued an all-points bulletin on Gloria."

~*~

Having seen more than my share of crime scenes and their aftermath the last year and a half, I recognized a stakeout when I came across one. Unmarked police vehicles might as well have flashing neon signs on their roofs. In my opinion, law enforcement should drive around in a variety of makes, models, and colors to better blend into traffic and neighborhoods. As far as I was concerned, men (or women) dressed in black suits and hunkered down in black sedans and SUVs screamed cops, funerals, or Mafioso. Well, maybe not Mafioso women. They tend to dress more flamboyantly.

I spotted several unmarked cars as I turned onto my street, including one at the corner, one parked in front of my next-door neighbor's house, and one two doors down on the far side of the McMansion. No doubt, there were others on the street behind us in case Gloria cut through a neighbor's yard to her back door.

I wondered if Spader had intel that she was on the move and headed home. He'd certainly pulled out all the stops, considering how he'd bemoaned a constant lack of manpower lately. Maybe he'd brought in officers from neighboring towns.

I pulled into the driveway behind Zack's Boxster and the Jeep Nick had inherited from his brother but was still several months shy of legally driving, now that Alex was in school up in Boston.

As I stepped from the Jetta, I caught sight of a drone hovering overhead. Had Spader also authorized arial surveillance? Unless he had conclusive information that Gloria had murdered her husband, that seemed like overkill to me. No pun intended.

I was halfway to my front door when a classic red Mustang convertible drove down the street and turned into the McMansion driveway. I watched as Gloria killed the engine, stepped from behind the wheel, and removed a brown paper grocery bag from the trunk.

Suddenly, the three stakeout vehicles, lights now flashing, converged and boxed in the Mustang. Gloria appeared startled, then confused. When the officers jumped from their vehicles, guns drawn, she screamed. "Don't shoot!"

"Drop the bag. Hands in the air," demanded one officer.

She started to bend her knees to place the grocery bag on the ground, but the officer yelled, "I said drop it. Hands in the air."

Halfway squatting, she opened her arms, letting the bag slide to the ground. As it toppled over, assorted food items spilled out. A bottle of wine and several cans rolled down the driveway, landing in the gutter. Boxes of cereal and cookies and bags of chips and pretzels remained scattered around her feet.

Gloria kept her upper arms plastered to her torso, raising them from her elbows. A key fob dangled from one hand. Her purse hung on her shoulder.

"All of it. Now!" ordered the cop. "Keys and purse. Hands over your head. Don't make me tell you again."

She opened her palm, and the keys fell from her hand. With her arms still only partially raised, she dipped her shoulder until the purse strap slid into the crook of her arm. At that point she seemed confused as to how to proceed. Finally, she pleaded, "I need to move my arm to get my purse off."

"Slowly. No sudden moves."

She nodded, then lowered her arm to let the purse fall to the driveway. Still crouching, she then raised both arms above her head.

Her entire body shook. Fear etched across her face. Her jaw flapped open and closed, but no words came out. At least none that I could hear. The poor woman looked like she'd collapse into a quivering mass at any moment.

While one officer remained with his gun trained on her, a second grabbed her arms, yanked her to a standing positioned, then cuffed her behind her back. The third cop retrieved her purse and keys but made no attempt to corral the groceries.

One officer stood with his back to me but appeared to be speaking to her.

She shook her head violently. "He's dead? How?" Her eyes widened as she stared at the officer. "Murdered? "No! I didn't kill him! I wasn't even here. You have to believe me."

Obviously, they didn't. One of the other officers then spoke to her, presumably conveying her Miranda rights. When he'd finished, she stared in disbelief at each in turn before finally lowering her head and nodding. The officer who had cuffed her then escorted her to one of the vehicles and placed her in the back seat.

Within seconds, all three officers slid behind the steering wheels of their vehicles and drove off.

I walked across the street, collected the bottle of wine and cans of chili, salsa, and Spam, and carried them to where the brown paper bag lay discarded on the driveway. After depositing the wine and cans in the bag, I added the other items. On the off chance that Gloria quickly made bail, I left the bag on her stoop.

Zack opened our front door before I reached it. "What was that all about?"

"How much did you witness?"

"Just you placing a grocery bag at Gloria's front door." He eyed the Mustang. "Is she home?"

"She was for about a minute before the cops hauled her off in handcuffs. Pour me a glass of wine, and I'll tell you all about it."

I followed him into the kitchen where a bottle wine and two glasses already waited on the island. "I'm surprised you and Nick didn't hear anything."

Zack poured two glasses of Sauvignon Blanc and handed me

one. "Nick is blasting evil alien warlords across the universe. I was in the basement trying to figure out why your ancient washing machine suddenly decided to give up the ghost."

"Did you figure it out?"

"The motor's shot. We're buying a new one after dinner."

"Ouch!" I downed my wine to numb the pain of a major household expense.

Zack refilled my glass. "Don't worry about it."

"Easy for you to say."

"Yes, it is. We're married now. I'm paying for it. Along with a new dryer because that will probably go next. I should have thought to include them when I purchased the new kitchen appliances."

I still had trouble coming to terms with Zack paying the bulk of our household expenses. He'd also offered on numerous occasions to pay off the remainder of my Karl-induced debt, but I drew the line at that. Zack already did more than his share, and my guilt runneth over. He wasn't responsible for what Karl had done to me and our kids.

However, now that most of my salary went to paying down the remaining debt, I was making considerable headway. Once I finally paid off the last outstanding bills, I'd insist on contributing more to household expenses.

He broke into my thoughts. "Are you going to tell me what happened across the street?"

I shrugged. "Not much to tell, really. As soon as I turned onto the street, I realized Spader had a stakeout in progress. I told you he'd issued a BOLO earlier. He must have known Gloria was on her way home. Right after I pulled into the driveway, she drove up in that Mustang. Given her screams and loud denial, I assume they arrested her for murdering her husband. The whole thing seemed extremely heavy-handed, considering Spader had said he only wanted her brought in for questioning."

"Looks like he discovered some incriminating evidence that pointed to her."

~*~

I consider appliance shopping as bad as car shopping. Too many choices make my head spin. It's one thing to dither about which brand of shampoo or dog food to buy. If the shampoo leaves my hair frizzy or Leonard turns his nose up at the kibble, I'm only out a few dollars. Not so with big ticket items.

The last thing I wanted to do this evening was figure out which make and model washer and dryer to purchase. However, after pronouncing my nearly twenty-two-year-old washing machine dead, Zack had done some research and narrowed the choices down to two, both highly rated from multiple sources, priced within a few dollars of each other, and in stock at the nearest appliance center. My hero!

Shortly after finishing dinner, I stood in the washer and dryer aisle, Option One to my left, Option Two to my right. I turned to the saleswoman helping us. "Give me a reason not to go with the eeny-meeny-miny-moe method."

She placed her hand on the washer to my left. "This manufacturer offers a slightly better warranty."

"Done," I said.

Zack whipped out his credit card. After scheduling delivery, we exited the store as the sun began to set.

We arrived home to find the Crime Scene Unit, several patrol cars, and Detective Spader's unmarked vehicle parked on our street.

SEVEN

The detective stood on the sidewalk in front of the McMansion. Much to my surprise, Gloria stood beside him.

As we exited Zack's Boxster, his phone dinged an incoming text. He glanced down at the screen, then across the street. In the waning light I noticed Spader looking our way. Zack caught his eye and nodded.

"What's up?" I asked.

"Not sure but Spader said he'd stop by as soon as his team finishes up the search."

I glanced back across the street, zeroing in on Gloria. As much as I knew about police procedures after constantly tripping over dead bodies and getting sucked into multiple murder investigations, there was still much I didn't know. However, I thought it odd that the police would bring someone arrested for murder less than three hours ago back to the crime scene during the execution of a search warrant. Even odder still that she wasn't handcuffed.

If Gloria had made bail, shouldn't her attorney accompany her during the search to make sure she didn't inadvertently incriminate herself? What defense attorney in his right mind would allow the detective assigned to the case unrestricted access to his client?

Was it possible Gloria hadn't secured an attorney? And if not, why not?

Or did Spader jump the gun in arresting her? I didn't think he'd make such a rookie mistake. The guy was methodical to a fault. All his little duckies always had to line up in military precision before he'd move to make an arrest.

Twilight had set in, but from what I could see as the sky grew darker, Gloria wasn't seething as she stood next to Spader. Nor did she look worried. Although neither spoke to the other, nothing about their body language suggested any friction between the two. Gloria's posture was neither ramrod stiff nor slouched but somewhere in-between.

Spader looked the way he always did, a still slightly overweight and more than slightly overworked detective in a rumpled dark suit.

~*~

I didn't have long to wait for answers. Fifteen minutes after we arrived home, our doorbell rang. Zack ushered Spader inside and waved toward the living room. "Have a seat. Care for something to drink?"

Spader consulted his watch before settling into one of the chairs opposite the coffee table. "I'm officially off duty. An ice-cold beer would hit the spot. The humidity is brutal this evening."

"For heaven's sake," I said, curling up on the sofa. "Do you need an invitation? Take off your jacket and roll up your sleeves."

He grinned. "Don't mind if I do." He removed his notepad and a pen from his jacket pocket and placed them on the side table before hanging his jacket on the back of the chair. Then he loosened his tie, unbuttoned his cuffs, and rolled his sleeves toward his elbows.

Zack returned with two bottles of beer and a chilled glass of white wine for me, then joined me on the sofa. I allowed Spader to take a large pull of his beer before I asked the question uppermost on my mind. "I thought you were only bringing Gloria in for questioning. What changed?"

"Nothing."

My wide-eyed stare conveyed my disbelief. "I witnessed her arrest. It wasn't pretty. Three officers drew their guns on her in the driveway. Which was totally unnecessary. She posed no threat to them."

Spader grimaced. "I know. Chalk it up to a major communications SNAFU."

I pressed. "She didn't kill her husband, did she?"

Spader inhaled, then released a huge rush of air. "No, Mrs. Barnes. Once again, you were right. The poor woman had no idea he was dead."

"I figured as much from what I saw and heard."

Spader reached for his notepad and pen. "Tell me what you observed."

"Does it matter now?" I asked.

"It might."

"Are you worried she'll sue for false arrest?" asked Zack.

Before answering, Spader grabbed the beer bottle and took another swig. He scowled as he deposited the bottle back on the coaster. "Unfortunately, that's always a possibility."

With his pen poised to begin taking notes, I related what I'd observed earlier this evening. When I'd finished, I waved toward him. "Your turn."

Spader first drained his beer. "Gloria Forester has an ironclad alibi. She dropped her car off for repairs first thing Thursday morning before the movers arrived. She said someone had backed into it in their apartment complex parking lot sometime Wednesday night. Smash and run."

"Did she file a police report?" asked Zack.

"No, but she did report it to her insurance company. We have confirmation from both the insurer and the body shop. But here's where it gets interesting. The guy I spoke with at the body shop said he believes the damage was from vandalism, not one car backing into another."

"How so?" I asked.

"Both rear lights were smashed, but there was no other damage to the back of the vehicle."

"Sounds like someone used a baseball bat or tire iron," said Zack.

"Exactly my thought," said Spader. "Then late Friday Gloria received a call from the summer camp her son is attending in the Catskills. The kid fell off a horse and sustained a concussion."

I cringed. Talk about bad Karma. "Is he okay?"

"He's fine. The concussion was minor, but Gloria freaked out. As soon as the body shop opened Saturday morning, she picked up the Mustang and drove to the camp. She stayed overnight at a motel, then returned home earlier this evening. Her alibi checks out. I not only spoke to the camp director, but she showed me her gas, food, and motel receipts. EasyPass surveillance footage also captured her Mustang both ways."

"There was no kid with her when she arrived home," I said.

"He insisted on staying at camp. I spoke with both the camp director and the hospital. Her son never lost consciousness, but they kept him overnight Friday for observation. As an added precaution, he spent Saturday night in the camp infirmary. The camp has a nurse on staff and a doctor on call. By Sunday, the kid was fine, so Gloria allowed him to stay."

"No one ever contacted her about her husband?" asked Zack.

Spader shook his head. "She learned of his murder when she was arrested. There was no communication between them Saturday or Sunday. She heard about the fight at the street fair and his arrest from me."

"How did she react?" I asked.

"Neither surprised her. She said he developed anger issues after sustaining a head injury ten years ago. He sometimes picks fights with people for no reason but only when he forgets to take his meds."

"Did he ever take his anger out on his family?" asked Zack.

"Not according to his wife. He broke a lot of glasses and plates over the years until she switched to plastic, and once destroyed a TV when his team lost. For the most part, though, he zeroed in on inanimate objects."

"Like Mustang taillights?" I asked.

"The thought had occurred to me," said Spader.

That probably also explained the worn furniture the movers had delivered to a million-dollar-plus home.

"No one Sumner assaulted ever pressed charges?" asked Zack.

"If anyone had, the charges were dropped. We couldn't find any recent records."

"Don't you find that strange?" I asked.

"I do. I also found it strange that she didn't mention the motorcycle accident until I pressed her on the nature of his head trauma. She finally admitted what had happened when I accused her of hiding something."

I shook my head. "She's still hiding something. Rowena told us he always had anger issues."

"Assuming Rowena isn't hiding something," said Spader. "I haven't had a chance to interview her yet."

"Victims of abuse are often in denial and cover up for their abusers," said Zack.

Ralph flew in from the kitchen. He alighted on Zack's shoulder, let out a loud squawk, then said, "*In thine own person answer thy abuse. Henry the Sixth, Part Two.* Act Two, Scene One."

As Zack fed Ralph a sunflower seed, Spader said, "I wouldn't be surprised if someday that bird solves a crime for me."

I eyed Ralph. "Too bad he wasn't looking out the window Saturday night," I said, then asked, "Did Gloria show any outward signs of abuse?"

"Not that I noticed," said Spader. "In any case, we checked. Neither she nor their son ever showed up at a local hospital or urgent care with injuries that would raise suspicions. By law, health care providers are required to report suspected abuse."

I was impressed. Spader had collected quite a bit of information in a few short hours, especially considering the county staffing shortage.

As I sipped my wine, I thought back to what I'd observed of Mr. and Mrs. Stoop Sitter from the moment they'd moved in across the street four days ago. "They certainly exhibited odd behavior, but that alone doesn't indicate an abusive marriage. By any chance, did you ask her about his dirt mowing obsession?"

"I did," said Spader. "After she brought up the behavioral changes that occurred following the motorcycle accident. She said she knew it was weird, but the routine calmed him, and the doctors told her it was a harmless outlet."

I stared into my wine glass. "Unlike gambling."

When I lifted my head, I found both Zack and Spader staring at me. Had I uttered those words out loud? Their expressions indicated I had. I shrugged an apology. "Some wounds take longer to heal."

Zack reached over and squeezed my hand. "Perfectly understandable."

"And now," I said, moving the conversation back away from me, "that poor woman has to return to the Catskills to tell her son his father is dead." I knew what that was like, too.

"Since you haven't mentioned it," said Zack, "can we assume nothing turned up in the search of their home?"

"Nothing of much interest. We already had the victim's phone. It was in his pocket when he was killed and wasn't password protected."

"That's strange," I said. Or stupid. Who doesn't password protect their phone?

"His wife said he had a hard time remembering even the simplest of passwords, but when pressed, she admitted she monitored his calls and search history."

I scowled. "How trusting of her. Is that how she found out about Tonya?"

Spader nodded. "The husband had anger issues. The wife has trust issues. They made for quite the dysfunctional couple."

As much as I felt sorry for Gloria and glad she hadn't killed her husband, I wondered if she was still somehow culpable in his death. "You've established Gloria couldn't have kill her husband," I said, "but given their toxic marriage, have you considered the possibility that she hired someone to kill him? She has the money."

"I'm one step ahead of you," said Spader. "First thing tomorrow morning we're looking into her finances to see if any large sums, other than the new house and moving expenses, have been withdrawn from her bank accounts or the trust."

"Or maybe someone killed him for another reason," I suggested. "One that didn't involve any payment. Who's to say Gloria wasn't also having an affair, and her lover decided to eliminate her husband?"

"Another stone we're looking under," said Spader. "Something interesting might pop up when IT finishes going through her phone. We also have more interviews to conduct and leads to track down from Saturday's melee at the park. That bayonet didn't drop from the sky into the victim's heart. It belongs to someone."

"And it's not a weapon anyone other than a reenactor or collector would own," I said. "Are you sure it didn't belong to Barry?"

"We found his bayonet in the house on the kitchen table, along with his musket."

"He owned only one?" asked Zack.

"One musket according to his wife."

I raised an eyebrow. "And you believe her?"

Spader chuckled. "Do I look like I fell off a turnip truck, Mrs. Barnes? He owned a small collection of colonial weaponry. At this point, we have no way of telling if anything is missing. Most were still packed in sealed cartons that showed no evidence of having been opened and resealed. That's why we need to continue interviewing the other reenactors to find out what they knew about him and his collection. We can't go by the wife's statements alone. If she was in cahoots with someone, she may have given him a bayonet."

"What about fingerprints?" I asked.

"None found. Either the killer wore gloves, or he wiped the weapon clean afterwards."

"Most collectors keep documentation of their collections." said Zack.

"We haven't found anything so far," said Spader. "The team searched through all the still packed moving cartons but found nothing of any significance. Mostly household items, clothing, and lots of worthless junk."

"No computer?" I asked.

Spader shook his head and spit out a derisive laugh. "That would make my life way too easy. I suspect the kid has a laptop he took with him to camp. What kid doesn't have one these days? But Gloria claimed the only tech she and her husband owned were their phones."

I offered Spader a look I hoped came across as sympathy because I really did feel sorry for him. I'm sure whatever restful respite he'd gotten on his recent vacation had now evaporated, thanks to this case. "You have your work cut out for you, Detective. You need a clone."

"Which brings me to a request," he said.

Zack and I both eyed him suspiciously. "Regarding?" asked Zack.

"The medical examiner hasn't released the body yet, but when he does, Gloria plans a viewing and funeral. I wouldn't mind a few extra eyeballs at both if we haven't solved this case beforehand."

"We've never even met," I said. "Wouldn't that look odd?"

"She knows Nick discovered her husband's body, and that you alerted the police. Under the circumstances, I think she'd feel grateful for you paying your respects."

Zack turned to me. "How do you feel about that?"

"The question is, how do you feel about it? What if the killer shows up?"

"He probably will. That's why Detective Spader wants help keeping an eye on attendees."

I turned to Spader. "Just observation? No interaction?"

"None. I don't want you speaking with anyone other than to offer your condolences to the widow and her son. Mention nothing about the case to anyone."

"As long as it's okay with Nick."

"It's okay with me, Mom." He stepped into the living room from the foyer.

I glared at my son. "How long have you been spying on us?"

"Ever since Detective Spader arrived." He turned to the detective. "I found the body. I should offer my condolences, too. Besides, I want to help."

"I don't mind," said Spader, "as long as your mother doesn't."

My eyes shifted from Spader to Nick to Zack. "I'm not sure about this, Nick. Aren't you the kid who keeps making me promise I won't get involved in any more murders? The one who berates me every time I break that promise, whether intentional or not?"

"Face it, Mom, you're a dead body magnet. It's never going to stop, no matter how much I want it to. Besides, Zack will be there, and he's got a gun. So does Detective Spader."

"That's not the point."

"What is the point? That it's okay for you to place yourself in danger but not me? If it's safe for you to be at the funeral home, why wouldn't it be safe for me?"

I opened my mouth to answer him, but the words wouldn't come because I had none to counter his argument. Nick had already lost his father and through no fault of my own, nearly lost me on more than one occasion since Karl died. Finally, I said, "I'll discuss it with Zack later."

"What's to discuss?" asked Nick.

"Quite a bit. I'm your mother. It's my responsibility to keep you safe."

"How are you keeping me safe if you get yourself killed?"

"Nick!" The one word from Zack conveyed a stern warning.

Nick's eyes grew wide. His expression said it all. He knew he'd pushed too far and began to stammer. "I...I...I'm sorry, Mom."

Tears swam in my eyes. "It's okay, Nick."

"I...I...I think I'll take Leonard out for his evening walk."

Afraid to speak, I simply nodded.

Nick crossed the living room but stopped in front of me, bent down, and enveloped me in a huge bear hug.

"I'm sorry," said Spader after we heard Nick leave through the back door.

I waved his apology away. "It's not your fault. This has been an ongoing tug of war. Nick is right, and he's scared that something might happen to me. As much as I've promised to stay away from dead bodies, they keep showing up in my life. Even when I'm not involved, I get drawn in."

"Then I take back my request," said Spader. "I don't want to cause you more problems."

"I'm afraid the cat is out of the bag. This time Nick found the body. I understand why he wants to help. His father's duplicity robbed him of so much, and not just materially. He may not voice it, but I know at times he's struggled with a sense of hopelessness and helplessness."

How could he not? Hadn't I dealt with those same emotions countless times? Life had improved greatly, thanks to Zack, but betrayal leaves permanent scars.

I turned toward Zack. "Maybe allowing Nick to attend the viewing and funeral will offer him a sense of control."

Zack grew thoughtful for a moment before speaking. "I think we can safely assume this was a targeted murder. We're not dealing with a serial killer. No one is going to open fire in a funeral home, especially with the presence of law enforcement." He addressed Spader. "There will be other officers on scene, right?"

"Absolutely."

Zack reached for my hand. "Ultimately, it's your decision, but Nick will be safe. We all will. And hopefully, he'll wind up so bored that he'll quickly lose interest in crime-solving."

I had my doubts. Nick was too much his mother's son, but hope always springs eternal.

EIGHT

Spader phoned me as I arrived at work early Tuesday morning. The medical examiner had released Barry Sumner's body to the Gray Funeral Home in downtown Westfield. "A viewing is scheduled for Wednesday evening at seven o'clock," he said.

"Did the autopsy show anything out of the ordinary?"

"From the physical evidence at the crime scene, cause of death was evident," said Spader. "The victim drank himself into a stupor and while passed out, someone plunged the bayonet into his heart." After a pause, he asked, "Were you expecting something other than that?"

"I'm not sure. Suffocation? Signs of poisoning, perhaps?"

"There was no sign of a struggle, nor petechial hemorrhaging to indicate he was first smothered. Poisoning usually leaves observable evidence. Burns or redness around the mouth. Vomit. A chemical smell. I'm guessing whoever killed him knew him well enough to know his habits and simply bided his time until the victim passed out."

"Now all we need is to find that person."

Spader exhaled a harrumph. "Stating the obvious, Mrs. Barnes. Unfortunately, we have nothing to go on so far. With no moon that night and no lights illuminating the front of the house, your surveillance camera only picked up a dark shadow moving up the steps, then descending within seconds. Whoever it was made sure no one could identify him. Or her."

"You found no other DNA besides Barry's on the beer cans?"

"None. And no other fingerprints on the cans. The perp didn't stick around long enough to have a beer or even grab one to go. All twelve empty cans were scattered on the landing."

"None of my neighbors' security cameras picked up anything?"

"Neither of your next-door neighbors have security cameras. If there's nothing else, I've got a pile of paperwork staring at me. I'll see you tomorrow evening."

I assured the detective we'd be there, assuming he hadn't found and arrested the killer before the viewing. Then I said goodbye and hung up.

~*~

Zack, Nick, and I arrived at the funeral home a few minutes after seven o'clock Wednesday evening. The widow stood at the foot of the casket, a boy of about twelve or thirteen in an ill-fitting suit, too short for his lanky frame, fidgeted beside her. Detective Spader and a woman he quietly introduced as Officer Bella Halston, lingered in the foyer outside the viewing room. To me, they came across as a couple of plainclothes cops trying to blend in and look like an ordinary couple, but I wasn't an unbiased observer. I had insider information.

Maybe they'd fool everyone else. So far, though, we were the only ones who had arrived to pay our respects. Talk about awkward!

Gloria observed us with glassy-eyed uncertainty as we approached. I suspected she was trying to place how she knew us. Once we stood in front of her, Zack eased her puzzlement. "We're your neighbors from across the street." He rattled off our names, then added the requisite, "We're so sorry for your loss."

When recognition dawned, Gloria ignored Zack and me. Instead, she zeroed in on Nick. "You're the kid who discovered my husband's body, aren't you?"

Nick stared down at his shoes and mumbled, "I was walking my dog. He started barking and pulled me across the street."

"That was brave of you."

More curious than brave. At first, Nick had no idea Barry was dead. And none of us realized he hadn't died of natural causes until Zack took a closer look.

Nick glanced back up at Gloria and shrugged. "I did what anyone would've done." He then turned to the boy beside her. "I'm sorry about your dad. Mine died nearly two years ago."

The boy cocked his head toward Zack. "Then who's he?"

"My stepdad." Nick grinned at Zack, then added, "But he's cool."

Gloria spoke to her son, "Billy, why don't you take Nick to the refreshments table."

After the boys had exited the viewing room, Gloria frowned into the casket. Barry wore his Continental Army uniform. Several faint stains remained. I guessed blood. Someone had also attempted to mend the hole made by the bayonet. Under the circumstances, the attire seemed like an odd choice. Was Gloria making a statement by her selection of his burial attire, or was she honoring a directive spelled out in her husband's will?

Still focused on the body, she said, "I always thought he'd drink himself to death one day. I never expected this. Although, maybe I was fooling myself."

Her comment surprised me, but it also served as the sort of conversational opening I needed not to sound like a prying neighbor. "Do you have any idea who would have wanted to kill him?"

She spit out an ironic laugh. "Probably most of the people he knew. My husband had trouble controlling his mouth. Among other things. Most people didn't understand it wasn't his fault."

"How so?" asked Zack.

The corners of her mouth dipped. "Not all handicaps are visible."

I suppose this referred to the aftermath of his head injury, but both Zack and I played dumb. We weren't supposed to know about the motorcycle accident, and Gloria didn't provide any further explanation. Instead, at the sound of other people arriving, she pulled her attention away from the casket and stared across the room.

I glanced over my shoulder to follow her gaze. A group of reenactors, all in full period attire, minus muskets, had entered. Most wore the uniform of the Continental Army. A few dressed as Redcoats. Many were accompanied by women. As I turned back to Gloria, I noted her expression had hardened.

"The killer could be any one of them," she said, jutting her chin in the direction of the newcomers. "I understand they got into a brawl Saturday."

"Do you know what caused the fight?" asked Zack.

She shrugged. "Beats me. I steer clear of most of those guys. They all drink too much and play with guns. Not a great combination."

Said the widow whose breath proclaimed she was no teetotaler. But could I blame her for needing something to numb the pain of a difficult marriage that had ended both abruptly and tragically?

Her mouth curved into a scowl as she added, "I'm not too fond of their wives and girlfriends, either."

I followed her gaze and saw that Tonya had entered the room. A man decked out as a Redcoat accompanied her. I wondered if he was the guy Barry had decked to start the melee. His face still showed signs of Saturday's brawl. As did those, in various degrees, of the other men. Only Barry's face appeared unscathed, thanks to a talented mortuary cosmetologist.

Zack and I stepped to the side of the room as the growing group swarmed toward Gloria and fell into a ragged line that snaked down the side of the room. As each approached the widow, one by one they took a quick look into the coffin, then offered brief condolences. No one lingered more than a few seconds. All gave off an uncomfortable vibe, some even resentful, which made me think everyone had shown up out of obligation rather than friendship or respect.

Afterwards, they stepped into the foyer to help themselves to refreshments before returning to the viewing room and breaking into small groups.

Spader and Officer Halston had entered the room behind another group, none in costume. I was surprised to see that Rowena Milford was one of them. She either hadn't noticed me or chose to pretend she hadn't as she stepped to the end of the queue.

As the other newcomers headed toward the receiving line, Spader and Halston began to mingle. They moved casually from cluster to cluster, always standing on the periphery of each small gathering as they eavesdropped on various conversations without appearing to do so. Zack and I split up and followed their lead.

Wandering from group to group, I kept one eye on Gloria, watching as she interacted with those offering their respects. One of the men stood out to me. He appeared to be in his late sixties, about six feet tall with a full head of salt and pepper hair. Unlike the reenactors, he alone had taken Gloria's hands in his and showed genuine concern for her, lingering longer than any of the reenactors and their wives. Before moving on, he placed a chaste kiss on her cheek. Maybe he was a relative.

When Rowena reached the front of the line, I maneuvered to a spot where I could eavesdrop on her conversation with Gloria but positioned myself in a way that I remained out of her line of sight.

"I'm sorry for your loss," she said, "I'm Rowena Milford, Barry's ex-wife."

Gloria had operated on autopilot to this point. As she nodded and mumbled her thanks, her mind appeared elsewhere and not really focused on their words. Rowena's words hit her like a bucket of ice water. She stared at Rowena, saying nothing for the longest time.

"I...I'm sorry," said Rowena. "You didn't know?"

Finally, Gloria found her voice. "I don't know what kind of con you're playing, slut, and I don't want to know. I've had my fill of scam artists. He's dead. The cash cow died with him. Whatever your game is, you'll get nothing from me."

"I'm not—"

Gloria's tone grew menacing. "Get out. Now. Or you'll be sorry you ever set foot inside this building."

Rowena paled and immediately rushed for the exit.

I checked to see if either Zack or Spader had caught the interaction, but I spied neither through the thickening crowd. As I continued to weave around the room, listening to the various conversations, it became apparent that Barry's murder was the only topic of conversation. The room buzzed with speculation about who had killed him. People began pointing fingers. Voices rose. Tempers flared.

Over the increasing din, I heard someone say, "It's not like the creep didn't deserve it."

Another chimed in. "He'd been asking for it for years."

Someone barked out a laugh. "Well, he finally got it."

One man's gaze darted around the room. "Yeah, but from who?"

"My money's on Brock," said one man. Those two have gotten into it for years."

Another offered a differing opinion. "I wouldn't be surprised to learn the wife killed him."

"You think?"

The man shrugged. "Heck, I'm surprised she waited this long."

The conversations continued to grow louder and more heated as people took sides. Heads began to turn until eventually everyone had focused their attention on the widow. Above all the chatter, one woman's voice rang out. "She did it. She killed him."

I stood on my toes and craned my neck in the direction of the voice. Over the shoulder of a Redcoat standing in front of me, I saw Tonya, her arm outstretched, pointing toward Gloria.

The room erupted in a simultaneous gasp, then grew silent enough to hear the proverbial pin drop until Gloria broke the silence. "Liar!"

She then launched herself at Tonya. The two women fell to the floor and began rolling around, pulling each other's hair, slapping, punching, kicking, spitting, and biting.

Nearly everyone else in the room formed a ring around the two women, egging them on. The man who had showed Gloria some kindness tried to push his way through the crowd but made no headway. However, Zack and Detective Spader managed to muscle their way through the perimeter. After pulling Gloria and Tonya apart but keeping them face-down on the floor, Spader shouted for Officer Halston to cuff them.

Tonya and Gloria were then pulled to their feet. "Make way," said Spader.

The circle broke, opening a path to the exit. Nick and Billy stood at the entrance to the room. Billy locked eyes with his mother as Spader marched her past him. His voice filled with tears he had trouble choking back. "Why, Mom?"

Gloria raised her chin and practically spit out her answer. "Because she deserved it."

As Spader and the crowd started to disperse, Zack and I made our way to the boys. Nick cast pleading eyes toward me. "What about Billy?"

I placed my hand on Billy's shoulder. "Why don't you spend the night with us? I'll make sure your mom knows where you are."

Uncertainty clouded Billy's face. He searched the room, his gaze finally settling off to my left. I turned to see the man I'd observed earlier with Gloria. He nodded to Billy before turning to leave.

The dam broke. Tears rained down Billy's cheeks. "Why are you being so nice to me?"

"Why shouldn't we?" asked Zack.

Billy lifted his chin. It trembled as he spoke. "Because most people aren't."

Zack and I stared at each other over Billy's head. I thought my heart would break.

On the ride home, I texted Detective Spader to let him know Billy would spend the night with us. Even if Gloria was released, I didn't want to run the risk of her taking her anger out on her son. She'd already proven she, too, had anger issues.

As if reading my mind, Billy said, "My mom's not like that. I don't know what got into her. She never even spanked me when I was little."

I twisted in my seat to face him. "She's under a lot of stress right now, Billy. Sometimes people reach a point where they can no longer control their emotions, and they lash out in inappropriate ways."

He scowled. "Like my dad. For as long as I can remember, she's covered up for him."

Zack and I exchanged a quick look before I turned back to Billy. "Because of his accident?"

His eyes widened. "You know about that?"

Oops! I covered by saying, "I heard some people talking about it at the viewing."

He shook his head. "She uses the accident as an excuse. I was only about five when it happened, but I remember stuff from when I was younger. He was always crazy."

"In what way?" asked Zack.

Billy hesitated. "Maybe I shouldn't be talking about this."

Nick had remained silent to this point but now jumped in. "Your father was murdered, Dude. If you have information that will help catch his killer, you can't keep it to yourself."

Billy's eyes grew wide with fear. "Is that true?"

"It's called withholding evidence," said Nick. "You can go to jail for that."

"Nick," I warned, using my mom voice.

"No one is throwing Billy in jail," said Zack.

Billy heaved a ragged sigh. "My mom pays people off not to file charges whenever he gets in a fight with someone. My grandfather would give her the money. Sometimes I'd hear them talking. My grandfather always said everyone has a price. Find out what that price is, and the problem goes away."

How cynical, I thought, but kept the comment to myself. Instead, I asked, "How often did your father get into trouble?"

He shuddered a ragged sigh. "A lot. I think Mom's paid off just about everyone who showed up this evening. She warned me something might happen tonight. She said, with my dad dead, so is the cash cow, and that's going to piss off lots of people. She called them leeches. They'd go out of their way to pick fights with my dad just so they could threaten to press charges, knowing she'd pay to keep them quiet."

I wondered if Spader knew about this. Instead of narrowing the pool of suspects, the number had now grown to include everyone Gloria had ever paid off over the years. Although, killing the guy whose wife paid out the bribes made about as much sense as killing the goose that laid the golden eggs.

Spader had his work cut out for him. I'm sure no one would admit to blackmailing Gloria. In addition, if she'd had an ounce of brains, she'd paid the bribes in cash. Meaning, no money trail for Spader to follow.

When we arrived home, Billy accompanied Nick on Leonard's final walk of the night. This gave Zack and me a chance to discuss what we'd learned on the short drive home. "Chances are, Spader knows nothing about the blackmail," I said.

Zack raised an eyebrow. "Now that's the understatement of the year."

"Very funny. We need to tell him what we learned."

"I'll send him a text, asking him to stop by on his way home."

I thought about that for a moment. "I don't think it's a good idea for Billy to overhear us speaking with the detective."

"Agreed. I'll tell him to text me when he arrives, and we'll meet him in the apartment. I expect it's going to be a long night. By the time he finishes up at headquarters, the boys should be in bed. Hopefully, asleep."

"Especially Billy. The poor kid looked exhausted. My guess is he hasn't slept much since he learned of his father's murder."

~*~

Two and a half hours later, Spader finally entered the apartment. "Fun evening," he said, punctuating his comment with a grimace.

"Care to share anything else?" I asked.

In the past, I'd always received the standard cop response about how he couldn't divulge any information about an ongoing investigation. However, given staffing shortages, Spader's overload of cases, my intuitive sleuthing talents, and the bro link he'd forged with Zack, Spader had recently unofficially deputized Zack and me to pick our brains. My gut told me Zack's inclusion had to do with privileged information the detective knew about my husband but that I only suspected.

Spader collapsed into the chair across from the sofa and waved off an offer of either a potent or non-potent potable before he began speaking. "The widow claims Tonya Benedetto lured the deceased into an affair to get her hands on what she thought was his money. Benedetto claims Gloria killed Barry to keep him from leaving her and taking half the money Gloria had inherited. She said she and Barry planned to marry once the divorce was finalized."

"Tonya arrived on the arm of another reenactor," I said. "He was dressed as a Redcoat, and I think he may have been the guy Barry punched to start the brawl."

"He was," said Spader. "We verified that. He's also Benedetto's husband Rocky."

"Does Rocky know Tonya was having an affair with Barry?" asked Zack.

"If so," I said, "That should place him at the head of the suspects list."

Spader's jaw tightened. "He's already there."

"As a reenactor," said Zack, "he'd own a bayonet. Maybe more than one."

"Exactly," said Spader. "We're following up on that. Although Tonya claims her husband had no idea of the affair and still doesn't. She was waiting until Barry filed for divorce. Then she'd file."

I noticed Zack roll his eyes.

So did Spader. He chuckled. "Hard to believe. I plan to interview him further tomorrow."

"Something doesn't add up," I said. "I heard Gloria tell Tonya that in New Jersey, inheritances aren't included in divorce settlements."

"Looks like Tonya didn't believe her," said Zack.

I turned to Spader. "Were Gloria and Tonya booked or released?"

He shook his head. "Neither. But since they both blew well-over the legal limit, I decided to let them cool their heels in adjoining cells overnight. Maybe by tomorrow morning, one of them might feel more like talking."

"They didn't lawyer up?" I asked.

"Both waived their rights."

I squinted at Spader. "Don't you think that's strange?"

He shrugged. "Doesn't matter what I think. We did everything by the book. Neither was incoherent. They both said they understood their rights but continued to talk, pointing the finger at the other. Not that we got anything of much use out of either of them."

He checked his phone, then changed the subject. "It's getting late. Sorry to keep you both up so long. You said on the phone you had information for me."

Zack and I proceeded to tell Spader what we'd learned from both Gloria and Billy. "Can we assume Gloria never mentioned she's been paying off blackmailers for years?" I asked.

Spader grimaced. "News to me. I suppose it slipped her mind." He reached for his notepad and pen. "I don't suppose Billy mentioned any names."

"Assuming everyone who entered the funeral home signed the guest book," said Zack, "you've got a long list of suspects right there."

When Spader raised his eyebrows, I added, "According to Billy, Gloria had paid off nearly everyone at the viewing at one time or another. But," I added, "we don't know that all the blackmailers showed up this evening. There could be others."

"Anything else stand out to you?" asked Spader.

"There was one man who stood apart from the crowd," I said.

"In what way?"

"He showed concern for Gloria and Billy." I explained what I'd observed. "Billy appeared to either need or want his approval when we offered to let him spend the night."

"Describe him."

"About six feet tall, average build, salt-and-pepper hair. Probably in his mid to late sixties. He was in the group that entered the viewing room in front of you and Officer Halston."

Spader finished jotting notes, pocketed his pen and pad, then stood. "I'm tired of running around in circles, getting nowhere with this case. First thing tomorrow morning, I'm going to demand Gloria come clean about everything. Let's see what she has to say once she knows I'm aware of the blackmail. Because right now, she's also at the top of my list."

"What about her alibi?" I asked. "Unless she's overcome the space/time continuum and figured out a way to time travel, she couldn't be in two places at once."

"She may not have plunged the bayonet into her husband's heart," said Spader, "but she could have orchestrated his death. Either Rocky killed Barry for having an affair with his wife, or Gloria killed her husband to stop getting bled dry by blackmailers. If neither of those leads pan out, we'll start focusing on the people at the viewing, but my money is on one of those two."

"Or not," I said.

"Meaning?" asked Spader.

"I overheard some of the reenactors' conversations. Lots of speculation about who may have killed Barry. One person suggested someone named Brock, but I don't know if that's a first or last name."

"Anything else mentioned about him?"

"Just that he and Barry had a long history."

Spade scribbled another note.

"What about the interment?" I asked. "Do you still want us to attend?"

Spader shook his head. "Not necessary. After this evening's events, Gloria has changed her mind and opted for a private ceremony. No one besides her and Billy."

"What if others show up?" asked Zack.

"They'll find the deceased already laid to rest."

As Spader rose to leave, I remembered something else. "Did you notice that Rowena Milford showed up this evening?"

"I did. When I interviewed her, she said she might attend the viewing to pay her respects. Did you speak with her?"

"No, but I did overhear her conversation with Gloria."

Spader plopped back onto the chair and removed his notepad and pen. After he flipped to an empty page, he made eye contact with me. "And?"

"It wasn't pretty. Apparently, Gloria had no idea Barry was previously married. She accused Rowena of trying to scam her."

"How did Rowena respond?"

"She didn't. Gloria threated her if she didn't leave immediately."

Spader mumbled, "Interesting," as he jotted a few notes.

"You don't think Rowena's a suspect, do you?"

"I haven't ruled anyone out at this point, Mrs. Barnes. She doesn't seem to have a motive, but she also doesn't have an alibi for Saturday night after your brother-in-law brought her home."

NINE

I was in a quandary as I dressed for work the next morning. Zack had a meeting in D.C. and had left earlier to catch the Amtrak Acela. Nick wasn't scheduled to go into work until four o'clock. If Gloria didn't return home before he left the house, I didn't want Billy wandering around our home by himself for hours.

It wasn't that I didn't trust him. He seemed like a nice enough kid, but I really didn't know him, and recent experiences with the seamier side of humanity had made me overly suspicious of anyone I didn't know well.

I wasn't quite sure how old Billy was, but he had to be at least twelve or thirteen from the slight peach fuzz I'd noticed on his upper lip. He was certainly old enough to spend the afternoon alone in his own house, but did he have a key?

As much as I hated to wake both boys so early, I saw no other solution. I quickly scrambled some eggs and popped slices of bread in the toaster before heading to Nick's bedroom.

However, instead of the bedroom, I found both boys already

awake and seated on the couch in the den where they were engrossed in destroying space aliens. "Breakfast is on the table," I said.

They paused their game and followed me back to the kitchen. Once they were seated, I asked, "Billy, do you have a key to your house?"

He nodded. "Why?"

"If your mother isn't back by the time Nick has to leave for work later this afternoon, you'll have to go home."

His face clouded with worry. "She didn't come home last night?"

"I don't think so, but Nick is working the late shift today. I'm sure she'll be home before he leaves if you want to stay until then."

I had no idea what would transpire after Detective Spader interrogated Gloria this morning, but I didn't want to worry Billy further. We'd deal with that if or when it occurred.

But Billy pressed. "What if she doesn't come home?"

"I'm sure she'll be home sometime this morning."

"Will she?"

Nick stepped up. "Of course, she will, dude. Why wouldn't she?"

"Because the cops arrested her."

Nick glanced my way. "Mom?"

"As far as I know, your mother isn't under arrest, Billy. The detective in charge of the case knows you're staying with us. I'm sure he'd contact us if he pressed charges, but even so, she'd be released."

"For murder?"

That caught me off-guard. "Why would you think that?"

Billy stared intently at the eggs on his plate as he pushed them around with his fork. "Someone killed my dad," he mumbled.

Nick's eyes grew wide. He stared at Billy. "Do you think your mother killed him?"

Billy raised his head and turned from Nick to me. "I really don't know." Then he bowed his head again and mumbled, "Maybe."

To me that sounded like Billy had many more secrets inside him, but if I pressed too hard, he might shut down. Besides, I needed to get to work. Finally, I said, "Billy, if you don't feel comfortable being alone, I'll come home from work before Nick leaves. You're welcome to stay here until your mom returns. I'm sure there's no need to worry."

When he raised his chin, I saw the tears swimming in his eyes. "Thanks, Mrs. Barnes. I'd like that."

~*~

On my way to work, I mulled over the breakfast conversation. Thinking about the worst possible scenario, I wondered if Billy had any relatives living nearby. Or any relatives at all for that matter. I had hesitated to ask. I didn't want to give the impression that his mother might not come home for quite some time, but depending on the outcome of Gloria's interview with Spader this morning, that might be the case.

However, if Gloria had relatives in the area, where were they last night? Why hadn't they attended the viewing? From what I'd observed, except for that one gentleman, I doubted any of the people at the viewing were Gloria's friends, let alone relatives. Not from the comments she'd made about the people who showed up or the conversations I'd overheard.

This led me to wonder about the terms of the trust. I had assumed, without any evidence, that Gloria had recently inherited the trust upon her father's death, but she never mentioned his death during her angry confrontation with Tonya last Friday. Although, she had alluded to it when she mentioned that inheritances were exempt from joint property in New Jersey.

The trust may have come from a grandparent with her father administering it until she gained control upon reaching a certain age. Gloria may have had control of the money for some time.

However, if that were the case, why were she, Barry, and Billy living in an apartment in a working-class town until last week? And if one or both of her parents were still alive, why weren't they standing beside their daughter last night to support her and their grandson?

Once I pulled into a parking space at work, I sent Detective Spader a text, asking him to call me when he got a chance. To my surprise, my phone rang before I stepped from the car. I pulled a Spader and instead of answering with a hello, said, "That was quick."

"What can I do for you, Mrs. Barnes?"

I told him about Billy's comment at breakfast. "I think he knows more than he's saying. He's scared you're going to arrest his mother for his father's murder."

"That's still a possibility, but she's on her way home now."

"He'll be relieved. At least for now. Do you know if they have any other family?"

"You don't care for your houseguest?"

"On the contrary. He's a sweet kid. He and Nick have bonded with Nick taking on a big brother role. But I'm concerned about what will happen to Billy if you arrest Gloria."

"Right now, I don't have definitive evidence for an arrest. Of anyone. She came clean about the blackmail. It didn't seem to faze her, other than she wanted to know how I found out about it."

"You didn't tell her, did you?"

"Of course not. I told her police interviews work one way. We do the asking, and she does the answering. That put a stop to her questions."

"And she still had no lawyer with her?"

"We asked again. She declined again."

"Your certain she understood her Miranda rights?" I didn't want to jump to conclusions about Gloria's intellectual acumen based on a few brief observations and one extremely short conversation. Looks and first impressions are often deceiving. For all I knew, Gloria had a PhD and enjoyed reading Proust. In French.

"Positive. Said she had nothing to hide."

I gasped. Had the woman never watched a single episode of any police drama on TV? You don't need a law degree to know you always, always, always keep your mouth shut until you have an attorney present. And then, you let the lawyer do the talking for you. I pointed out the obvious. "Except years of being blackmailed by various people."

"Exactly."

"Odd. It can't be for lack of money."

"Makes me wonder what else she's hiding," said Spader.

It made me wonder why Gloria had stayed with a loser like Barry for all those years. What kind of example was she setting for her son?

I'd like to think that if I'd known what Karl was doing, I'd have immediately taken control of all our assets and insisted he get help for his gambling addiction. Or else. But as the saying goes, hindsight is twenty-twenty. Maybe the signs had always been there, but I was too blind or too busy or too trusting to see them. Until I knew Gloria's full story, I'd try not to pass judgment.

"Did you ask her about the older man I mentioned?"

"His name is Lance Melville. He was a family friend and her father's accountant. Her father's will designated him as the trustee of the fund she inherited. Gloria said her father didn't trust Barry and wanted to make sure he couldn't blow through her money."

I voiced my irony. "But it was okay to pay off blackmailers continually?"

Spader chuckled. "I suppose that didn't count. After all, according to what Billy told you, the grandfather spent years forking over money for that very purpose. Even though he didn't like his son-in-law, he liked scandal even less."

"And he apparently had plenty of money to keep that from happening."

"Millions," said Spader. "But Gloria wouldn't come into any of it until her fortieth birthday or upon his death, whichever came first."

"Maybe he hoped she'd wise up and leave Barry before then," I suggested. "So, which came first?" Gloria had such a haggard look about her that it was hard to determine her age. Either circumstances had accelerated the aging process, or she'd lost out in the gene pool lottery.

"Neither. He died four months ago. On her fortieth birthday."

"Quite the odd coincidence."

After ending my call with Detective Spader, I sent off a quick text to Nick: *Billy's mother released. On her way home.*

As I rounded the corner onto the path that led to the main entrance of our offices, my phone rang again. I checked the screen, at first hesitating to answer, but delaying the inevitable solved nothing. I stepped away from the entrance and tapped my screen. "Good morning, Doctor."

"Good morning, Mrs. Pollack, I have news regarding your mother-in-law's tests."

I braced myself. "Yes?"

"All came back negative. She also aced every cognitive test we gave her. Putting aside the mini-stroke last year, she's in excellent health for a woman her age."

Which is what I'd expected once the tests ruled out anything serious. "You're releasing her?"

"We have no reason to keep her any longer. How soon can you get here?"

Reading between the lines, they wanted to get rid of Lucille as soon as possible. Hospital staff weren't paid nearly enough to put up with the likes of my mother-in-law twenty-four/seven. I could hardly blame them.

Having just arrived at work, however, I wasn't about to turn around and drive to Summit to pick her up, then deliver her back home. The day would be half-over before I set foot in my cubicle.

"Unless she can arrange transportation with one of her friends," I said, "she's going to have to wait until this evening. I'm at work, and my husband is out-of-town." Nick was still several months away from getting his probationary license, not that I'd ever saddle him with such a task. Both Shane and Ira would gladly offer to pick up Lucille if I asked, but knowing my mother-in-law, she'd refuse to go with either of them.

The doctor's tone changed. And not for the better. "If we need the bed, she'll have to wait in the hospital lobby until someone arrives for her."

"I understand."

I didn't want to be a spider under Lucille's hospital bed during that conversation. Then again, I wasn't looking forward to the tongue lashing I'd receive once I arrived at the hospital. Maybe the Goddess of Unappreciated Daughters-in-law would take pity on me and arrange other transportation for her.

I still didn't know the extent of Harriet Kleinhample's injuries, but the EMTs had suggested she may have sustained a leg or hip fracture. Possibly both. Either one would prevent her from driving.

To my knowledge, none of the other Daughters of the October Revolution still owned their own vehicles. They always crammed themselves like sardines into Harriet's VW minibus. I had to admit, it was looking exceedingly doubtful that I'd receive a bailout from the Goddess of Unappreciated Daughters-in-Law.

I thanked the doctor and disconnected the call. As soon as I entered the building, I made a beeline upstairs to the break room. I was in serious need of a chocolate anything and an infusion of caffeine.

A large bakery box sat in the middle of the round table that took up most of the floorspace in the break room. Cloris stood at the counter, pouring herself a cup of coffee. I lifted the lid to find a dozen enormous chocolate croissants. "If I had any money," I told her, "I'd put you in my will."

"Rough morning?" she asked, holding up the coffee pot.

I grabbed a clean cup and held it as she poured. "You have no idea."

We settled at the table, and as I grabbed a croissant, I told her about my conversation with Dr. Pavlochek. "But at least you brought chocolate." I took a bite of the flakey, buttery, chocolate pastry and closed my eyes, savoring the decadent mouthful. "This is divine. Maybe both my luck and the day have decided to improve."

At which point, my phone rang again. One look at the display told me the gods had fallen to the floor and were rolling around, laughing hysterically. I groaned. "I have a bad feeling about this."

When I answered the call, Dr. Pavlochek said, "Mrs. Pollack, I'm afraid we have a problem."

"Has something happened to my mother-in-law?"

"You could say that. She's disappeared."

"What do you mean disappeared? She couldn't just disappear. Maybe someone brought her down for more tests and didn't tell the nurse on duty."

"She's not in the hospital. We checked. She's gone."

"Doctor, she needs a cane or walker to get around without falling. Even if she somehow managed to leave the hospital on her own, she couldn't have gotten far. You and I just spoke."

"I called you before making my rounds."

"What about the floor nurses? When was the last time someone saw her?"

"No one is sure. Probably sometime last night during the last shift. There was an incident on the floor very early this morning before shift change. It looks like she slipped out during the disturbance. Security cameras show her leaving through the main entrance and getting into a waiting vehicle. Another woman was with her."

This all sounded extremely suspicious. Not to mention completely orchestrated. "What sort of disturbance, doctor?"

"About a dozen elderly women barged in at the crack of dawn. They carried picket signs and made so much noise that everyone on duty came running to see what was going on."

"Was security alerted?"

"Yes."

"What happened to the women?"

"When someone told them security was on the way, they dropped their picket signs and fled."

The incident that had landed my mother-in-law and Harriet Kleinhample in the hospital had occurred a week ago. If Harriet had sustained one or more fractures, she'd now either be recovering at home or in a rehab facility. If she hadn't broken anything, the hospital may have kept her overnight for observation but released her in the morning.

I suspected the latter. Harriet had either gotten her VW out of impound or secured another one from whatever no-questions-asked commie used-car dealer provided her with wheels. No doubt, once they knew Lucille had made her escape off the floor, Harriet and most of the other Daughters of the October Revolution had headed for the parking garage, while Lucille, with the aid of another member, hopped into a waiting Uber.

"Sounds like my mother-in-law's Bolshevik Brigade pulled off an Entebbe-type rescue," I said.

"Really, Mrs. Pollack. How in the world could you possibly know that's what happened?"

"Simple. I know my mother-in-law and her commie cohorts."

What I didn't know was where Lucille had gone. I hoped she'd opted for either Harriet's apartment or my home. If Lucille blew the coop hours ago, she would have arrived at the house before I left for work. However, that didn't mean she and her troops wouldn't descend on my home later.

Since Dr. Pavlochek had nothing more to impart, I thanked him for his call, hung up, and alerted Nick. "Do I have to let them in?" he asked.

"She has a key, Nick."

"No, she doesn't, Mom. When I got home the night she went to the hospital, I saw her purse sitting on the floor alongside the coffee table in the den. Harriet's, too. I stuck them both on Grandmother Lucille's dresser."

The first good news I'd heard all day.

Now that I thought about it, the EMTs had loaded Lucille and Harriet onto gurneys and driven them to the hospital. Since I had all of Lucille's health insurance information on my phone, I never thought to grab her purse. I hadn't given a thought to Harriet. I suppose her daughter had copies of her insurance and handled the paperwork when she arrived to pick Harriet up at the hospital.

"In that case," I said, "if they show up, don't answer the door. They'll think no one is home and leave."

Before he hung up, Nick mentioned that Gloria had returned, and Billy had gone home.

"Have I mentioned lately how proud I am of you, Nick?"

"For what, Mom?"

"For lots of things. Like the way you befriended Billy."

"He's an okay kid. I sort of knew some of what he's going through."

"Which is why I'm proud of you."

I could almost sense his blush through the phone. Before I got too maudlin, I told him I needed to start work. He seemed relieved to have an excuse to end the call.

"You do live an interesting life," said Cloris as I finally returned to my now-tepid coffee and half-eaten croissant.

I zapped the coffee in the microwave, then topped it off with what remained in the pot. "Not that I wish something horrible to befall her, but a part of me had hoped the hospital would find something that required Lucille move to rehab for a month or two. A week's respite from her isn't nearly enough." I glanced at Cloris. Does that make me a bad person?"

"Heck, no. You deserve a Purple Heart for all you've put up with from that woman, not to mention what her son did to you and the kids. Your problem is you've got too big a heart. You've been far too nice to her."

I laughed. "I doubt she'd see it that way."

~*~

Even though the day had gotten off to a rocky start, I managed not to dwell on the imminent return of my mother-in-law. I dove into work, checking off quite a few items on my morning to-do list. Then, with ten minutes to spare before the start of a working lunch with Cloris, Jeanie, and Danica, I sent out e-vites to friends and coworkers for a barbeque the Sunday of Labor Day weekend.

Cloris, Jeanie, and I had always worked well together, and we found Danica's partnership-like style seamlessly meshed with the way we were used to working. The first book in the series we had dubbed *American Woman Through the Decades: Crafts, Recipes & Decorating* was coming together faster than we thought possible.

We had wrapped up our meeting and were clearing the remains of our take-out lunch when I received a call from our receptionist. "A Gloria Forrester is here to see you, Anastasia." She lowered her voice to a whisper and added, "She looks like someone used her as a punching bag."

TEN

This couldn't be happening. Talk about a rollercoaster day. How did Gloria even know where I worked? Surely, Nick wouldn't have told her.

"Is she standing near enough to overhear you?"

"No, I told her to wait in the seating area on the other side of the lobby. She looks nervous, though."

"In what way?"

"Like someone might jump out of the shadows and finish what they started. She can't sit still. Keeps hopping up and pacing back and forth. When she does sit, she's always on the edge of the seat, bouncing one leg. Like she might have to dart for the exit at any moment. She's giving off a really sketchy vibe if you know what I mean."

I did. I'd seen Gloria's volatile personality firsthand last night. No telling how she'd react if approached by security or a well-meaning coworker.

"Is security in the lobby?" With the various incidents we'd had the last year and a half, the Trimedia tightwads had reluctantly splurged for a full-time security guard during business hours. When Hugo regained control of his company, he'd wisely decided to pick up the contract after Trimedia departed.

"Sitting beside me. He's keeping a close eye on her."

"Good. Tell her I'm not in my office, that I may be in a meeting."

"And then?"

"Stall her until I get back to you."

I scooted out the conference room and made my way to my supply closet, the one place where I knew I had privacy. After locking the door, I placed a call to Detective Spader.

Thankfully, he answered his phone. "I need advice," I said.

"On what?"

"Gloria Forrester showed up at my office. She's waiting for me in the lobby."

"Are you afraid she'll become violent?"

"The receptionist described her as looking scared and nervous, but after what I witnessed last night? Who knows?" Gloria had gone from mild-mannered widow to vicious attacking hyena in seconds.

"Maybe she just wants to thank you for taking her son overnight."

"She didn't have to drive all the way to Morristown to do that. She could have waited until I got home this evening."

Spader agreed. "It does seem odd. Does she know you're in the building?"

"She may have seen my car in the parking lot, but I suppose I could have the receptionist tell her I took the train into the city for a meeting."

"Since we don't know what she wants," said Spader, "do that. Better to play it safe. With your track record, I'd rather your husband was by your side when you speak with her."

I couldn't disagree with him. Although I'd proven on more than a few occasions that I'm capable of taking care of myself, each time I had wondered if my luck would hold long enough for me to make it out alive. Then again, several times, Zack had arrived in the nick of time.

This wasn't the first time someone with ulterior motives had shown up looking for me at work. Whether Zack was a certified member of some government alphabet agency or not, he'd saved my tush more than once, and I wasn't too proud to have him standing beside me when Gloria showed up at our door tonight. Which I assumed she'd do after failing to speak with me now.

I hung up from Spader and called down to the receptionist. "Tell her I'm at a meeting in the city, and you don't know when I'll be back."

"Sure. Is everything okay? She's the wife of that guy who was killed across the street from you, right?"

Between social media and watercooler gossip, too many people at work knew too much about my life. Especially when it concerned dead bodies. "How do you know that?"

"She's creeping me out. I decided to Google her and saw a clip of her arrest after she got into a fight at the funeral home last night."

Long ago, I'd become the darling of the local news media. Whenever a murder occurred in or around Westfield, the press flocked to my house, assuming I had some connection to the crime. I always refused to speak with them, but that didn't stop them from constantly writing about the woman they'd dubbed

Westfield's own Jessica Fletcher.

I think they saw my standard "no comment" as a challenge. For all I knew, some entrepreneurial reporter or photographer had even set up a pool among the members of the Fourth Estate, betting on which one would finally score an interview with me first.

"Yes," I said. "She's the wife of the murder victim."

I then added, "Look, this is probably nothing, but I don't like the idea of people I barely know popping in to disrupt my workday whenever they feel like it."

"Don't worry," she said. "I'll send her on her way. Diplomatically, of course. If she resists, I've got Mr. Muscle with a Badge and Gun seated beside me."

After thanking her, I unlocked and opened the closet door. Cloris, Jeanie, and Danica stood on the other side, blocking my exit. Cloris grabbed one of my arms, Jeanie the other. They push me back into the closet. Danica followed, closing and locking the door behind her. Then all three surrounded me.

"Out with it," said Cloris. She stood feet apart, her arms crossed in quintessential Stern Mother Mode, as if she'd just caught me denying I'd raided the cookie jar when the evidence was stuffed in my cheeks. "What's going on?"

"Do you have another stalker?" asked Cloris.

Danica's eyes grew so wide I thought they'd pop out of their sockets. "*Another* stalker? When did you have a stalker?

"Should we call the police?" asked Jeanie.

I held up both hands to stem the onslaught of questions. "I don't know what's going on, I don't think I have a stalker, and I already called the police. Everything is under control."

Cloris smirked before reminding me, "Your life is never under control."

She had a point. Today had become a perfect example.

"We need details," demanded Jeanie.

"Like why you called the police," said Danica.

I knew I wouldn't have a moment's peace until I filled them in. "Fine. But I need coffee first." I turned to Cloris. "And you'd better have some to-die-for chocolate something or other stashed in your office."

Danica's body threw off an involuntary shudder. "*To-die-for* chocolate? You have a strange sense of humor, Anastasia."

Cloris came to my defense. "It's her coping mechanism." Then she turned to me and grinned. "Have I ever let you down in a chocolate emergency?"

I knew I could count on her.

~*~

After sating my need for caffeine and chocolate while sating Cloris, Jeanie, and Danica's need for details, the remainder of the workday ended without further disruptions or drama. Still, not knowing Gloria's motive for popping in to see me at work, I wanted to make sure she wasn't lying in wait for me in the parking lot.

I called down to the receptionist. "Did that woman who was looking for me leave?"

"As soon as I told her you weren't in the building and that I had no idea if you'd be returning today."

"Would you log into the security cameras? I don't want her ambushing me when I leave."

"We already did. I wanted to make sure she got into her car and drove off. I also had security walk the perimeter several times. We checked again a few minutes ago to verify that she hadn't returned.

The coast is clear."

I thanked her and headed toward the elevator. Throughout my drive home, I puzzled over why Gloria had driven to Morristown instead of walking across the street once I arrived home. Did she not want her son to know? Or did she not want Zack around when she spoke to me? And if so, why?

I was certainly no threat to her. If anything, besides Lance Melville, my husband, son, and I were the only people who had shown her any compassion at the viewing.

I thought back to Billy's heartbreaking question last night. *Why are you being so nice to me?* Maybe Gloria was so used to people baiting her husband, then blackmailing her, that she couldn't believe anyone would treat her kindly without having an ulterior motive.

Maybe I shouldn't wait for her to come knocking on my door. Perhaps, after arriving home, I should pay her a visit.

Rounding the corner onto my street, I was glad to see that Zack had beaten me home. I'd discuss Gloria's visit to my office with him before I decided anything.

However, when I walked through the front door, I no longer had to mull over how to handle the situation. Gloria Forrester sat tensed on my living room sofa, her right leg bouncing up and down. I followed her gaze across the room to where Ralph had locked eyes with her.

Over the cool jazz of John Batiste emanating from the sound system and a video space invasion drifting in from the den, I assured her, "He won't hurt you."

"So your husband said."

Both her expression and her voice told me she wasn't convinced.

Her body wore the evidence of last night's brawl. The receptionist hadn't done justice in describing the extent of Gloria's injuries. Both eyes were blackened. Bruises and scratches covered her face and arms. A line of sutures ran diagonally along her forehead above her right eye. A bandage wrapped around the palm and top of her left hand.

She grabbed the arm of the sofa with her right hand and began to hoist herself to her feet.

I held up my hand. "Please, don't get up." I feared she'd lose her balance and topple head-first onto the coffee table.

She collapsed back into the cushions and offered me a wan smile as Zack entered from the kitchen. He carried a bottle of wine and three stemmed glasses. After dipping his head to plant a kiss on my lips, he said, "I invited Gloria and Billy to dinner this evening."

"If that's okay with you," said Gloria.

I smiled at her. "Absolutely."

After Zack poured the wine and passed around the glasses, he and I settled into the chairs across from the sofa. Ralph flew over to his favorite human and nuzzled his cheek in anticipation of a sunflower seed.

I turned to Gloria. "I understand you came to see me at work today. I'm sorry I missed you." Hopefully, she wasn't adept at discerning white lies.

Zack tilted his head ever so slightly, and we momentarily locked eyes. Then he turned to Gloria. "You didn't mention that."

"I'm sorry." Her fingers nervously twisted the stem of the wine glass as she stared at the liquid rippling slightly from the motion. "My father used to complain that sometimes I'm too impulsive and don't think things through. The way I look, I think I scared your receptionist half to death, but I wanted to thank you for taking Billy overnight. I got it into my head that it was important to speak with you as soon as possible."

She offered a slight smile and shrugged. "Stupid, right? The police first brought me to the hospital before they decided I should be their guest for the night. I think the painkillers the doctor gave me messed with my brain."

"How did you know where I work?"

She laughed. "Are you kidding? You're all over the Internet. After they returned my phone, it took me less than a minute to find your office address."

She then grew serious, narrowing her gaze at me. "You work with the police to solve murders, don't you?"

I didn't like the direction this conversation had suddenly taken. "Not really."

Technically, that was stretching the truth. I had helped to solve more than a few murders, but I wasn't a paid consultant or on retainer with county law enforcement. I didn't so much work *with* the police as I worked *adjacent* to them. And then, only when circumstances had forced me to get involved.

Except, even that was no longer true. Not since Detective Spader had wheedled Zack and me into allowing him to pick our brains.

Gloria wasn't buying it. "The newspaper reports I read say otherwise. They claim you've helped solve quite a few murder cases."

Zack jumped in. "One of the homicide detectives is a good friend of ours. He sometimes finds it useful to bounce ideas off us. That's all. Where are you going with this?"

She scowled, suspicion clouding her features. "Which

detective?"

"Samuel Spader," I said.

Gloria gasped, nearly spilling her wine. "That's the detective trying to frame me. He thinks I had something to do with my husband's murder." Her eyes filled with tears. "I swear I didn't. Barry had lots of faults. Too many, really. But I loved him. He was the father of my son. I'd never do anything to hurt him. Billy would never forgive me."

Ralph squawked once, then got to the heart of the subject as only he could. "*Truth will come to light; murder cannot be hid long. Merchant of Venice*, Act Two. Scene Two."

Gloria's eyes grew wide, but I ignored her shock. My thoughts had landed elsewhere. Did she believe we'd taken Billy home with us last night to pump him for information to incriminate his mother?

Rather than explain Ralph's Shakespearean talents, I said, "Gloria, I assure you, we're not working with Detective Spader to find evidence against you. He's an honest, honorable, by-the-book cop. He follows leads until he finds the truth. He doesn't manufacture evidence."

Still focused on Ralph, she said, "I want to believe you. Billy said you were the kindest people he'd ever met." She pulled her attention from Ralph and stared directly at me. "That's why I'd like to hire you to find my husband's killer. I know you could use the money."

My jaw dropped. Surely Nick had not divulged such information to Billy. "How do you—?"

"On my drive to your office, I listened to the first episode of that podcast about you."

Something else she'd probably discovered while scrolling

through the vast information about me on the Internet. I wished Alex and Sophie had never created the Sleuth Sayer podcasts about my reluctant crime-solving exploits. They had wanted to help pay down the debt Karl had saddled me with. A noble sentiment, albeit misguided.

I did appreciate their desire to help, but I didn't appreciate the added exposure. Local notoriety as the Jessica Fletcher of Westfield was bad enough, but that podcast had placed me on the radar of every true crime junkie from the Redwood forests to Long Island Sound and all points in-between.

Much to the kids' surprise and delight, the Sleuth Sayer became so successful that a production company had wanted to option it for a television series. However, when the owner of the production company was gunned down in front of my house last month, the TV series died along with him.

Thankfully, Alex and Sophie going off to college had heralded the end of the podcasts. But that hadn't deterred the true crime junkies who couldn't get enough of my reluctant sleuthing adventures in the land of murder and mayhem.

"I have money," said Gloria. "A lot of money. I can pay you."

"No," said Zack.

Gloria turned her attention to him. "I don't understand."

"My wife is not putting herself in danger to help you or anyone else."

Ignoring Zack, Gloria shifted her attention back to me. "But you need the money. I'm willing to pay anything. Name your price. I can wipe out your debt with the stroke of a pen."

I heaved a sigh. So could my husband if I'd let him. Money wasn't the issue. I wouldn't get involved in Gloria's problems no matter how much money she offered me. I had confidence that

Spader would figure out who killed Barry and whether Gloria was an accomplice to his murder.

I wasn't some vigilante amateur sleuth. I had no stake in Barry's murder, no pun intended. A cat may have nine lives, but I only had one, and I wasn't about to risk it on a case that didn't involve me or my loved ones.

I wasn't about to tell her that, though. Instead, I asked, "Gloria, do you know who my husband is?"

Her gaze bounced from me to Zack, then back to me. "What do you mean?"

"Zack is one of the top photojournalists in the world. He's paid extremely well for his work. We don't need your money."

Puzzlement creased her brow. "But the podcast said—"

"My financial situation has changed."

"There are plenty of excellent private detectives who would be willing to take your case," said Zack. "I suggest you call one of them. And while you're at it, get yourself a good defense attorney."

Gloria's voice grew steely. "I don't need an attorney. I've done nothing wrong."

"That's exactly why you do need one," he said.

"Why?"

"To protect yourself."

"From what? I have the truth on my side. I wasn't even in the state when Barry was murdered."

"That only proves you didn't wield the weapon."

She puzzled over Zack's words for a moment. Then her eyes bulged in realization of what he'd inferred. "Are you suggesting I hired someone to kill Barry?"

"We're not," I said, "but the district attorney might. As you said, you have plenty of money." I caught myself before adding that she'd already used some of it to pay off blackmailers. Gloria didn't know that we knew about the blackmail. Although, Billy may have told her that he'd mentioned it to us. Instead, I added, "That's why you need a lawyer."

Her lips trembled. "I...I guess I never thought about that."

From the brief interaction I'd noticed between Billy and Lance Melville, it was obvious the man was more than just a numbers guy sitting behind a desk in an accounting office. Billy had looked to him for guidance. I would have thought he'd insist on Gloria retaining counsel, even provide an attorney for her. Maybe he'd tried.

Some people are loathe to accept advice, no matter how well-intentioned and correct. I didn't know if Gloria fell into that category, but I was beginning to lean in that direction. The trait seemed to pair well with someone prone to sudden outbursts of anger.

When the timer on the kitchen stove went off, Zack rose, putting an end to the discussion. "Dinner is ready."

~*~

Both Gloria and Billy praised the dinner of roasted chicken, mashed potatoes, and zucchini cheese casserole so effusively that I wondered when either of them had last eaten a nourishing homecooked meal. For Billy? Probably his last night at camp. For Gloria? If the groceries I'd retrieved from their driveway were any indication, she probably subsisted primarily on junk food.

Throughout dinner, neither of them brought up Barry's murder or Gloria's recent overnight stay as a guest in the Westfield lockup. As curious as I was, I refrained from asking the numerous questions rattling around in my brain. Conversation was pleasant enough, but it never advanced beyond small talk, and after we'd finished our meal and the small talk had petered out, mother and son departed.

Zack and I were in the kitchen cleaning up from dinner when he casually brought up Gloria's visit to the magazine as he loaded the dishwasher. "I get the feeling there's more to the story."

I scraped a plate into the trash can, then handed it to him as I answered, "Much more. I've had enough uncomfortable surprise visits at work the last year and a half. I wasn't about to run downstairs and greet Gloria with open arms."

"What did you do?"

"I called Spader for advice." I then filled Zack in on how I'd handled the situation.

"I'm not sure what to make of Gloria," I added.

"In what way?"

"All ways. I can't nail down her personality. She's either equal parts erratic, volatile, ignorant, nervous, childlike, naïve, stubborn, and caring, or she's an extremely talented actress who devised what she thinks is a foolproof plan to get away with murder."

He placed the last plate in the dishwasher. "We know she has an ironclad alibi for the time of the murder. She was up in the Catskills overnight. She'd need an accomplice or a hired killer."

"Maybe Lance Melville is her accomplice. If Gloria had confided to him that Barry had a habit of drinking himself into a stupor on their tiny front porch, all he'd have to do is lay in wait until Barry was out cold, then creep up the steps and plunge the bayonet into him. Who would suspect a mild-mannered elderly accountant and funds manager of murdering someone he had little connection to?"

Zack stared at me.

"What?"

"You just did."

"I did, didn't I? Maybe I should mention this theory to Detective Spader."

He wiped down the counter as I rinsed out the sink. Once we'd both dried our hands, he wrapped an arm around my waist. "It can wait until morning."

I had a pretty good idea what he had in mind, but I reminded him that Nick hadn't yet returned from walking Leonard, and Ralph needed to be tucked into his cage for the night. "Killjoy," he muttered.

"Good things come to those who wait."

"I'm going to hold you to that."

"You'd better."

At that moment my phone began to vibrate where I'd left it on the kitchen table. We both turned and stared at the screen, finding an incoming call from Spader.

I grabbed the phone, swiped to answer the call, and placed Spader on speaker. "Pulling an all-nighter again, Detective?"

"Afraid so, Mrs. Barnes. We've had another murder of a reenactor."

ELEVEN

Even though there were hundreds of reenactors from High Point to Cape May in New Jersey, my gut told me there had to be a connection between this latest murder and Barry Sumner's death. "Who?"

"Rocky Benedetto."

I gasped. "Tonya's husband? I suppose that eliminates him as Barry's killer."

"Not necessarily," said Spader. "He still could have killed Barry because he found out about Tonya's affair with him."

"Then who killed Rocky?" I asked.

"Could be another reenactor who had a beef with both Barry and Rocky," suggested Zack. "Or maybe just Rocky. He may have seen Barry's murder as the perfect opportunity to eliminate Rocky with a copycat crime that misdirected the investigation."

I mulled that over. "I suppose. Judging from the way the reenactors went after each other Saturday, Rocky's killer could be any one of them. And for reasons not connected to Barry." I addressed Spader. "Detective, other than dressing up to play war, what else did Barry and Rocky have in common?"

Spader grunted. "As far as I know at this point, only Tonya."

Which left Gloria as the prime suspect in her husband's murder. And possibly Rocky's if Lance or someone else was doing her bidding.

I hated to add another checkmark in the Gloria as Suspect column. Not because I believed in her innocence so much as I didn't want Billy to lose both his parents. Still, I couldn't let sentimentality cloud my judgment.

I told Spader about my newest theory concerning Lance Melville. "He may have killed both Barry and Rocky, or he could have handled the payment for Gloria taking out a hit on both men."

"Why would she want Rocky dead?" asked Spader.

"To get back at Tonya," I suggested. "After all, hell hath no fury like a woman scorned."

"Hmm...I had planned to question Melville in the morning," said Spader. "But before I do, I'm going to bring Gloria in for further questioning."

"Has the M.E. determined Rocky's time of death?" asked Zack.

"He's narrowed the window to less than two hours ago. Rigor mortis hadn't started to set in when he arrived at the scene. Why?"

"Because Gloria Forrester and her son had dinner with us this evening," I said. After glancing at the clock, I added, "They were here when I got home from work around six o'clock and left about half an hour ago."

"Did you learn anything new?" asked Spader.

"Other than my insight about Lance Melville? Gloria tried to hire me to find Barry's killer."

"How did she know about your side gig?"

Side gig? He made it sound like I'd hung up a Sleuth for Sale shingle on my front lawn. "Same as half the country at this point. She Googled me to find my work address and came across the Sleuth Sayer podcasts. Said she listened to the first episode on her way to Morristown."

"And?"

"She offered to wipe out my remaining debt."

Spader's voice took on a menacing edge. "You didn't accept, did you?"

"Of course not! But she was quite persistent. Until I played the Zack card."

Spader let loose what sounded like a cross between a sigh and a yawn. "Tired as I am, Mrs. Barnes, I'll bite. What's the Zack card?"

"I told her my financial situation had dramatically changed since marrying one of the world's leading photojournalists."

"At least this time she didn't suggest I was also a government operative," added Zack.

Spader barked out a laugh. I certainly hoped his amusement didn't indicate an inside joke between the two of them. Changing the subject, I asked, "Who found Rocky's body?"

Spader sobered back into cop mode. "Tonya. She said she'd gone to the supermarket and found him dead in his recliner when she returned. No sign of forced entry."

"Meaning he likely knew his killer," said Zack.

"Maybe." But my mind had veered toward something more sinister. "Or perhaps Tonya deliberately left the door unlocked for the killer to enter and surprise Rocky."

"Someone definitely surprised him," said Spader. "Impaled

him from behind through the back of the recliner. He never saw it coming."

"Another bayonet?" asked Zack.

Spader shook his head. "This time the killer used a replica of a Revolutionary War saber."

"Close enough that we could be dealing with a serial killer. Were there a large number of empty beer cans scattered around the recliner?" I asked. Maybe Rocky and Barry had something else in common—drinking until they passed out.

"Not a one."

Scratch that idea. But it didn't mean that Rocky hadn't passed out through some other means. And maybe not by his own hand. "Tonya might have drugged him before she left the house."

"Always a possibility," said Spader. "He may have ingested something at some point before he was killed. We'll know more once the M.E. performs an autopsy."

~*~

We woke Friday morning to a pounding on the front door. I pried open one eye and stared at the alarm clock. It read ten minutes to six. "What in the world—?"

Zack grabbed his phone. I propped myself up on one elbow and squinted at his screen. "Lucille?"

"Spader." He jumped out of bed and reached for his bathrobe.

"What could he possibly want this early?"

"I guess we'll soon find out."

Not before I peed and brushed my teeth. While Zack headed down the hall to the foyer, I darted into the bathroom. Three minutes later, I joined them in the kitchen. Zack stood at the counter, preparing a pot of coffee. Spader sat at the table, his arms crossed, his face one huge glare of annoyance.

"What's going on?" I asked.

"That's what I'd like to know," said Spader, sounding more like the old Spader from back when he and I belonged to the same mutual animosity club. "Gloria and Billy are missing. Tell me you didn't mention I planned to bring her in for more questioning today."

Zack turned to face him. "Is that what this is all about? Of course not."

"How could you think such a thing?" I asked. "After all we've been through together, do you really think we'd stab you in the back like that?"

When his eyes narrowed at me, I realized what I'd said. I cringed. "I suppose that wasn't the best choice of words."

He raised one of his bushy eyebrows and grunted. "You think?"

I tried unsuccessfully to tamp down a yawn. "Chalk it up to being jarred awake at the crack of dawn."

"Noted." He unknotted his arms and ran his hands through what was left of his hair. Then he heaved a frustrated sigh. "This isn't looking good for your new neighbor. Any idea where they ran?"

"Where who ran?" asked Nick as he entered the kitchen. He stared at Spader while he punctuated his question with a loud yawn, then added, "Why is everyone up so early?"

"Your new friend Billy and his mother," said Spader, answering Nick's first question and ignoring the second. "You wouldn't happen to know where the hell they disappeared to, would you?

Nick rubbed his eyes. "Sure. Billy didn't want to miss the last few days of camp. He said they were leaving really early this morning to beat rush hour traffic. He wanted to arrive by nine o'clock for the first day of Color War."

I pulled a frying pan from the cabinet and held it aloft. "How would you like your crow served this morning, Detective?"

He scowled. "I suppose I deserved that."

This time I tilted my head toward him and raised one of my eyebrows. "You think?"

His face set in a tight frown, Spader rose to leave.

"Sit," I said.

"You'd serve me breakfast after I barged in and accused you of abetting a suspect?"

"I'm chalking your behavior up to dealing with another murder, pulling an all-nighter, and being extremely hangry."

He plopped back onto the chair and grimaced. "You're a good person, Mrs. Barnes. And an excellent observer of human nature."

"Remember that the next time you accuse my wife of something," said Zack, handing Spader a cup of coffee.

Spader muttered into his mug. "Noted again."

I opened the refrigerator. "Oh, look at that."

"What?" asked Zack.

I grabbed a few items from the fridge and held them up. "I'm afraid we're all out of crow this morning, Detective. You'll have to settle for bacon, eggs, and toast."

He responded with a huge belly laugh.

~*~

Forty minutes later, I was showered and dressed and had decided to head into work early to make a dent in my various deadlines. August had flown by so quickly that I hadn't realized until this morning that our monthly staff meeting was this coming Monday. With all the time I was devoting to the craft book series, I'd completely forgotten I needed a presentation for the January issue we'd start brainstorming in three days.

I had just settled behind the steering wheel of my Jetta when a car that wasn't Gloria's classic red Mustang pulled into her driveway. Instead of starting my Jetta's engine, I watched from the rearview mirror as Lance Melville stepped from an ice blue Hummer pickup truck that probably cost nearly as much as Karl and I had paid for our house twenty-two years ago. He bounded up the front steps, unlocked the door, and stepped inside.

Why would Gloria's trust fund manager have a key to her house? I grabbed my phone, opened the Notes app, and tapped out the license plate number. Then I placed a call to Detective Spader before backing out of my driveway. At the last minute, I stepped on the brake and snapped a photo of the Hummer, capturing the license plate just in case my still-not-quite-awake brain hadn't correctly translated the mirror image of the letters and numbers.

I knew I wouldn't run the risk of waking Spader. Even though he'd left my house looking in desperate need of a week's worth of forty winks, he'd only planned to run home to shower and change clothes before returning to headquarters. I hoped he'd stop to get a large to-go cup of decent coffee on his way back. He was going to need constant infusions of caffeine to stay awake today. What passed for coffee at the police station looked, smelled, and tasted like week-old reconstituted motor oil.

Spader answered on the first ring. "Forget to tell me something, Mrs. Barnes?"

"I don't think so, but I thought you'd want to know what I just observed."

"I'm all ears."

After I told him, he whistled under his breath. "Interesting. I think I'll drop in on him under the pretext of needing Gloria to answer a few more questions. He doesn't need to know that I know she's not home." Before he hung up, he remembered his manners. "Thanks for the tip, Mrs. Barnes."

He disconnected the call before I could say, "You're welcome."

I spent the next forty-five minutes of my commute puzzling over why a) Lance Melville had a key to Gloria's home and b) what he was doing inside the house. Nothing I came up with made any sense. Planting evidence against her? Removing any possible evidence the police had inadvertently overlooked? I discounted both theories, knowing the crime scene team had a stellar reputation and wouldn't make such rookie mistakes. If they'd discovered definitive evidence pointing to Gloria, she would have already been charged in Barry's murder.

I pulled into the parking lot at work just as perplexed as I was the moment Melville entered Gloria's house.

Having beat every other *American Woman* employee into the office, I started a pot of coffee and hoped Cloris arrived with some morning goodies. Spader wasn't the only one who'd need a caffeine drip this morning. In my case, though, I'd also need a chaser of chocolate.

I was frowning at the barren table when our food editor strolled in, a pink bakery box tucked under her arm. She tilted her head and eyed me quizzically. "Who are you, and what did you do with my perpetually late BFF? You never arrive before me."

"Blame it on Spader nearly banging down my door before the early bird left its nest to go worm-hunting this morning."

"He was that desperate for one of Zack's homecooked breakfasts?"

SEAMS LIKE THE PERFECT CRIME

I poured two cups of coffee and handed her one. "In full-blown hangry meltdown but that wasn't his primary reason for showing up so early." I filled her in on the events of last night and this morning.

We settled into two of the molded plastic chairs around the table. I lifted the lid of the bakery box. The moment my gaze settled on the chocolate French crullers topped with chocolate ganache and sprinkled with crushed dehydrated raspberries, my salivary glands began to work overtime. I lifted one droolworthy confection from the box and took a bite. "Yum!"

"Good, huh?"

"I had no idea taste buds could have orgasms."

"I'm thinking of featuring them for our February issue, but let's get back to the more important topic at hand."

I took another bite, then held up the now half-eaten cruller. "What could be more important than this?"

Cloris air-swatted my hand away from her face. "You and dead bodies. I realize I only play Watson to your Sherlocking abilities, but I've learned a few things from you over the last year or so."

"Such as?"

"I've developed my own Spidey senses, and I have a bad feeling about this Lance guy. I don't know why, but for some reason, he brings to mind your former stepfather."

"Which one? I've had five."

"The only one who laundered money for the mob and handed out assignments to hitmen."

"I'll admit a few red flags had popped up in my brain when I saw Melville this morning, but you've never even seen the man, let alone met him. What makes you think he's a carbon copy of Lawrence Tuttnauer?"

Cloris shrugged. "I don't know. I just got this tingly feeling up my spine when you mentioned him. Call it woman's intuition."

"You sure it wasn't a French cruller-induced tingle?"

"This was more a creepy tingle than a pleasurable one. Promise me you'll steer clear of the guy."

"Believe me, I have no intention of getting involved in this investigation."

Cloris scowled. "I've heard that before. Somehow, though, you always manage to get drawn in."

I popped the remainder of the cruller in my mouth and shook my head, savoring the perfect mélange of tastes before saying, "Not this time. You have my word."

~*~

My phone rang two hours later. I checked the screen, saw the caller was my mother-in-law, and decided to let her call go to voicemail. I had assumed her phone was in the purse still sitting on the dresser in her bedroom. I assumed wrong. She must have slipped it into one of her pockets before her altercation with the police.

Several seconds later, she called again. Then again. I silenced the ringer and went back to work. The phone continued to vibrate in my pocket, the calls coming in every twenty to thirty seconds. I no longer bothered to check the screen.

"Spambots?" asked Cloris from across the hall.

"Worse. Lucille."

After about half an hour and dozens of calls, my mother-in-law finally gave up and left a voice message. In a shrieking tone she demanded, "Anastasia, where are you? We can't get into the house. Come home immediately to let us in."

Not going to happen. I got up to stretch my legs and walked across the hall. "Listen to this," I said, then played the message for

Cloris.

"What's wrong with her key? You didn't change the locks on her, did you?"

"Tempting, but no. She and Harriet left their purses in the house when the police hauled them to the hospital last Thursday. I have no idea where she spent last night. Probably at Harriet's apartment, assuming her daughter supplied her with a spare key."

"You're not planning to drive home, are you?"

"Not until the end of the workday."

"Smart woman. I take it Zack and Nick aren't home?"

"Nick should be at work already. Zack had to run back down to D.C. again this morning. Halfway through their meeting yesterday, the head archeologist he was meeting with was called away on a family emergency."

"You believe him?"

"Do I have a choice?" Someday, my husband may come clean and tell me what he really did for a living, along with taking photographs around the world. Or not. I wasn't holding my breath. It was the one bone of contention between us. No matter how much he insisted he wasn't a spy, I couldn't let go of my suspicions. But every time he flew off to some dicey locale at a moment's notice—a much too frequent occurrence—I lived in fear of a phone call from the State Department.

At that moment my phone rang again.

TWELVE

If I claimed I wasn't freaked out, I'd be guilty of a whopper. And if I said I released a huge sigh of relief upon viewing Robyn Konopka's name on my phone's screen, that would be the understatement of the century.

"Good morning, Robyn."

"Sorry to bother you at work, Anastasia, but I just drove down your street and thought you'd want to know what's going on."

"Please don't tell me there's been another murder."

"No, but you might be tempted to commit one. Your mother-in-law is holding a press conference on your front lawn. She's surrounded by a dozen other elderly women. Check the local news online."

"Which network?"

"Any one of them. They're all parked in front of your house."

I thanked Robyn for the heads-up and disconnected the call.

"What's up?" asked Cloris.

"I don't know, but I'm about to find out." I crossed back to my cubicle and brought up the Action News live feed. Cloris followed and leaned over my shoulder. The chyron at the bottom of the screen blared, "Westfield Resident Accused of Elder Abuse."

After muttering something that would have led to my mother washing my mouth out with soap, I copied the link and shot a text to Detective Spader: *Does this qualify as justifiable homicide?*

A minute later, I was shocked to see Spader stride into view of the cameras. Had he spent all morning speaking with Lance Melville at Gloria's house? He elbowed his way to the mic, then reminded the press they'd been warned about trespassing on private property.

"I gave them permission," growled Lucille. "I live here."

Spader turned to her. "Only as a guest of the homeowner. You have no claim on this property."

Lucille's face turned purple as she continued to bluster. Spader ignored her to address the gaggle of reporters. "You should all be ashamed of yourselves. Don't you have anything better to do than report of the rantings of a delusional woman?"

"She's claiming she's the victim of elder abuse," said one of the reporters.

Spader barked a laugh. "Really? The only abuse that's gone on in this house is the abuse the homeowner has taken from this woman." He shot a stubby index finger in Lucille's direction. "She's a career criminal who's been arrested countless times for everything from destruction of property to filing false police reports to assaulting law enforcement personnel."

The reporters grumbled their skepticism.

"Don't believe me? Check the court records."

"How dare you!" yelled Lucille.

"Police brutality!" yelled Harriet Kleinhample.

The other Daughters of the October Revolution chimed in.

One of the reporters shouted, "What are you doing here, Spader?"

"My job."

"How is this your job? You're a homicide detective," yelled another reporter.

"Your point?" asked Spader.

Another reported asked, "Has there been another murder?"

"Not since yesterday. Now, I suggest you all find some real news to report." He turned back to Lucille and her minions. "And the rest of you stop causing trouble."

"She locked Lucille out of the house," said Harriet. "That's elder abuse."

"No one locked anyone out. Mr. and Mrs. Barnes are both at work. I suggest you go back to wherever you came from and return this evening when someone will be home to let you in the house."

The cameras continued to roll as a standoff set in between Spader and the women. Finally, he said, "You're pressing your luck, ladies."

"We refuse to leave," said Lucille.

Spader threw up his hands. "Fine. But you'll do it without press coverage."

"You can't make us leave, either," shouted one of the reporters. "All you can do is force us to keep to the sidewalk."

"Feel free to waste your time, then," said Spader. "I'm sure all your advertisers will be thrilled to see how your networks are spending ad revenue."

One of them groused, "That's hitting below the belt, even for you, Spader."

"Is it? Let's talk about hitting below the belt. You people are worse than jackals and hyenas. You keep harassing a private citizen, and when she refuses to relinquish her privacy for your ratings, you turn on her by giving airtime to a raving communist lunatic with an agenda."

He pointed a finger at Lucille. "This woman would be out on the street if not for the compassion and generosity of Anastasia Pollack. And this is how she thanks her. By making false accusations about the character of a woman who has never been anything but kind to her, no matter how little this nasty, hateful woman deserved it. You should all be ashamed of yourselves."

A moment later, the Action News feed went black.

"Wow!" said Cloris. "You've got yourself a real champion. I'll bet that news clip goes viral."

"I hope not. If it does, it will have the completely opposite effect." But I didn't mention that when I shot Spader a text: *Watched the live feed. Thanks. I owe you.*

He wrote back: *Didn't know we were keeping score.*

"Remind me never to complain about my mother-in-law," said Cloris.

We both went back to work. An hour later, the receptionist called. "There are thirteen angry, elderly women in the lobby. They're demanding to see you."

"Tell them I'm not here. If they refuse to leave, have security escort them from the building."

A moment later, my phone rang again. "They've whipped out cans of spray paint and are threatening to use them."

"Call the police."

I ran down the hall to alert Naomi to the situation. "I'm sorry. I probably should have run home to unlock the door for them."

"It's not like you live around the corner. Sounds to me like your mother-in-law deliberately set you up."

That hit me like a bucket of ice water. Had she? Was Lucille that premeditating and devious? "What should I do?"

Naomi stood. "Nothing. Stay here. I'll handle it."

As I followed Naomi out of her office, I said, "I never expected anything like this. She's really crossed the line this time."

Naomi's response heartened me. "Yes, she has. Perhaps it's time you moved your mother-in-law out of your home and into a supervised setting. You don't deserve this treatment, Anastasia."

I wish I had access to the security cameras. I'd love to see Naomi in action, but I'd have to settle for an after-the-fact account.

Twenty minutes later, Naomi stepped into my cubicle. "They've gone."

"With or without the help of the police?"

"In concert with. I told them they had two choices. They could leave peacefully, and I'd forget they were ever here. Or the police would haul them off, and Reynolds-Alsopp Media would press charges for trespassing and disorderly conduct. They opted to leave on their own but not before accusing me of harboring an abuser. I don't envy you this evening, Anastasia."

I didn't envy me, either, but at the moment, I was more concerned with any possible damage to the building. "They didn't spray paint anything in the lobby?"

"Not a drop."

I breathed a sigh of relief.

~*~

My relief was short-lived, though. I arrived home to find someone had spray-painted *An Elder Abuser Lives Here* in large black letters on my teal front door. I called the police.

"We're aware of the vandalism," said the desk sergeant, "and have already apprehended the suspects. All thirteen of them. They were booked and released after a hearing was scheduled."

"My mother-in-law and her cohorts?"

"Yes, ma'am. The responding officers caught them red-handed." I heard him bite back a chuckle. "Or black-handed in this case."

"Who reported it?"

"The gentleman directly across the street from you."

"That's not possible. He was murdered last week. Do you have a name?"

"Yes, ma'am. Hold on while I check." A moment later, he came back on the line. "The police report lists a Lance Melville."

I thanked the desk sergeant and hung up.

After changing into a pair of old jeans and a T-shirt, I hunted through the various cans of leftover paint on a shelf in the basement. We had last painted the exterior of the house twelve years ago. I held little hope of finding any usable teal paint. However, once I found the can and broke through the solid skin of paint, I found about two inches of usable latex. Not enough to repaint the entire door but hopefully enough to cover up the words.

I carried the can, a stir stick, a rag, some sandpaper, and a brush outside. Before setting to work, I took a picture of the offensive commentary in case I needed to preserve a record of the evidence. Then I sanded down as much of the black lettering as possible.

Paint quality breaks down over time, and as I stirred, I quickly discovered the remains of the can consisted of lumpy goop. I added some water from the garden hose and continued to stir, which resulted in transforming the goop into a watery soup of floating clumps.

Undeterred, I began to paint but soon discovered I'd need several coats to cover the black paint. Not having nearly enough soupy latex, I tackled the most offensive word first, cursing Lucille with each stroke of the brush. Part of me wanted to lock her out permanently. *How dare she?* If not for me, she'd be living in some rat-infested subsidized hovel in Camden.

"Anastasia?"

I turned to find Gloria walking down my front path. She stared at the words and shook her head. "I'm so sorry. Lance told me what happened."

My thoughts jerked from Lucille to Lance Melville. *Gloria knew he was at her house?* What she didn't know was that I knew who Lance was. I played dumb. "You know him? The police said someone named Lance Melville reported the vandalism."

"He's my trust fund manager."

"I'm confused. He just happened to be driving down the street at the time?"

She chuckled. "Sort of. I was halfway to the Catskills this morning to drop Billy off when I realized I couldn't remember if I'd turned off the oven. I think my brain is still fuzzy from the pain meds, even though I'm no longer taking them. I asked him to drive over to the house to check."

"He has a key?"

"My father always said it's a good idea to give a spare key to someone you trust." She shrugged. "I don't have anyone I trust more than Lance."

That explained what I'd seen this morning. Nothing nefarious. Just a friend doing a favor. But why had he hung around all day? The vandalism took place after the press conference. Most likely, even after Lucille and her minions had shown up at my office. I hadn't bothered to check out the security cameras when I arrived home. What difference would it have made to know when the graffiti had occurred? "And was it?"

Her brow creased in puzzlement. "Was what?"

"The oven. Had you left it on?"

"Oh, yes. Good thing I called him. I might've burned down the house."

She pointed to the door. "Why did those women target you?"

I dipped the brush in the can to sop up more latex. Alex and Sophie had painted Lucille in broad strokes in the podcast, mentioning her only when necessary and avoiding political commentary. Not wanting to dive into the weeds with Gloria, I kept details about Lucille to a minimum as I stroked the brush across the door. "My mother-in-law didn't have her housekey. Apparently, she decided I'd deliberately locked her out of the house as a form of elder abuse."

Gloria's eyes grew wide. "Your mother-in-law accused you of abuse because *she* forgot her key?"

I shrugged. "We've never gotten along."

"But she lives with you, right?"

"How do you know that?"

"From some of the news articles I read. Why would you allow someone like that to live with you?"

"I couldn't exactly kick her out after her son died."

"And this is how she repays you?"

I frowned at the words on my front door. "I'm afraid so."

"Someone should nominate you for sainthood."

Gloria's comment opened a conversational door that might gain me more insights into what made her tick. "What about you?

What kind of relationship do you have with your in-laws?"

"I never knew them. They both died when Barry was in his teens. He bounced around in foster care for a few years before he turned eighteen and enlisted."

"And your family?"

"They tried to break us up." She pulled a face. "I probably should've listened to them, but I was stubborn. No one was going to tell me what to do."

She grew thoughtful for a moment before continuing, "We met the summer I turned nineteen. He was twenty and stationed at Fort Dix. I don't know why I fell for him." She grinned. "Hormones, probably. I suppose it's hard to believe, but Barry was quite the stud back in the day. He swept me off my feet. We were like Danny and Sandy in *Grease*."

How did Rowena's brief marriage fit into the timeline of this puzzle? "Did you marry right away?"

She shook her head. "My parents insisted we wait until after I graduated college."

"Did you?"

"Reluctantly. Shortly after I went back to school, Barry was deployed overseas. He was wounded in combat and spent time at a VA hospital."

She mumbled as she stared at her feet. "Even before the motorcycle accident, he suffered from PTSD. But for all his faults, I knew he loved me and Billy. He didn't deserve what happened to him."

"Do you have any idea who killed him?"

"Like I told you at the viewing, it could have been any of the reenactors or their wives. Or others."

I decided to go out on a limb. "Billy said people deliberately goaded your husband into fights, then blackmailed you to keep them from filing charges."

She inhaled deeply, then nodded as she exhaled a sigh. "He mentioned he told you. I was angry at first, but it was bound to come out during the investigation. That detective friend of yours suggested I killed Barry to stop the blackmail." She forced an ironic laugh. "I told him I have more money than I could spend in three lifetimes. Paying them off was better than dealing with assault charges. Barry never would have survived prison."

I waited for her to say more, but she only added, "I should get home. Lance offered to bring takeout for dinner."

"Before you go, did you speak with Detective Spader today?"

"You mean about Rocky Benedetto?"

"Then you heard?"

"Lance told me. The detective showed up at the house this morning while I was on my way to the Catskills."

"Did he give Lance any details?"

"Only that Rocky was murdered last night around the time Billy and I were having dinner with you."

"Anything else?"

Gloria thought for a moment. "That he was also stabbed to death."

"Can you think of anyone who would want both Barry and Rocky dead?"

Gloria narrowed her eyes. "I thought you weren't working with the police."

"I'm not."

"Sure sounds like you are."

"I like solving puzzles."

She stared at me for a moment before saying, "It might pay off for you."

"What do you mean?"

"I've decided to offer a reward for information leading to the arrest of Barry's killer."

I knew where this was going. "Are you dangling a carrot in the hope of getting me involved in the investigation?"

She shrugged. "I really don't care who solves the murder. I want my husband's killer caught, and I'll do whatever it takes to make that happen."

"Just make sure you don't cross the line," I warned her.

Her eyebrows shot up. "What does that mean?"

"The police don't take kindly to people impeding their investigations."

"I'll keep that in mind. Meanwhile, tell your cop friend to take a closer look at the other reenactors. Especially Axel Brock. Maybe he'll listen to you since he doesn't seem to believe anything I tell him. It doesn't take a rocket scientist."

"What doesn't?"

"To figure out the killer." When I continued to look puzzled, she added, "Two reenactors were murdered. Both stabbed to death."

"Are you suggesting the killer is another reenactor?"

"Exactly."

I shook my head. "Not necessarily. The murderer might be someone who wanted to frame a reenactor."

Gloria sighed. "I suppose you have a point. But it would still be a reenactor, wouldn't it?"

"Or not. Were both Barry and Rocky involved in any other activities besides the battle reenactments?"

"They both bowled in the same league, but most of the other

bowlers were also reenactors."

At that moment, Zack pulled into the driveway. Gloria spun on her heels and hustled down the walkway toward the street before Zack exited the car.

He scowled at the door as he crossed the lawn. "I'm guessing you already know what happened."

"Robyn alerted me to the press conference. I watched the live feed. Spader was there. He certainly didn't mince any words speaking to the press."

"And this?" he asked indicating the door with a tilt of his head.

"Lucille and her cohorts showed up at my office. They were brandishing spray paint. When Naomi threatened to press charges, they left." I stared at the door, the words still evident under several layers of paint, despite my efforts. "I'm guessing they returned to the house to take their revenge."

We both focused on the door. The graffiti now read, *An eld lives here.* I'd had just enough paint to somewhat cover *er* and *abuser*, but the offensive graffiti still faintly showed through the paint. I dropped the paintbrush into the empty can and fought unsuccessfully to stem a shaky sigh. "I've run out of paint."

"We'll pick some up on our way home tonight."

"Home from where?"

"We're going out to dinner."

"What are we celebrating?"

He drew me into his arms. "You surviving the day."

"The day isn't over yet."

He bent to pick up the empty paint can. "I'll set this in the basement to dry out before we toss it and soak the brush. Why don't you freshen up?"

"What about Nick?"

"He's going out to dinner with some coworkers. We have the evening to ourselves."

~*~

Zack had made a reservation at a newly opened restaurant in downtown Cranford. He waited until we were seated and had ordered before he brought up Lucille. Reaching across the table, he clasped both of my hands in his and in a somber tone said, "Today was the last straw. I don't want to come home one evening to find she's bashed in your skull with her cane."

"I agree."

He stared at me. "You do? I thought I was going to have to browbeat you until you gave in."

The sommelier returned with the bottle of wine Zack had chosen. I waited until he'd opened the bottle, poured two glasses, and departed before I spoke. "I've had enough. More than enough. I can't take her spitefulness anymore. She was a bitter, nasty woman before Karl's death, but every week since, she grows exponentially worse."

I hadn't wanted to come to this conclusion, but Zack was right. Who knew when Lucille would finally snap? "Dr. Pavlochek said she aced all her cognitive tests. Maybe she's not experiencing the onset of dementia. Maybe negative character traits simply increase with age, but I'm tired of living in a war zone. She's sucking the joy out of our lives. I want her gone from our home."

He lifted his glass in a toast. "And here I thought it would take at least two bottles of wine. You haven't even had your first sip."

I clicked my glass against his. "Don't get too cocky. We still need to figure out how to convince her to move in permanently with Harriet or relocate to a senior facility. She's never going to agree to either, and no judge is going to sign off on commitment papers just because she's got a mean streak a mile long. Besides, even though she's spending more and more nights with Harriet, our home is still a revolving door with an all-you-can-eat pantry for her and her minions. She won't willingly give that up."

"Willingly or not, she's got to go," said Zack. "You hold her medical power of attorney. Her behavior today should enable you to have her moved to assisted living, even if she goes kicking and screaming."

"Harriet and her other minions will spring her just like they did at the hospital."

"Perhaps, but by then we'll have changed the locks on the doors. I also think you should take out a restraining order on her."

I stared wide-eyed at him. "Seriously?"

"I've never been more serious. That woman is on a trajectory to cause severe bodily harm to someone. I'll do everything in my power to make sure that someone isn't you, the boys, your mother, or any of our friends."

His expression left no doubt that he meant it. Feminism aside, sometimes a girl just needs a white knight. I wasn't too proud to admit this was one of those times, and I welcomed Zack's forcefulness regarding our Lucille problem. Without his insistence, I doubt I'd have had the courage to reach this decision on my own.

"First thing Monday, I'll speak with Dr. Pavlochek. He said Lucille aced her cognitive tests, but perhaps there are others he didn't perform that might give us more of an insight into what's going on with her."

"We should ask Spader how to go about getting a restraining order," he said. "Given all their interactions with her, the police should have plenty of documentation to present to a judge." He whipped out his phone.

"You're calling someone now?"

"I don't think we should wait until Monday. I'm texting Spader to let him know we need to speak with him at his earliest convenience."

Afterwards, while we ate dinner, I filled Zack in on Lance Melville's arrival at Gloria's house early that morning and how he had called in Lucille's vandalism this afternoon.

~*~

To my surprise, an hour later, as the waiter cleared our dinner dishes, I saw Spader enter the restaurant, scope out the room, then head for our table.

THIRTEEN

Zack sat with his back facing the front of the restaurant. "Did you ask Spader to meet us here?"

He offered a sheepish grin. "No time like the present."

"Were you afraid I'd change my mind?"

"Never."

"Pretty confident, aren't you?"

His eyes teased. "It's one of my many superpowers."

"Right. At some point I'd like a full list, please." By this time, Spader had arrived at our table. "Have a seat, Detective. You're just in time to join us for coffee and dessert."

He pulled out one of the two remaining chairs as the waiter returned with dessert menus and hovered off to the side as we perused them.

When I glanced up from my menu, the waiter asked, "Has madame decided?"

As much as I disliked being called ma'am, I had no problem with madame, especially when spoken with a French accent, even though far from authentic. I handed him the menu. "Madame would love a slice of your Black Forest cake and a vanilla latte."

Zack ordered an Irish coffee. "And an extra fork."

I raised an eyebrow. "Did I agree to share?"

He waved his hand toward some of the other tables. "Look around. Have you noticed the size of the desserts?"

I scanned the room, zeroing in on the tables where dessert was being served. I nearly gulped. Every cake, no matter the flavor, was seven layers tall and at least three inches thick. Even I, the Chocoholic Queen of Desserts, couldn't eat that large a slice of cake. "Two forks," I told the waiter.

"Coffee for me. Black," said Spader.

"Make that three forks," I added.

The waiter returned minutes later with our coffees and the most ginormous slice of Black Forest cake I'd ever seen. After savoring a bite, I turned to Spader. "Before we discuss the reason Zack invited you to join us, I'd like to know what you learned about Lance Melville. Apparently, he didn't just drop in to check Gloria's oven, as she led me to believe. Either he came and went throughout the day or spent the entire day at her house. She also mentioned they planned to have dinner together this evening."

Spader helped himself to a forkful of cake. "He was unpacking some of her cartons when I arrived."

"Not a typical item under the Terms of Service for a trust fund administrator," said Zack.

"Did you ask him if he also washes windows?" I asked.

Spader nearly choked on his cake. Once he recovered, he said, "No, but I did ask him exactly what his relationship was with Gloria. He swore it was purely platonic, that he'd known her most of her life. When her father was dying, he promised he'd look after her."

"Does looking after her include eliminating a problematic husband?" I asked.

Spader shot me a give-me-a-break look. "I was a bit more tactful in my questioning, but let's just say he's now definitely moved to the top of the Persons of Interest column in our investigation. He knew about the ongoing blackmail, and after her father's death, he continued giving Gloria cash from the trust to pay off the blackmailers."

"What about Rocky?" I asked.

"That's where it gets interesting," said Spader. "He seemed genuinely shocked to hear of his murder."

"He could have been acting," suggested Zack.

Spader shook his head. "If so, he's a damned good actor. I've investigated enough murders over the last two decades to spot the tells of a suspect who's lying. I saw none with him."

"Where is the investigation at this point?" I asked, knowing that with each passing day, the odds grew against finding the killer or killers of both Barry Sumner and Rocky Benedetto. Spader knew his stuff. He had an impressive record, but no detectives ever solve all their cases.

"We're in the process of requestioning everyone who attended the viewing and those reenactors who didn't. Someone might trip up, remember something, or point us to another connection between the two victims."

"Gloria mentioned both men bowled in the same league," I said.

"I already have a list of the league members."

Zack leaned forward, placed his elbows on the table, and addressed Spader. "I'd like to change the subject to what occurred at our home this afternoon."

Spader jumped right in, as if he had prior knowledge of the event. "That woman is a genuine menace. One day, she's going to go too far, and seriously injure someone. Or worse."

"Agreed," said Zack.

"What can I do to help?"

"What are the statutes concerning restraining orders?" I asked. "Lucille hasn't physically attacked any of us. At least not yet. But she makes constant threats. Could we get one against her based on her behavior?"

"In my opinion?" said Spader. "Yes, but it's up to a judge. New Jersey requires a recent act of domestic violence. That's defined mostly as assault, harassment, or terroristic threats. The abuse doesn't have to be physical. It can include various forms of verbal abuse. Anything from destructive criticism, shouting, name-calling, mocking, or verbal threats. Her actions to this point would fall under harassment. You need to provide proof, but I don't think that's a problem in your case. You have witnesses, news footage, and prior police reports that document her various run-ins with the law, which back up your accusations."

"Where do we file?" asked Zack.

"Either the police station or the county courthouse. A judge will determine if you qualify for a temporary restraining order. If so, a date will be set for a hearing for the final protective order."

"Then what?" I asked.

"After you receive the TRO, the police will serve your mother-in-law with the papers and remove her from the premises if she refuses to go willingly. She won't be allowed back during the TRO and will be prohibited from making any form of contact with you. She'll have to appear in court for the hearing, at which time she'll have a chance to defend herself."

"Is there a jury?" I asked.

Spader shook his head. "The judge makes the final determination."

"How long will all this take?" asked Zack.

"Usually within ten days from the time the TRO is issued until the hearing."

Zack turned to me. "I suggest we head over to the police station this evening. I see no point waiting until court opens on Monday."

"Monday wouldn't work for me, anyway," I said. "I can't miss our monthly issue planning meeting."

"Then it's settled." Zack reached out to shake Spader's hand. "We owe you."

Spader accepted Zack's hand. "As I told your wife earlier today, I didn't know we were keeping score." He then turned to me and punctuated a grin with a wink.

After we finished our dessert and Zack paid the bill, we stopped at police headquarters to fill out the paperwork for the temporary restraining order. Before returning home, we made one last stop at the home center for a can of paint.

As we waited for the clerk to formulate and mix the color, Zack asked, "Are you sure you're still okay with filing a restraining order?"

I didn't hesitate. "I am. Surprisingly, I feel no guilt."

"You have no reason to feel guilty. You did your best."

"I know, but I also know that my best will never be good enough for Lucille. I'm finally at peace with that. It's her loss."

"Prepare yourself, though."

"For what?"

"It could get ugly if she's at the house when the order is served."

"Hopefully, it will occur while I'm at work, but I have a suspicion she won't dare show up after the stunts she pulled today. Even she has to know she finally went too far. I suspect she's hiding out at Harriet Kleinhample's apartment."

~*~

After breakfast the next morning, Zack and I grabbed the new can of paint and supplies and headed outside to tackle the front door. "That's interesting," I said.

He followed my gaze as I stared across the street. Lance Melville's Hummer sat parked in Gloria's driveway. "How many trust managers make house calls early on a Saturday morning?" I asked.

"Probably not many, but I don't think he ever left last night. I noticed his pickup still parked in her driveway before we went to bed. Maybe there's more to his relationship with Gloria than she led us to believe."

"If so, it raises a host of questions that add credence to Spader's suspicions about them."

Zack began to sand the door to remove the lumps I'd added during yesterday's attempt to cover up the graffiti. "What does your gut tell you, Nancy Drew?"

I crouched over the can and stared at the teal ripples as I slowly stirred the latex. "I don't think Gloria had a hand in Barry's death. Even with the difficulties of their marriage, she seems to have truly cared about him. She could have divorced him, but she didn't. Why would she kill him? It wasn't over money, and unless both she and Billy are lying through their teeth, Barry never raised a hand to either of them."

"And Lance?"

"Since we've never interacted with him and only have Gloria's word about who he is and their relationship, the jury's still out, as far as I'm concerned. Maybe he's had a crush on her for years and finally decided to get rid of the one impediment to a happily-ever-after with her."

"I suppose..."

He didn't sound convinced, but I refrained from pointing out the obvious, how a guy who'd graced the cover of *People* magazine on more than one occasion could fall for a slightly overweight, pear-shaped middle-aged me. Instead, all I said was, "Life is full of mysteries."

"There's another possibility," he suggested.

I stopped stirring and looked at him. "Which is?"

"What if he's really after the trust? He first gets rid of Barry, then arranges an accident that takes out both Gloria and Billy, thus inheriting millions of dollars."

"That's cold. And devious."

"Prisons are filled with greedy people who thought they could get away with committing the perfect crime."

Not always. "Plenty of murders are never solved. Or solved long after the perpetrator has died a natural death."

Across the street, Gloria's door opened. She and Lance Melville exited the house and made their way to his Hummer. She waved and called out, "Good morning," as she opened the front passenger door. Zack and I replied with a wave of our own before she stepped inside the truck.

Lance ignored us, not even glancing in our direction. A moment later, they pulled out of the driveway and drove down the street.

That's when I noticed a black sedan parked at the end of the block. As the pickup turned onto Central Avenue toward the

Parkway entrance, the sedan pulled out onto the street and slowly followed. When it drove past our house, I recognized Bella Halston, the officer who had accompanied Spader to the funeral home the night of Barry's viewing. Maybe he was grooming her for a rise in the ranks once next year's budget took effect.

"I'm not sure that's the best use of strained resources," I said motioning to the car. "I don't want to tell Spader how to do his job, but it's obvious where Gloria and Lance are headed."

"I'll bite, Ms. Claire Voyant. Where are they going? Out to breakfast?"

I shook my head. "Maybe as a stop along the way to pick up Billy at camp. Although..."

"What if they're fleeing to Canada?"

I love when we're on the same wavelength. I never had that with Karl. It adds another dimension, one I never knew possible until meeting Zack, to a relationship. "Exactly. If they keep heading north after they leave the camp, someone will need to alert the authorities to pick them up before they cross the border."

Maybe Spader wasn't wasting precious county resources after all.

~*~

Except later that afternoon, Billy knocked on the door. Scratch a run for the border.

Nick was about to leave the house. "I'm headed to the pool, then out for burgers with some friends."

From down the hall, I heard the disappointment in Billy's voice. "Okay, maybe I'll see you tomorrow."

I arrived in the foyer as he turned to leave, but Nick stopped him. "Want to come?"

Billy hesitated. "Your friends wouldn't mind?"

"No way, dude. The more the merrier."

"I'll have to ask my mom."

"Go ahead. I'll wait."

Nick shut the front door as Billy raced toward the street. When he turned around and saw me, he shrugged. "He's really desperate for friends, Mom."

"You're racking up Good Son points, Nick. I'm proud of you."

A few minutes later, Billy returned, dressed in swim trunks and carrying a change of clothes and a towel under his arm. He and Nick headed off for the pool.

Mama called a few minutes later. "Nordstrom is having an end-of-summer sale. I thought we could drive up to the mall, do some shopping, and have dinner. Just the two of us."

She could do some shopping—with the credit cards Ira had given her and paid each month. I could think of dozens of places I'd rather be than the Mall at Short Hills on a Saturday afternoon with my shopaholic mother. And dinner for two? That was code for an interrogation. When it came to mother/daughter relationships, Mama wielded a mean guilt trip, and I usually caved.

However, Zack had planned to spend the day making inroads on several deadlines. Helping me tackle the front door had eaten precious hours. Therefore, I managed a forced excitement into my voice and said, "Sounds like fun, Mama. I'll pick you up shortly, but Zack and I have dinner plans."

Sometimes her internal lie detector didn't work as well in non-face-to-face interactions, especially when I wasn't stretching the truth too much. I hoped this was one of those times. After all, Zack and I did have dinner plans for the evening. We fully intended to eat—somewhere at some point.

Mama sounded disappointed, but if she planned for me to be

her pack mule as she tried on dozens of new suits and dresses she didn't need, I'd require a clean break after a few hours. And possibly a Moscow Mule to numb the pain.

I used to enjoy an occasional trip to the mall. That was prior to falling out of the middle class and getting roped into a failed sting operation that involved a trip to the Burberry store and hours sitting in a ladies' room stall, both of which resulted in my first near-death experience.

Mama's mall memories of late weren't much better. On a trip to have her Tiffany diamond engagement ring appraised for insurance purposes, she'd discovered the ring her deceased fiancé had given her was a third-rate, seriously flawed stone. Only the classic robin's egg blue box had come from Tiffany. I'm not sure which bothered her more, finding out the true value of the ring or the humiliation she sustained upon hearing it from a pompous salesperson.

Less than an hour later, with a smile permanently frozen on my face, I followed Mama around Nordstrom as she pulled one outfit after another from the racks, held it up in front of her, and awaited my nod of approval before handing the garment to me to hold for her. Only after I'd collected a massive armload of assorted suits and dresses and could barely see over the top of the teetering pile, did she steer me into a fitting room.

One by one, Mama removed a garment from the pile and placed it on the hooks on either wall alongside the mirror. I shook the circulation back into my arms. "I'll wait for you in the seating area, Mama."

"You're not going to help me?"

"Mama, you live alone. If you need my help getting in and out of an outfit, it will remain unworn in your condo bedroom closet."

She frowned at a lemon-yellow silk sheath with a row of buttons up the back of the dress. "I suppose there's no point even trying this one on, then."

She removed the dress from the hook and handed it to me. "Would you mind hanging this on the discards rack, dear?"

One down. Dozens to go. I accepted the dress, stepped from the fitting room, and headed for the waiting area in anticipation of the long fashion show and even longer decision-making process to come.

Rounding the corner, I nearly collided with Gloria Forester.

FOURTEEN

"Anastasia! What a coincidence."

I certainly hoped so. I'd hate to think that Gloria was stalking me. "Yes, isn't it? I'm here with my mother."

Gloria carried an assortment of pants, tops, and dresses, mostly casual except for a few fancier garments. It's one thing to run out to buy a sedate black dress for a funeral if you have nothing appropriate in your closet. It's another to head to Nordstrom for a sale a week after your husband is brutally murdered.

Seeing me eyeing the clothing she clutched to her chest, Gloria offered a shrug with an explanation. "Lance decided I needed a diversion to help me cope with Barry's death. I haven't bought any new clothes for myself in ages."

Lance Melville certainly went above and beyond the norm in his role as trust fund manager. Did he harbor ulterior motives? Had the two of them been carrying on an affair behind Barry's back? Their relationship certainly suggested more than that of someone looking out for the financial well-being of a deceased friend's daughter.

Not knowing how else to respond, I said, "I hope it helps. I'll leave you to it."

She blocked my path. "I should introduce you to Lance first. He's sitting in the waiting area." She pivoted and reversed direction. I followed.

We found Lance Melville, looking bored as he absent-mindedly leafed through the pages of a magazine without really looking at it. He glanced up and frowned as we exited into the waiting area. "Gloria, you couldn't possibly have tried on anything yet."

She tittered. "Of course not." She motioned toward me. "This is Anastasia Pollack, the neighbor across the street who's been so kind to Billy. And me."

Lance discarded the magazine, stood, and offered his hand. "A pleasure, Mrs. Pollack. And quite a coincidence."

"My exact words to Gloria, Mr. Melville." As I shook his hand, I added, "And it's Barnes, not Pollack, but please call me Anastasia."

He didn't suggest I call him Lance. Instead, he turned questioningly to Gloria.

"My mistake," she said. "I guess I still have that podcast swimming around in my brain."

"Ah, yes," said Lance. "The podcast." He focused back on me. "Gloria told me all about your exploits. Are you aiding the police in their investigation into Barry's murder?"

I certainly didn't want to say anything that would lead him to believe I had questioned whether he or Gloria had a hand in Barry's death. "I don't aid the police. They're quite capable of solving crimes on their own."

He frowned. "That's not what I've heard."

I forced a chuckle. "Don't believe everything you hear. Especially on unauthorized podcasts."

"What do you think of this one, dear? Isn't it stunning?"

I turned to find Mama had exited the dressing room into the waiting area. She twirled in front of the set of full-length tryptic mirrors that stood opposite the chairs. A garland of large roses encircled the full hem of a pale pink tea-length sleeveless shirtwaist dress with a scooped neck.

Before I had a chance to utter an opinion, Mama zeroed in on Lance Melville standing beside me. "Oh, hello, are you one of my daughter's friends or coworkers?"

I quickly made introductions. "Mama, this is my neighbor, Gloria and her friend Lance." I deliberately refrained from adding last names, hoping Mama wouldn't make the connection to the recent murder that had occurred across the street from me.

Ignoring Gloria, Mama held her hand out to Lance. Her eyes sparkled. I knew that look. Mama had shifted into husband-hunting mode. "Flora O'Keefe."

That caught me by surprise. When had she decided to drop Tuttnauer from her long list of former husbands?

Mama must have sensed me eyeing her because she shot me a pointed look before continuing to speak to Lance and Gloria. "I didn't catch your last names."

"Melville," said Lance, still holding Mama's hand. Or was she holding his?

Mama turned to Gloria. "And yours, dear?"

"Forester."

"Oh." Mama segued into sympathy mode. "The widow. I'm so sorry for your loss."

Gloria stared at the floor as she mumbled her thanks.

I needed to break up this impromptu meet-and-greet. "Mama, the dress is lovely, but you have many more to try on, and we have limited time."

Lance extricated his hand from Mama and turned to Gloria. "You still haven't tried on anything."

She studied the pile of clothes in her arms. "I suppose I should start."

Unlike Mama, who shopped 'til she dropped, Gloria sounded like Lance had dragged her unwillingly to the mall. However, she followed Mama into the dressing room, leaving me alone with Lance Melville. After a brief awkward silence, he grabbed the magazine he'd earlier tossed aside and returned to his seat. This time, he opened to a random page and buried his nose in whatever article had appeared.

I took out my phone and shot Zack a text. Maybe Cloris had been onto something when she compared Lance Melville to Lawrence Tuttnauer. The vibes Melville sent off were anything but friendly. I didn't expect trouble, but trouble often found me anyway. It wouldn't hurt to alert Zack to the situation.

A few minutes later, Mama returned wearing another dress, this time a V-neck peach shantung sheath with capped sleeves. The dress hugged her figure, making me wish, as I had for most of my life, that I'd inherited more of her genes and less of my father's.

Lance Melville's attention remained riveted on the magazine he held in front of his nose, but I noticed he hadn't flipped a page since he'd first returned to the magazine.

Mama sighed as she stepped into the corridor that led to the dressing rooms. Seconds later Gloria returned to the waiting area.

"Finished already?" asked Lance.

The corners of Gloria's mouth dipped. "I've changed my mind. Nothing here appeals to me."

Lance stood. "Why don't we try some of the other stores?"

She shrugged. "Sure. Why not?" She started to walk away but stopped, turned back, and offered me a smile that never reached her eyes. "Nice seeing you, Anastasia."

Lance Melville inclined his head toward me. "A pleasure meeting you, Mrs. Barnes." He then took Gloria's arm and led her toward the store exit.

"What an odd duo," said Mama the moment the two were out of sight. She still wore the peach sheath. "Are you sure one of them didn't kill that woman's husband?"

"Mama, were you spying?"

"Of course, dear."

Why didn't that surprise me? "I'm not sure of anything, right now, except that I have faith Detective Spader will figure it all out."

She cocked her head and raised an eyebrow. "Without your help?"

I wasn't sure of that, either, but it wouldn't hurt to let him know about this odd encounter.

Mama spent the next hour trying on the other outfits she'd chosen, then decided she couldn't make up her mind. Never one to employ the eeny-meeny-miny-moe method, rather than narrowing down her choices, she bought them all.

I wondered if Ira would bat an eye when he opened his credit card statement. Probably not. His guilt runneth over from having introduced his father-in-law to my mother, and Ira always assuaged his guilt with his AmEx card. No rosary or worry beads for him, only ka-ching, ka-ching.

Mama and I departed Nordstrom with both of us laden down by her purchases. While we rode the escalator to the first level, I thought I caught a glimpse of a full-figured, big-haired over-bleached blonde wearing a glittery, low-cut emerald-green Spandex top and matching Spandex hotpants. The same outfit Tonya Benedetto had worn the day Gloria accused her of having an affair with Barry. Even though New Jersey was awash in full-figured, big-haired bleach blondes, what were the odds that two of them owned the exact same glittery, low-cut emerald-green Spandex top and matching hotpants?

As the escalator descended, I scanned the lower level, searching for Gloria and Lance, but the first floor was packed with shoppers. I didn't find them anywhere before the escalator descended farther, cutting off my bird's eye view.

The odds of all of us at the mall at the same time stretched both coincidence and probability. For all I knew, Gloria and Lance may have been only a few steps ahead of Tonya. Was it possible Tonya was stalking Gloria? And if so, why?

I admit, paranoia had set in, and I repeatedly checked my rearview mirror throughout the drive from Summit to Mama's condo. I saw no evidence of either a classic red Mustang or an ice-blue Hummer following us, which provided me with a modicum of comfort.

However, Lance Melville's quasi-hostile attitude sent too many red flags waving around in my brain. Given Gloria's countless experiences with the reenactors and others who took advantage of Barry's handicap, maybe Melville was simply overly suspicious of anyone who offered Gloria a kind gesture. Those blackmailing incidents had to breed strong cynicism, souring the milk of human kindness.

Or was Melville a psychological abuser? Had he systematically insinuated himself into every aspect of Gloria's life until he'd assumed total control over her and Billy?

Then there was Tonya Benedetto, assuming Tonya had been the person I saw at the mall. I hate to form an opinion based solely on looks, but Tonya didn't come across as someone who shopped for upscale designer brands at one of the most exclusive malls in the country. Even during end-of-season sales. Not if that glittery, low-cut Spandex top and matching hotpants were any indication of her taste in clothing.

The woman I spied was headed for the exit, with not a single shopping bag dangling from her arm. If I had only stepped on the escalator a few seconds earlier, I may have spied Gloria and Lance several steps ahead of Tonya. If so, I could firmly place her in my Tonya Is Stalking Gloria column.

But why? What did she have to gain by following Gloria? Was she trying to intimidate her, or did she have a more sinister motive?

~*~

By the time I had dropped Mama off at her condo and returned home, I'd convinced myself that Tonya was the Spandex woman at the mall and that I should mention my suspicions about her to Detective Spader.

I didn't have long to wait. As I turned onto our street, I noticed his unmarked black sedan parked in front of my next-door neighbor's house. I wasn't surprised. I suspected Zack had contacted him after receiving the text I sent from the mall.

I also noted that Melville's Hummer pickup was once again parked in Gloria's driveway. No surprise there, either.

I found Zack and Spader camped out in the living room. Each

179

held a bottle of beer. Both men rose as I entered, but only Zack kissed me hello.

"How'd it go with Flora?" He held me at arm's length and eyed me for what I assumed were signs of wear and tear.

"Let's just say we needn't worry about a recession while Mama has Ira's limitless AmEx credit card at her disposal. The woman singlehandedly keeps the economy on a solid footing."

Spader chuckled.

I turned to him. "Hey, I'm serious."

"Keeps her out of trouble," he said. "Which is more than we can say about your mother-in-law."

"Any word on her whereabouts?"

He shrugged. "Not my beat but I haven't heard anything through the blue grapevine. At least we can assume she hasn't killed anyone or died at the hands of someone she royally pissed off."

Zack headed into the kitchen, returning seconds later with a glass of white wine for me. I kicked off my shoes and curled up in the corner of the sofa. "At the rate Lucille's going," I said, "it's only a matter of time before one of those scenarios comes to pass. Her behavior grows more erratic with each passing day."

The doorbell rang the moment Zack settled next to me on the sofa. "That should be our dinner. I ordered Thai." He bounded back up and headed for the front door.

While we passed around cartons of Pad Thai, Khao Pad, and Pad Kra Pao Moo, I told Zack and Spader about my encounter with Gloria and her trusty trust fund manager. "I don't know what to make of their relationship, but I'm convinced there's more to it than overseeing investments and account distributions."

"I suspect we're all in agreement there," said Spader.

"But we can't necessarily assume it's a suspicious relationship," added Zack.

"No," I said. "Their odd personalities don't automatically make them complicit in Barry's death. Even if the two were carrying on an affair, it doesn't mean either of them killed Barry."

"But neither does it rule them out," added Spader.

I paused, my chopsticks halfway to my mouth. "Ever feel like you're a hamster on a wheel?"

He scooped up a mouthful of noodles with his chopsticks. "More and more, especially on this case," he said, dropping noodles into his mouth.

I knew the feeling. "There's also something else I haven't mentioned yet."

Both men stared at me. "As Mama and I descended the escalator, I'm almost certain I noticed Tonya Benedetto."

"Doing what?" asked Spader.

"Heading toward one of the exits. I think she may be stalking Gloria."

"Are you sure it was Tonya?" asked Zack.

"About ninety-five percent sure. She was wearing the same outfit as the day Gloria accused her of having an affair with Barry."

"I'm sure there are other women who own that outfit," said Spader.

"Not many who shop at that mall."

When he frowned, I added, "If you'd seen it, you'd understand."

"I'll take your word for it. What else can you tell me?"

"Not much. I wish I'd gotten more of a glimpse of the crowd exiting the mall in front of her, but the place was wall-to-wall shoppers. You'd think it was Black Friday. I couldn't tell if Gloria and Melville were somewhere in the mix, but I find it far too coincidental that she happened to be at the mall at the same time as Gloria and Melville, especially since she wasn't carrying any shopping bags."

"Even if all three were at the mall at the same time, it could still be coincidence," suggested Zack. "Tonya may have gone to the mall to return an item, not to shop. Or purchased something small enough to place in her purse."

I indicated Spader with a wave of my hand. "Except our friendly neighborhood homicide detective over here doesn't believe in coincidence."

The man in question shrugged. "I suppose they do occur occasionally. Rarely in my investigations, though."

"Anything new to report?" I asked, changing the subject.

Spader sighed. "As a matter of fact, once again you were right, Mrs. Barnes."

Even though I had no idea what I was right about, I forced my face to remain passive. Whatever it was, it appeared Spader was bracing himself for an I-told-you-so on my part. Although he should know by now, I'd never gloat. Instead, I simply asked, "About?"

He grimaced. "Rocky Benedetto. He had massive amounts of Benadryl in his system. Someone knocked him out before the killer struck. The guy never knew what hit him."

FIFTEEN

I'd heard of addicts getting high on cough syrup and other over-the-counter medicines. Maybe Rocky was one of them. "Is it possible Rocky was chugging Benadryl?"

"CSU didn't find an empty bottle near the deceased. The Benadryl was probably dumped into something he ate. It would be easy enough to bake into a cherry pie or add to a cherry beverage."

"Which means someone deliberately knocked him out," said Zack.

"Looks that way. Which brings us back to the other part of one of your wife's theories."

I turned to Spader, tamping down the urge to grin. "You think I'm right about Tonya setting Rocky up?"

"Yeah, it would be easy for someone to enter the house and kill him while she was out or do it herself when she returned. It's looking like a strong possibility, but I need proof that she drugged him."

"The Crime Scene Unit found no Benadryl in the house?" I asked. "What about pills?"

"Once we learned of the Benadryl today, we went back to do a more in-depth search of the home. There was one bottle of Benadryl in the medicine cabinet, but it was still sealed. No pills. No empty bottles or boxes in the trash, either inside the house or in the outside trashcan. Nothing hidden anywhere else in the home. The team searched from basement to attic and came up empty."

I mulled this over for a moment. "I don't know how smart Tonya is, but if I were plotting to drug someone, I'd dispose of the evidence somewhere other than in my own trash. Maybe in a neighbor's trashcan." But then I remembered something. "Didn't Tonya say she went to the supermarket?"

Zack piggybacked on my thought. "What if she dumped the evidence in a supermarket trash bin or in one of their Dumpsters? Do we know which supermarket?"

Spader pulled out his notepad and flipped through the pages. "ShopRite. I'll have someone check their surveillance cameras."

He picked up his phone and sent a text, then said, "If we can catch her on tape tossing something, we may get lucky."

"Assuming ShopRite didn't have a trash pickup yesterday or today," I said. "If so, I pity the Union County employees who pull the short straws for searching through the landfill."

Spader raised both his eyebrows. "What?" You mean to tell me you're not volunteering, Mrs. Barnes?"

"Heck, no, Detective. You don't pay me enough."

Spader snorted. "I don't pay you at all."

"Exactly!"

~*~

Yardwork is one of my least favorite chores. Now that Alex was away at college, we had one less able-bodied family member available to mow, weed, and rake. However, I'd learned that no matter how undesirable the task, at some point, I had to grit my teeth and plunge my hands into the dirt. This morning, with a lack of humidity and a gentle breeze heralding the coming of autumn, was that day.

While Nick ran the mower, Zack tackled pruning the shrubs. I crawled around on my hands and knees, convincing myself I was burning calories and toning muscles as I removed a summer's worth of weeds and assorted muck from around the azaleas, rhododendrons, and hydrangeas.

While engrossed in the mindless chore, I forced myself to concentrate on coming up with an idea for the January issue. I was running out of time. Our monthly staff meeting was scheduled for eleven o'clock Monday morning.

I was so engrossed in scooping, digging, yanking, and wracking my brain for an idea that I yelped, toppling onto my backside, when Gloria came up from behind me and called my name.

She jumped a step back, her hands flying up in surrender. "Sorry, I didn't mean to frighten you." She then bent and offered me her hand.

I accepted, and after she aided in hauling me to my feet, I brushed the dirt from my gardening gloves, then my knees and tush. Once my adrenaline rush had subsided, I asked, "What's up?"

She hesitated, worrying her fingers into knots as she stared at her sneakers. Finally, she mumbled, "I was wondering if I could ask you a huge favor."

I scanned my small yard, but both Zack and Nick had finished in the front, the sounds of the mower and trimmer now emanating from the back of the house. Not knowing what Gloria wanted, I would have preferred my husband by my side, but I didn't see how I could pause the conversation to fetch him without raising her suspicions. Instead, I offered her a shrug and a noncommittal, "Doesn't hurt to ask."

She inhaled a deep breath, then motioned across the street. That's when I noticed Tonya Benedetto halfway hidden behind a maple tree on the edge of Gloria's property. "She wants to talk to me. I'd prefer to have a witness. Do you mind?"

"Not at all." If nothing else, she'd triggered my curiosity. What could Tonya possibly have to say to Gloria after publicly accusing her of killing Barry? "Tell her to join us."

Gloria waved Tonya over. As she headed our way, Gloria said, "She showed up a few minutes ago. I told her I had nothing to say to her, but she begged me to listen. When I told her I wanted a witness, she agreed. Didn't even hesitate a split second. I don't think she plans to sucker punch either of us."

"Good to know."

I thought Gloria probably would have preferred Lance as a witness, but his Hummer pickup no longer sat in her driveway. Then again, maybe Gloria knew that Lance would never agree to her speaking with Tonya.

Tonya took her time sauntering across the street and up the path to where Gloria and I stood at the front of my house. Once again, she wore body-hugging glittery Spandex, but today's outfit featured a neon orange ombre top trimmed with gold piping at the neckline and matching capri-length leggings instead of hotpants, most likely a nod to the morning's cooler temperature.

Once she stood in front of us, she eyed me up and down,

squinting as if trying to place me. "Do we know each other?"

I certainly knew who she was, but she didn't know that, and I planned to keep her unaware. "Perhaps you noticed me at Barry's viewing."

She shook her head. "I think it's more than that. I know I've seen you somewhere."

I shrugged. "Possibly around town? In one of the shops or restaurants?"

"Maybe that's it." But she didn't sound convinced.

Gloria broke in. "What did you want to say to me, Tonya?"

Tonya turned from scrutinizing me to confront Gloria. Her voice grew forceful. "I didn't kill Barry, and I didn't kill Rocky, but the cops think otherwise."

Gloria raised an eyebrow. "No, you accused *me* of killing my husband."

Embarrassment suffused Tonya's neck and face. "Sorry about that. I was under a lot of stress that day."

Like she's not now?

Gloria crossed her arms, resting them on her ample bosom, and narrowed her eyes. "Is there anything else?"

Tonya shifted a quick side-eye toward me. "Yeah, since we're both under suspicion—"

Gloria's mouth dropped open. "What makes you think I'm under suspicion?"

Tonya smirked. "A little birdy told me."

Gloria shoved her hands onto her hips and leaned in, her nose inches from Tonya's face. "Who?"

Tonya took a step back. "I don't know his name."

"How convenient."

An awkward stare-off commenced, finally broken by Tonya.

"Look, it was the cops, okay? They suggested we were in this together. They joked about it being like some old movie where two strangers got together to kill each other's wives. They think I killed your husband, and you killed mine."

Gloria gasped. "That's crazy! Why would I kill Rocky?"

"Because he was blackmailing you."

"You were both blackmailing me. So were most of the other reenactors, but none of them are dead. Just Barry and Rocky."

"Tell that to the cops, not me. But it got me thinking."

Gloria snorted. "First time for everything."

Tonya evil-eyed her. She opened her mouth to spew a retort of some sort, but then paused. After inhaling a deep breath, she said, "Look, maybe we should bury the hatchet and work together to find out who really killed Barry and Rocky."

Gloria issued another snort. "That's even crazier."

"Is it? I don't know about you, but I don't want some eager-beaver D.A. railroading me into spending the remainder of my life in prison." She waved her hand across her body. "I know I look amazing in orange, but I'm not wearing jumpsuits for the rest of my life."

I'll admit, I hadn't a clue as to what Tonya might say to Gloria, but in my wildest imagination, I wouldn't have come up with this conversation. Gloria's expression told me she was equally gobsmacked. She turned to me. "What do you think, Anastasia?"

Was she seriously considering teaming up with Tonya? To do what? Between the two of them, I wasn't sure they possessed half a brain. Best-case scenario, they'd wind up in jail for obstructing an investigation. Worst-case scenario, they'd wind up dead—either at the hands of the real killer or as collateral damage in a standoff between the cops and the real killer.

I took a deep breath and exhaled slowly before answering. "I think it's a terrible idea." I turned to Tonya. "Have you spoken with your attorney about your theory?"

Tonya nearly spit out her next words. "That pimple-faced public defender already told me to cop a plea. Before I'm even charged! A plea for what? I'm innocent, but he's already decided I'm guilty. No way am I listening to him."

"Whoever murdered your husbands is dangerous," I reminded them. "We don't know why Barry and Rocky were targeted. You don't want to be the killer's next victims. Leave the investigating to the professionals."

Tonya ignored me. She turned to Gloria. "You in or out?"

Gloria hesitated. "I...I don't know. Do you have a plan?"

"Not yet. I figured we'd come up with something if we put our heads together."

Gloria chewed on her lower lip. "I need to think about this. What else do you know?"

Tonya expelled a rush of exasperation. "I know no one's looking out for you or me. The cops just want to close this case, and from what I can see, they're not looking beyond us."

I started to object. "That's not—"

She glared at me. "Not what? True? You got some insider information, lady?"

"She's friends with the detective investigating the case," said Gloria.

Tonya's eyes widened as she threw her hands onto her hips and got in my face. "Is that so? What do you know that we don't?"

I stepped back. "He doesn't discuss ongoing cases with me. It's not allowed." Not exactly true but I wasn't about to offer her any information, even if I had some. I didn't care for her aggressive attitude. Or anything else about her, for that matter. I also suspected Tonya had some ulterior motive. Although at the moment, I couldn't come up with one that made sense.

"He's not allowed?" She cackled. "That makes him what? The one honest cop in the state? Don't make me laugh."

She turned her back on me and spoke to Gloria. "Take too long to decide, and you might find yourself behind bars for the rest of your life. I'll do whatever it takes to make sure that doesn't happen to me. Your choice. You know where to find me."

Was that a not-so-veiled threat? After this encounter, I had no doubt that if Gloria didn't agree to this unholy union, Tonya would have no qualms about trying to save herself by implicating Gloria. After all, hadn't she already accused Gloria of murdering Barry? And moments ago, she'd offered a motive for Gloria also killing Rocky.

After a dramatic pause, Tonya leveled a spear-like look of disdain, first at me, then Gloria. She then executed a hair flip and strutted down the path. At the sidewalk she hung a right and continued toward the end of the block.

As we both watched her strut her way to the corner, I asked Gloria, "You're not seriously considering her offer, are you?"

"Maybe I should. She has a point. No one really cares about either of us."

"Do you trust her?"

Her brows knit together. "I never have."

"And you shouldn't now. That woman will throw you under an eighteen-wheeler if she thinks it will help her."

Gloria pondered my words for a moment. "I suppose you're right." But she didn't sound convinced.

"Maybe you should talk it over with Lance," I suggested.

She hesitated. "I guess that's a good idea."

"And your attorney."

"I...I..."

"Gloria, don't tell me you still don't have a defense attorney."

"Only guilty people need lawyers."

"Who told you that?"

She shrugged. "It's true, isn't it?"

"No, it's not."

"Really? Look at what Tonya said. Her lawyer told her to take a deal before she's even charged with anything."

"She has a public defender. You have the money to hire the best defense attorney in the state. Besides, I wouldn't necessarily believe anything Tonya says. Remember, this is a woman who stood in a room full of people at your husband's viewing and without any proof, accused you of killing him. Have you ever wondered why?"

Gloria hung her head and mumbled, "Because she doesn't like me?"

"Any other reason?"

"I don't know. None of them ever liked Barry or me. Only the money they got from me to keep them from pressing charges against Barry. I figured she was angry that with Barry dead, she and Rocky couldn't blackmail me anymore."

"How do we know that Rocky didn't kill Barry, and she was trying to protect him?"

Her eyes widened. "Do you think that's what happened?"

"It's a theory."

"But why? It makes no sense. Rocky wasn't stupid. He'd have to know that the money would dry up once Barry was dead."

"I don't know, but I do know two things."

Her expression grew hopeful. "What?"

"You shouldn't trust Tonya, and you need an attorney."

Her entire body seemed to deflate in front of me. "Oh."

Was she expecting that I'd had a sudden aha moment and solved both murders? Was she that naïve?

I looked across the street and spied Billy. He stood on the small landing and was staring at us. Had he seen Tonya speaking with us? I pasted a friendly smile on my face and waved to him. As Gloria turned to follow my gaze, I said. "Don't be stubborn, Gloria. Please, if nothing else, think about your son. What will happen to Billy if you're convicted?"

"I can't let that happen."

"Then get yourself a good lawyer. Tonya won't help anyone but herself. Don't be fooled into thinking otherwise."

She sighed. "I suppose you're right. Thank you, Anastasia. I won't take up any more of your time." She then headed back to her home.

Once Gloria and Billy had both entered their house and closed the door behind them, I turned back to the remaining weeds. However, before I'd had a chance to squat in the dirt again, Zack rounded the corner of the house. "Do you think you got through to her?"

"I have my doubts. How much did you hear?"

"Enough. I thought they'd both clam up if I joined you, so I kept hidden and eavesdropped."

"Probably. Did you catch Tonya's reference to *Strangers on a Train*?"

"That was the first thing I heard. No matter how stretched the Union County Homicide Division is currently, I'm skeptical that anyone is stupid enough to plant such an idea in Tonya's head."

"I've come to realize that cops often employ a macabre sense of humor to cope with the grizzlier aspects of their job. I got the impression Tonya overhead two of them speculating about the possibility, not that it was an accusation made during questioning."

Zack nodded. "Makes more sense."

"Tonya wouldn't have been allowed inside the house when CSU returned to search for the Benadryl, right?

"Highly unlikely."

Maybe Tonya hadn't overheard anyone mention *Strangers on a Train*. "Do you think she's smart enough to come up with such a scenario on her own?" When Zack raised an eyebrow, I added, "I know I'm veering into stereotypical territory, but Tonya strikes me as more of a *Real Housewives* fan than a Hitchcock afficionado. Still, anything is possible."

Zack offered another possibility. "We know nothing about Rocky other than he was a reenactor and Tonya's husband. Maybe he was the Hitchcock fan, and Tonya knew about the movie from him."

"Not that we know much about Tonya, either, but you left something out. She and Rocky were both members of the Bait Barry Brigade."

Zack offered me a sheepish grin. "I thought that was stating the obvious. We should make our friendly neighborhood detective aware of this latest twist in his case."

I stared across the street. "Tell him to park in front of Rosalie's house and come through the backyards. We don't need Gloria noticing his car parked in front of our house right after Tonya dropped her bombshell proposal. I'll alert Rosalie so she doesn't freak out if she sees Spader traipsing across her property."

Given how often we cut through the azaleas separating the two properties lately, Rosalie Schneider should consider setting up a toll gate to supplement her Social Security checks.

Meanwhile, I still needed an idea for the January issue, which was a perfect excuse to leave the remainder of the weeding to the men in the family. "I'm abandoning nature," I told Zack. "I have work to finish before tomorrow morning."

He narrowed his eyes. "Then why are you out here digging in the dirt?"

Good question. One for which I had no answer other than saying, "January."

"What about January?"

"It's the worst month for coming up with a theme. Do you know what happens in January?"

"Besides snow?"

"Nothing."

"Then use snow."

"I've used snow. Every January. For years."

"Then use it again."

"I'm tired of using snow."

Zack shook his head and threw his arm off to the side. "There must be something else that happens in January. If not, make something up."

If all else failed....

After a quick shower, I settled in front of my computer and did a search of January holidays and observances. After passing on such gems as Fruitcake Toss Day, Clashing Clothes Day, and Dental Drill Appreciation Day, I stumbled upon a listing I'd never noticed before, Local Quilt Shop Day. Held the fourth Saturday of January, the day is designed to celebrate local quilt shops and their contribution to the world. I could work with that.

~*~

Not surprisingly, Detective Spader arrived at the back door shortly before dinner, but he came bearing a bottle of wine and a shopping bag filled with assorted—mostly healthy—finger foods. The bakery box filled with double-fudge brownies was the one exception.

After Nick filled his plate, he begged off to eat in the den. The Mets stood a good chance of making the playoffs this year, and if they won tonight's game, they'd tie the division leader.

"Hope springs eternal," Spader told him.

"If they don't blow it like they did last year," said Nick. "We've still got all of September to get through."

Once Nick departed, Spader said, "Given Nick's recent interest, I'm surprised he didn't want to take part in our discussion."

"Baseball over bodies," I said, filling a plate with various fruits, cheeses, and veggies. "And the Mama Bear in me is more than fine with that."

Spader heaped a large spoonful of artichoke dip onto his plate and shrugged. "We all have our priorities. Given the way this case is going, I'd also much rather watch the Mets, even if they lose."

As we ate, I filled the detective in on my conversation with Gloria and Tonya. I ended by adding, "My gut tells me Tonya has ulterior motives."

"I've learned to trust your gut," said Spader, "but I've come to the same conclusion."

"Any luck with the supermarket security tapes?" asked Zack.

Spader pulled a face. "Nothing. If she did trash the evidence, she was smart enough not to do so where surveillance cameras would capture her in the act. We even checked the interior supermarket cameras in case she ducked into the ladies' room to dump the evidence."

"I take it, she didn't?" I asked.

He shook his head. "Maybe Tonya Benedetto is smarter than we've given her credit for being."

"Or lucky," said Zack.

"At least no one had the unpleasant task of sifting through tons of landfill trash," said Spader. "Which spared me from becoming persona non grata with everyone on the force."

I reached for a small bunch of grapes. "There's another possibility."

Both men stared at me. "Which is?" asked Spader.

"If Tonya planned Rocky's death well in advance, she could have crushed up Benadryl pills weeks ago, stored them in a Ziploc bag somewhere, and sprinkled them into whatever Rocky ate for dinner Thursday evening."

"She'd still have to dispose of the bag that had contained the crushed pills," said Spader. "We found no empty plastic bags in her trash."

"If Rocky's death was premeditated," I suggested, "the prep could have occurred days or weeks prior to her trip to the supermarket Thursday night. She'd have countless places to dispose of a Benadryl bottle or a box and empty plastic bag."

I ticked off possibilities on my fingers. "Last Friday, when I eavesdropped on Gloria and Tonya arguing on the street, Gloria mentioned Tonya works as a cashier at Walmart. They certainly have plenty of places to toss trash. Or maybe she disposed of the evidence at a gas station when she stopped to fill her tank. Or at the nail salon. Or the hair salon. Or the mall." I paused and eyed him. "Need I go on?"

Spader groaned. "You've made your point, Mrs. Barnes. "The possibilities are endless. We'll never find the evidence we need to connect her with knocking out her husband."

I offered him a look of apology but added, "For all we know, she cooked the Benadryl into a cherry pie and froze it weeks ago, waiting for the perfect opportunity, and defrosting it when that opportunity presented itself."

"Serving him a slice before she left the house," suggested Zack as he topped off our wine glasses.

"That would've been quite the potent slice," said Spader. "And he wouldn't wonder why she didn't join him for dessert before running her errand?"

"Maybe Rocky loves cherry pie, but Tonya doesn't," I suggested. "Or she's allergic to cherries. Or she's dieting. What better way to mask an affair than by spoiling your husband with his favorite dessert?"

It hit me then that we were all focusing on a possible non-issue where the plastic bag was concerned. "Forget the plastic bag. If she crushed the pills, she may have used a storage container. All she'd have to do is run it through the dishwasher to get rid of any residual pill evidence after she added the Benadryl to the pie. But maybe she didn't use crushed pills. If she poured liquid Benadryl into the cherry pie filling, she could have done so and gotten rid of the evidence days or weeks prior to killing Rocky."

"What about the remains of Rocky's dinner?" asked Zack. "Were the dishes brought to the lab for testing?"

"They found no dirty dishes or containers in the house," said Spader.

"Not even in the dishwasher?" I asked.

"Completely empty."

I had a sudden flash of *aha*. "She ran a quick wash cycle, then emptied the dishwasher before she called 911."

Detective Spader stared wide-eyed at me, his mouth dropping open. "If she's that diabolical, she may have committed the perfect crime. Unless she confesses, we may never find enough evidence to charge her."

"Cheer up, Detective. I don't think Tonya Benedetto has enough smarts to be that diabolical. If she did kill Rocky and Barry or just Rocky, she'll slip up eventually. She's too cocky not to."

"I hope you're right," Mrs. Barnes." Then he quirked his mouth and pointed his fork at me, "Maybe you're the diabolical one. Ever consider writing murder mysteries?"

"I'll add it to my to-do list, Detective. Meanwhile, have you eliminated the other suspects and persons of interest on your list?"

Spader grimaced. "Hardly. I've added some."

SIXTEEN

I studied Spader's grim expression. "Care to share?"

"For one, a deep dive into Lance Melville's past turned up some questionable connections."

I didn't like the sound of that. "What sort of questionable connections?"

"The kind you'd expect in the Garden State. On his mother's side. His grandmother was a Gambino."

I scowled. "Show me someone in New Jersey who doesn't have a mob connection."

Zack dug deeper. "Any current connections?"

"None that we've unearthed so far. In high school he hung out with a group of wannabes who eventually went into the family business. Melville chose college, getting a degree in accounting and finance. Nothing suggests he's been in touch with any of them recently, but he did have some minor run-ins with the law in his teens."

"Which could either mean the guy turned into a fine and

upstanding citizen, or he's adept at disguising the fact that he's not," I said. "He struck me as extremely aloof and unfriendly."

Spader showed his concurrence with a nod. "I've come across enough of those guys. They're often the hardest nuts to crack."

I thought of another possibility. "Given the situation with Barry and all the blackmailers, perhaps Melville is just overly cautious and suspicious of anyone who enters Gloria's orbit. Add to that her often short fuse and very low self-esteem, and he's got an almost impossible task trying to fulfill his promise to her father."

"Which would be a heck of a lot easier if he got Barry out of the way," suggested Spader.

"What about Gloria's family?" asked Zack.

Spader opened his notepad and flipped through several pages before arriving at the information. "Gloria's mother grew up an army brat. She never lived more than a few years in any one place. Her father's family owned a string of supermarkets in the Midwest. The grandfather made a fortune when he sold out to some private equity investors in the late nineties. Afterwards, he set up trusts for his children and grandchildren."

"Those trust terms were extremely rigid," I said. "I wonder about the reasoning behind making his heirs wait until they turned forty to inherit."

Spader shrugged. "Maybe he expected to live a long life and wanted to control the purse strings as long as possible."

Zack rose to clear the dishes, returning with the bakery box of brownies and four plates. I placed two brownies on a plate and brought them into the den for Nick.

When I returned, I helped myself to a brownie and asked, "There's nothing to indicate any connections between Gloria's family and organized crime?"

"None that we've turned up."

"That doesn't mean someone in the family didn't hold a grudge," I said. "Maybe one of Gloria's cousins had a beef with Barry. If that's the case, the only connection between Barry and Rocky's murders might be an opportunistic copycat killer."

"Which means two separate crimes, and two different killers," said Zack.

Spader polished off the last of his wine before saying, "And the reason this case is driving me nuts."

I then remembered the name I'd heard at the viewing. "What about Brock? Who is he, and where does he fit in?"

"Axel Brock." Spader reached for a brownie but continued speaking before taking a bite. "He's a reenactor. According to others who were at the viewing, Brock was a no-show."

He took a large bite from the brownie. While he chewed, I posed another question. "Why were people speculating that he killed Barry?"

"Brock and Sumner grew up in the same neighborhood, but according to Brock, they never got along."

I raised an eyebrow. "He admitted that?"

"Freely." Spader continued. "They got into it a lot over the years. Mostly mutual schoolyard bullying and juvenile pranks. Nothing that rose to anything serious. Brock claims it all stopped after Barry's accident."

"Any particular reason?" asked Zack.

Spader consulted his notes. "Said he felt sorry for the guy, that Sumner was never right in the head afterwards."

"But according to Gloria and Billy, Barry had anger issues prior to the accident." I shook my head. "This makes no sense. If nothing was going on between Barry and Brock, why would some of the reenactors, as well as Gloria, suggest Brock may have killed Barry? Someone's hiding something. Or maybe more than one someone is hiding more than one something."

Spader cocked his head toward me and raised an eyebrow. "Ya think?"

"Was Brock one of the blackmailers?" asked Zack.

Spader scowled. "He claims he wasn't. Gloria claims otherwise."

"He said, she said," I muttered. "And I suppose there's no proof because all the blackmail payments were in cash."

Spader's expression telegraphed a *duh* as he said, "Of course."

"I think Lance Melville is either an idiot, an extremely incompetent accountant and financial advisor, or has some ulterior motive for not documenting the payoffs."

"What more do you know about Brock?" asked Zack.

Once again, Spader consulted his notes. "He bounced around in foster care after his mother OD'd when he was twelve. He's now forty-one, single, and works as an assistant warehouse foreman for a flooring manufacturer in Elizabeth. Owns a one-bedroom condo in Union, a CVO Road Glide ST Harley, and an F-150 pickup."

Spader reached for his phone and pulled up a website featuring photos of recent reenactments held around the state. He pointed to one man. "This is Axel Brock."

The guy's muscles had muscles. With a full head of bright red hair and matching beard, he looked like he should be wearing a kilt and taking part in the Highland Games instead of parading around dressed as a Tory soldier.

"Any priors?" asked Zack.

"One of his foster families turned him in for shoplifting and drug use when he was fourteen. It landed him a short stint in juvie. Maybe that scared him straight. He's got a clean record after that and went into the army when he aged out of the system. He was dishonorably discharged within a year, though."

"For what?" I asked.

"Misconduct."

I frowned. "Which tells us nothing. Anything else?"

"He's got two kids by two different women."

I raised an eyebrow. "Does he pay child support?"

"Only when his baby mamas scrounge up the lawyer fees to haul him into court."

"Does he have an alibi for the night of the murder?" asked Zack.

"A flimsy one."

"Why flimsy?" I asked.

"He claims he spent the evening drinking alone at a dive out on Route 9 in Elizabeth. Said he sat in a corner by himself and left at closing. So far, we haven't found anyone who can corroborate his alibi."

"What about the bartender?" asked Zack.

"He said he couldn't say one way or the other. The place was jammed with tennis fans watching the U.S. Open. When I showed a photo of Brock to the two waitresses on duty, they laughed in my face and said they were too busy taking orders and serving drinks to pay attention to anyone's face."

"What about security cameras?" I asked.

Spader pulled a frown. "It's a biker bar. They look the other way and don't keep records."

I snorted. "Seriously? How many bikers are into tennis?"

"Probably not many," said Zack. "Most likely it's a front for illegal activity."

"Like?" I asked.

"Gambling. Human trafficking. Drugs. Prostitution. Take your pick from the typical biker résumé."

I shook my head. "Okay, I know I'm veering off-topic, but why hasn't the Vice Squad shut them down?"

He shrugged. "I'm need-to-know with those guys, but if I were to guess, probably because there are way too many dives in the county just like it and too few resources. It's possible they have them under surveillance, or maybe they're concentrating on bigger fish."

"Bigger fish?" I stared at him. "Tell me you're not suggesting a trickle-down theory of law enforcement."

He grunted. "I suppose that's one way of describing it."

I offered him an eye roll and redirected the conversation back to Axel Brock. "Does the bar have a back door?"

Spader nodded as he chewed.

"And is that back door anywhere near the corner where Brock claimed he was sitting?"

"Down a corridor a few feet from his table."

The dominoes were lining up against Axel Brock. "Let me get this straight," I said. "The guy was once arrested for drugs, was dishonorably discharged from the army, and has two kids he rarely supports. I'm guessing the condo, Harley, and pickup are well above the pay grade of the average assistant warehouse foreman."

"Roughly three-hundred-fifty grand total," said Spader.

I eyed Zack and Spader. "Anyone know the average salary of an assistant warehouse manager in New Jersey, or should I Google it?"

"No need," said Spader. Brock makes just under sixty-five K a year."

"Definitely living above his means," I said. "And he's sitting in a packed biker bar with no security cameras and easy access to an exit."

I paused to let my words sink in, then added, "It doesn't take a nuclear physicist to suggest he's engaging in some illegal enterprise to pay for his boy toys. But more importantly, it also means he could have slipped out at any point, killed Barry, then returned without anyone ever seeing him leave or return."

"Exactly," said Spader. He grabbed another brownie. "Axel Brock is yet another suspect who may have committed the perfect crime, even without anyone corroborating his alibi."

"It also means he's likely dealing illicit drugs out of that biker bar." I glared at Spader. "Someone should do something about that."

"I'm Homicide, not Vice," he said, "but I get your point, Mrs. Barnes. My guess is the bar is on Vice's radar. They get touchy when another division steps on their toes or tells them how to run their investigations."

Typical Y-chromosome male egos. But considering I was currently outnumbered, I kept that thought to myself.

"More importantly," said Zack, "we now have two additional suspects, either one of whom may have committed the perfect crime."

"What about Brock's motive?" I asked.

Spader turned to me. "That's the million-dollar question, Mrs. Barnes. You got any ideas?"

"Only one, Detective. Axel Brock lied to you. Something was going on between him and Barry. Find that something, and you've got your killer."

Zack grinned as he helped himself to a second brownie. "Nothing like stating the obvious, Sweetheart."

Spader pushed himself away from the table. "I think I'll pay Gloria Forester another visit before I call it a night."

"To find out what she knows about Axel Brock?" I asked.

"As well as more about Lance Melville. Let's see what she says when I make her squirm a little."

"That will depend on whether she took my advice and hired a defense attorney."

Spader pulled a frown. "When was that?"

"This morning, after Tonya tried to strongarm her into teaming up."

He huffed a rush of air as he shook his head. "Gloria Forester is one stubborn woman. If I'm lucky, she once again refused to heed your advice."

After Spader thanked us for the information and we thanked him for providing dinner, Zack and I escorted him to the back door. A few minutes later, as I crossed from the dining room into the living room, I noticed his unmarked sedan pulling up in front of Gloria's house.

However, Spader neither, called, texted, nor showed up at our back door the remainder of the evening. "I'm guessing Spader learned nothing more earthshattering from Gloria," I said as Zack and I settled into bed.

"Or not. For all we know, he was called to the scene of another homicide."

I shuddered. "If so, I hope it's one that doesn't involve Revolutionary War reenactors."

~*~

Spader texted early the next morning: *Biker bar raided late last night. Brock arrested.*

I texted back: *For?*

Drug trafficking.

I tamped down the urge to text back *told you so*. No one likes a smart aleck, especially first thing in the morning. Instead, I showed Zack my screen. "Looks like Spader's visit to Gloria paid off."

He disagreed. "Or not. Could be coincidental. We don't know what Gloria told him, if anything. Remember, last night Spader suggested Vice may have had the bar under surveillance for some time."

"True." Too bad Spader hadn't divulged any further details, but I had to remind myself that we weren't on equal footing. As much help as I'd provided him, he still called the shots, and even though he'd shared considerably more the last few weeks, I still remained on a need-to-know basis.

As if reading my mind, Zack said, "He'll fill us in when and if he can."

A few minutes later Zack left to head into the city for a breakfast meeting with his agent and the director of the Museum of Arts and Design. Last month, the director had personally escorted us on a tour of the museum. I wasn't foolish enough to believe this was because she was interested in the article I planned to write for *American Woman*. Crafts editors at third-rate women's magazines never receive red-carpet treatment.

The moment I had introduced myself, she zeroed in on the guy standing beside me. Having immediately recognized Zack, she hoped to score points with him by being overly accommodating to me. Her goal? To secure a retrospective of his work. Today's meeting signaled her efforts had paid off.

After suffering through the usual bumper-to-bumper morning

commute, I arrived at work in time to snag a coffee in the break room. Unfortunately, I found only crumbs remaining on the plate of whatever goodies Cloris had provided this morning.

I popped my head into her cubicle and mumbled a half-hearted, "Morning."

She took one look at me and frowned. "Get up on the wrong side of the bed?"

I held up my coffee mug. "Notice anything missing?"

"Should I?"

"Mondays are bad enough, but starting the week without a Cloris confection is a violation of the United Nations ban on torture."

"Before you report me, check your desk."

I spun around and stepped across the hall. A ginormous apple muffin sat on a napkin beside my keyboard. I called across the hall to her. "You're now officially in my will."

Cloris snorted. "So, I inherit your debt?"

"You never know. I may win the lottery someday."

"You don't play the lottery."

"That could change."

"I won't hold my breath, but you're welcome for the muffin."

I blew her a kiss. "Best BFF ever."

Throughout the day, I multitasked. Part of my brain concentrated on whittling down my *American Woman* to-do list while the other part tried to whittle down Spader's suspects list.

Gloria was the only person I felt confident in scratching off that list. My gut told me she had nothing to do with Barry's murder. However, the rational side of my brain insisted that even if she hadn't wielded the bayonet, it didn't eliminate her as an accessory to the crime. Not if the murderer turned out to be Lance

Melville, and they'd plotted together.

Still, even that scenario refused to gain any traction in my brain. Gloria had no reason to kill Barry. His death had devasted both her and her son. She gained nothing by her husband's murder. Even if dealing with Barry's anger issues and idiosyncrasies had finally gotten to her, she could have divorced him. It would probably have been cheaper than paying all that blackmail money.

A few minutes prior to eleven o'clock, I forced myself to press pause on my murder mulling. Grabbing my notes and the inspiration board I'd created for my quilting theme, which featured memory quilts, I headed to the conference room for our monthly staff planning meeting.

An hour later, during a break for lunch, Cloris sidled up to me as I stood at the sideboard, filling my plate with a tuna fish on rye and some cucumber salad. "You've been very quiet all day," she whispered. "Anything happen over the weekend?"

"Spader added two more suspects to his list. One was arrested last night at a biker bar."

"For the murder?"

I shook my head. "Drug trafficking."

"How does that tie into Mr. Stoop Sitter's murder? Or that of the other reenactor?"

"No clue." I then changed the subject. Call me paranoid, but who knew if one of our fellow editors possessed super-human hearing or the ability to read lips? The last thing I wanted was to set off wagging tongues speculating about their Nancy Drew coworker.

After Cloris helped herself to a sandwich and salad, we returned to our seats around the conference table. The meeting resumed while the staff ate lunch on the company dime.

The good news? Naomi loved my idea to highlight Local Quilt Shop Day and include a memory quilt project in the January issue.

The bad news? I hadn't heard from Detective Spader all day. Was he busy interrogating Axel Brock? Had he discovered a motive for Barry's murder? Curiosity was like an itch that needed constant scratching, and right now my curiosity had reached full-body poison ivy levels.

~*~

Aside from no communication from Spader all day and not a single aha moment that shed light on either murder, as Mondays go, this one had not been too bad. However, that all ended when I started hearing the telltale flub-flub sound of a flat tire while driving through the winding roads of the Watchung reservation on my way home from work.

I slowed to a crawl and continued about a quarter of a mile until I arrived at a small dirt parking area for one of the walking trails on the opposite side of the road. I pulled in, and after cutting the engine, stepped from my Jetta to survey the damage.

Did I even have a spare tire? I checked the trunk. All I found was a tire repair kit. I squinted to read the directions on the package, realized immediately that the kit was useless. My tire needed more help than a plug and a shot of air.

Twilight was setting in. The woods were home to all sorts of prowling wildlife, including Copperhead snakes, coyotes, and bears. All of which I wouldn't want to encounter in broad daylight, let along as my back was turned and the sun was setting.

I returned to the relative safety of my car, cracked the window a couple of inches for ventilation, and placed a call to Zack. He answered on the first ring, but when I explained my predicament, he said, "I'm stuck on the train. Power's out."

"Since after your breakfast meeting this morning?"

"For about an hour. Ibba and I met with my publisher after our museum meeting. I didn't leave the city until nearly five o'clock. We haven't moved in an hour. Call Ira. He'll send a tow truck."

As much as I disliked asking my half-brother-in-law for a favor, at least he wouldn't rip open my car door and eat me for dinner. I hung up from Zack and called him.

"Stay in your car," said Ira. "Someone will arrive in about twenty minutes."

As I disconnected the call, another car turned into the dirt lot and pulled up alongside me. I stared in disbelief as Tonya Benedetto hauled herself from behind the wheel of a battered pickup truck and sauntered over to my passenger side window. "Isn't this a coincidence?" she said.

Was it? Even in the waning sunlight, the glint in her eyes told me otherwise. Had Tonya punctured my tire, causing a slow leak? Had she followed me home from work, waiting to strike? But why?

"Need some help?"

"No thanks. A tow truck is on the way."

She tugged at the door handle, her features darkening. "Unlock the door."

"I don't think so."

Tonya raised her arm. She held something that looked like a small black flashlight. With one swift move, she smashed the object against the corner of the driver's side window. The glass shattered, pebble-sized pieces pelting me like hail. They bombarded my face, my arms, my torso, landing in my hair, and piling up on my lap and throughout the interior of the car.

Shocked, I stared dumbfounded at her. "What the—?"

Tonya cut me off with a maniacal laugh. She had swapped the flashlight-looking device for a yellow and black object that emitted a crackling noise. Her voice dripped with malice as she said, "Say hello to my little friend."

My adrenaline kicked in as I realized what she held and what was about to happen. I grabbed the taser and tried to force it from her grip, but Tonya overpowered me. My entire body convulsed. Fire consumed me from the inside out. Screams ripped from my throat. Then everything went black.

SEVENTEEN

I came to in total darkness. Someone dragged me by my arms across a rough surface. I couldn't move. As sensation returned to my limbs, I realized my legs were trussed together, my arms cuffed at the wrists and extended over my head. My mouth was gagged, my eyes blindfolded. I had no idea how long I'd been unconscious. Minutes? Hours? All concept of time had deserted me.

My captor grunted and cursed as she yanked on the handcuffs securing my wrists and hoisted me backwards up several steps, my rump bouncing against the edge of each. One, two, three.

A moment later, I found myself flat on my back on a hard surface. At first, I thought my kidnapper was going to release my hands, but after unlocking the cuff around one wrist, it was immediately reattached.

I felt hot breath on my face as my blindfold was removed. After blinking my eyes into focus, I stared into Tonya Benedetto's crazed eyes.

She waved the taser in my face. "Here's how this is going down.

Try anything stupid, and you get yourself another date with my little friend. Each time you make me angry, I dial up the power another notch and make it last longer. Got it?"

I nodded.

"Good. I'm glad we understand each other. Make yourself comfortable." She laughed at what I suppose she meant as a joke, then switched off the overhead light. A moment later, I heard a garage door open. An engine revved to life, and a few seconds later, the garage door closed.

I tried to contort my body, attempting to bring my legs close enough to my hands to release the bindings that held my legs, but I was no contortionist. My wrists were cuffed above my head, around a massive table leg. I raised my trussed legs and maneuvered to prop up the table far enough to slide out my hands, but I couldn't budge the table.

As my eyes began to adjust to the dark, I realized why. I was in a kitchen, and the leg was attached to a stationary island, not a table.

Had Tonya brought me to her house? As the cobwebs faded from my brain, my memory began to return, and I took solace in the last thing I remembered before the taser jolted me into oblivion. When the tow truck arrived, the driver would see my broken car window and not find me. He'd call Ira who in turn would alert Zack, who would contact Detective Spader.

No matter how much time had passed, I knew the calvary was out looking for me. I just hoped they'd show up before Tonya returned. That woman was bat-poop crazy. I had no idea why she'd kidnapped me or what she planned to do with me. And I didn't want to find out, not until she was permanently locked away in a prison cell. Hopefully, with no chance of parole.

Since I had nothing better to do, I tried to harness some elusive Zen, taking deep calming breaths while forcing the remainder of the cobwebs from my brain. I tried to concentrate on getting into Tonya's head. She wasn't the first psychopath I'd come up against since Karl's death had turned me into a reluctant amateur sleuth. If I could figure out her plan, I could thwart her.

Overpowering her wouldn't work. The woman towered over me and outweighed me by at least fifty pounds. All that bedazzled Spandex didn't hold in rolls of flabby fat. It accentuated muscular arms and legs, leading me to believe Tonya worked out at least several times a week, if not daily. Even with the stubborn baby weight I still hadn't lost after nearly seventeen years, I had no doubt she could body slam me with little effort.

Which meant, I'd have to defeat her by relying solely on my gray matter. Meanwhile, I'd bumped both Axel Brock and Lance Melville down a few rungs on the suspects list, moving Tonya to Suspect Numero Uno. After my encounter with her this evening, I had no doubt she was quite capable of knocking off her husband, for whatever reason.

Had she also killed Barry? Too many loose threads still needed connecting in Barry Sumner's murder. Melville struck me as likelier when I considered motivation. Either he'd eliminated Barry for altruistic or avaricious reasons, for love or money. Both ranked high on the Murder Motivation Scale.

Brock made no sense as a suspect in Barry's murder unless I was missing a huge piece of the puzzle. Had he also eyed Gloria's money and planned to woo her after getting rid of Barry?

The more I pondered, the more convinced I became that Tonya had killed her husband, even if I didn't know her motive. Gut overrode reason, but I'd learned to trust my gut.

Maybe she'd also killed Barry Sumner. I didn't yet know why, but I'd faced enough killers since Karl's death to recognize the fevered look that comes over a coldblooded killer when someone like me gets in their way. I'd seen that look of evil in Tonya's eyes twice today.

I pondered various scenarios that might tie her to both murders. Maybe she killed Barry because he'd led her to believe that he, not Gloria, had inherited a fortune. Try as I might, though, I couldn't picture Tonya falling for Barry for any other reason. At least Gloria had claimed back in the day, Barry was quite the stud. My wildest creative brain cells had trouble picturing Barry as a youthful Romeo, but I suppose anything was possible.

Although, that didn't explain why Tonya would kill Rocky. Had she learned he knew she'd killed Barry and planned to turn her in to collect the reward Gloria had offered?

Or had Tonya killed Rocky to get back at him for killing Barry after Rocky had learned of the affair? Was it possible that Tonya had really loved Barry? That was another huge stretch of credulity for me, but either scenario worked.

However, neither explained why Tonya had kidnapped me. I was no threat to her.

Or was I?

Had Gloria praised my sleuthing skills to the point that Tonya worried I'd nail her for either Barry or Rocky's murders? Or both? Did she plan to murder me and dump my body somewhere to create a false scenario about a serial killer whose M.O. was impalement by reproduction antique weaponry?

Yet, if Tonya had wanted to kill me, she had the perfect opportunity earlier in the dirt parking lot of the hiking trail. With no security cameras and no other people around, no one would ever know who had killed me.

I clung to the hope that Tonya wanted me for some other reason, something she planned to force me to do that she couldn't do herself. Something I wouldn't agree to do otherwise. If so, I'd pull a Scheherazade and figure out a way to keep myself alive long enough to get out of this mess. I'd done it before. Yet, the more I wracked my mind to come up with a plausible reason for my abduction, the more my brain refused to cooperate.

As it turned out, I didn't have long to wait. The garage door soon rumbled open. Seconds later, a vehicle entered, the engine died, and the garage door rumbled closed. I braced myself for my next encounter with Tonya.

Overhead light flooded the room, and I once again squinted from the sudden blinding onslaught. Tonya entered the kitchen, but she wasn't alone.

"Who owns this house?"

I immediately recognized Gloria's voice, and my heart sank. She hadn't listened to my warnings, hadn't taken my advice. Instead, she'd allowed Tonya to prey on her insecurities and manipulate her into becoming a willing accomplice in whatever Tonya had planned.

Tonya's voice grew closer as she answered. "My cousin. She's out of town."

"Why are we here?"

"The cops trashed my house. I decided to camp out here until I clean up the place. Careful you don't trip."

"Trip? Over what?"

"I have a little surprise for you at the end of the island."

"I don't understand."

LOIS WINSTON

"You will in a second. Check out the floor."

A moment later Gloria stood over me and screamed. "Are you crazy? What have you done?"

"What I had to do. She's going to help us prove we're innocent, that Brock killed both Barry and Rocky, not us."

"I didn't kill anyone," said Gloria.

"It doesn't matter. I told you, the cops are going to pin Barry's murder on you and Rocky's murder on me."

Gloria stared down at me, her eyes filling with tears. "Why would Anastasia help us after what you've done to her?"

Tonya pulled the taser from her waistband and waved it in Gloria's face. "I've given her incentive."

Gloria's eyes grew wide as she stared at the gun. Her voice rose several octaves. "You tased her?"

"How else do you think I got her here? She wasn't going to come willingly."

"And why would she help us after what you've done to her?"

Tonya patted the taser with her other hand. "Because my little friend here is very persuasive. Want a demonstration?"

She then gripped the taser with both hands and pointed it at me. Unable to move out of her line of fire, I braced for the jolt.

"No!" Gloria swatted at Tonya's arms. "Stop it!"

Tonya whipped around and aimed the taser at Gloria. "Maybe I need to give you a little incentive."

Gloria stepped back and raised both hands. "Calm down. I told you I'd help you, but you should've let me convince Anastasia to help us."

"You tried, remember? It didn't work."

Gloria stared down at me. "Please, Anastasia, will you help us?"

I nodded. My only hope for getting out of this mess was to play

218

along.

She turned to Tonya. "See?"

"Well, sure. She already knows I'll zap her if she doesn't do as I say."

"Untie her."

"I'm not so sure that's a good idea."

"How can she help us if she's bound and gagged?"

Tonya eyed me skeptically as she again pointed the taser at me. "Try anything stupid, and I hit you with the highest setting. Understand?"

I nodded again.

She reached into her pocket, removed a small key, and handed it to Gloria. "Release her."

Gloria first unlocked the handcuffs. My shoulders screamed with pain when I lowered my arms from above my head. As I massaged circulation back into my wrists and hands, Gloria went to work on a series of bungee cords Tonya had used to bind my legs together.

Tonya kept the taser aimed at me throughout. When Gloria released the last of the bungee cords, then the gag, Tonya said, "Get up."

Easier said than done. I grabbed the leg of the island and pulled myself to a sitting position, but I stumbled and fell twice as I tried to hoist myself to my feet. My legs were completely numb and refused to bear my weight.

Tonya huffed out her annoyance and spat out an order to Gloria. "Help her into a chair."

Gloria positioned herself behind me, leaned over, and wrapped her arms around my torso. She slid me across the room to the breakfast nook, but when she tried to lift me onto a chair, she couldn't get enough leverage. I was dead weight. "I need help," she said.

"For heaven's sake," cried Tonya, "do I have to do everything myself?" She pushed Gloria aside and grabbed me under my armpits. After yanking me to my feet, she plopped me into a chair. "Now," she said, "let's get down to business."

I forced a calm that I didn't feel into my voice. "Do you have a plan?"

Tonya dropped into one of the remaining chairs and sneered at me. "Of course, I have a plan. That's why you're here." She turned to Gloria. "Tell her about Brock."

Gloria joined us at the table. She laced her fingers together in a prayerful manner and placed them on the tabletop. Staring at her clasped hands, she began to speak. "I...I think I'm responsible for Barry's death." She glanced up at me. Sorrow filling her face, and tears gathered in her eyes.

Tonya slammed her fist onto the table. Both Gloria and I jumped. "Get to the point. We haven't got all night."

Gloria emitted a ragged sigh. Returning her gaze to her hands, she continued. "Barry had no memory of his motorcycle accident, but ever since, he was plagued with nightmares that woke him up in a cold sweat most nights. The doctors called it a form of PTSD."

"What sort of nightmares?" I asked.

"Reliving someone forcing him off the road. But he never saw the vehicle. After years of these terrible dreams, a few months ago, the nightmare changed. He suddenly became convinced that his memory was returning after all these years and that another motorcyclist had cut in front of him, causing him to veer to his right to avoid a collision. When he did, he lost control and plunged down an embankment."

"Is that where he was found?" I asked. "At the bottom of an embankment?"

Gloria shook her head. "Not exactly. He was found unconscious in a small ditch on the side of the road. He'd hit his head on a large rock."

Tonya waved the taser in the air. "Move it along."

After another deep sigh, Gloria continued. "A few weeks ago, the dream changed again. This time, he saw the face of the other motorcyclist." Gloria hesitated, darting a glance at Tonya.

"Tell her who it was," demanded Tonya.

Again, Gloria hesitated, then said, "Axel Brock."

"Did Barry go to the police?" I asked.

Gloria shook her head. "He said there was no point. They weren't going to believe him over a dream."

"Did he confront Brock?"

Gloria's lips trembled. Again, she shot a glance at Tonya before answering. "I...I did. Brock got off on picking on Barry. It never stopped. Every time Barry took a swing at him, Brock leaned into Barry's fist, then demanded money not to press assault charges. About two weeks ago, I lost my temper and confronted him. I told Brock that Barry had proof he'd tried to kill him, and if he didn't leave us alone, I'd go to the cops."

"Even though you knew there was no proof?"

Gloria sniffed back some tears as she lifted her head. "Three days later, Barry was murdered. If I hadn't lost my temper, he'd still be alive."

"That's assuming Brock murdered Barry." Which I seriously doubted. Gloria's body language belied her words. Her hesitation and constant glances toward Tonya, as if she was looking for approval, led me to believe they'd concocted the story. If there was any truth to it, why wouldn't Gloria have mentioned it to the police before now? Or at least to me?

Tonya barked out a laugh. "Of course, Brock did it. Who else could it be?"

The woman sitting across the table from me came to mind. Tonya was a bat-poop psychopath, and I now believed, quite capable of murder. Perhaps two murders. I was ninety-nine percent certain that one of my theories about her would prove correct. Either she killed Rocky because he killed Barry, or she killed both men.

However, to avoid another taser zap, I played dumb and agreed with her. "It makes sense." Of course, there were two huge problems—a lack of evidence pointing to Axel Brock, and an accusation based on the dreams of a dead man who'd lost his memory regarding an accident that occurred nearly a decade ago.

And then, there was Rocky's murder. Why would Brock kill him? I knew I had to tiptoe around that huge gorilla in the room. "Do you think Brock also killed Rocky?"

As I suspected, Tonya pulled out a ready answer. "I don't think. I know. Rocky and Brock hung out together. Brock was stoned one night when he told Rocky that Barry planned to rat him out, and he needed to make sure that didn't happen."

"Rocky told you this?" I asked.

"Yeah, but Brock doesn't know he told me. That's why he only killed Rocky and not both of us."

"Or maybe he had planned to kill both of you," I said, "but you weren't home."

Tonya snapped her fingers and grinned in the same lunatic manner I'd seen previously. "Of course. That's probably what happened. If Brock gets released, he'll come after me. That's why we need to make sure that doesn't happen."

"How do you plan to do that?" I asked, dreading her reply. I figured this was where I fit into her fiendish scheme, whatever it was. Otherwise, why was I here?

"Brock kept an enemies list. He crossed off names as he eliminated people."

I gasped. "Eliminated? As in killed them?"

Tonya rolled her eyes. "That is what eliminate means, isn't it?"

"You're saying Brock is a serial killer?"

"You catch on quick."

"Did he tell you about the enemies list?" I asked.

"Rocky told me." She stood and walked across the kitchen to where she'd left her purse on the island. After removing a folded piece of paper, she returned and handed it to me.

I unfolded the sheet and studied the list. Barry and Rocky's names were the only ones I recognized, but several others also had lines drawn through them.

However, anyone could have created that list. It was computer generated, not handwritten, and I suspected a search of Axel Brock's computer wouldn't find the file. I also suspected that Tonya was smart enough that she hadn't used her own computer to type the list. From where I sat, I saw a small office situated off the kitchen, a desktop computer in full view.

I was about to ask Tonya how she'd gotten hold of the list when the doorbell rang. She checked her phone. "I ordered pizzas and beers for us. We're going to wait until after midnight before we put my plan into action."

When she rose to answer the front door, I whispered to Gloria, "How much of what you said about Barry's dream and Brock is true?"

She shook her head. "Only that Barry suffered from PTSD from the accident. Tonya made up everything else I told you."

"Why did you go along with her?"

"She said it was the only way to keep the cops from charging both of us." She hung her head. "I'm sorry, Anastasia. I had no idea she planned to kidnap or harm you."

"Don't worry," I assured her. "We're going to get out of this."

"How can you be sure?"

"Trust me." As if on cue, at that moment we heard an ear-splitting scream.

EIGHTEEN

I smiled at Gloria. "Sounds like the cavalry has arrived."

A moment later, I heard Detective Samuel Spader call out, "Mrs. Barnes, you here?"

"In the kitchen, Detective."

Gloria's mouth gaped open. "How did he know?"

Before I had a chance to answer, Spader strode into the room. He carried two pizza boxes. Zack followed close behind, sidestepping Spader the moment he saw me and racing to where I sat.

When I didn't stand to step into his arms, he leaned over me, his face clouded with concern. "Are you okay?"

I offered him a weak smile. "I will be. Just not sure I can stand on my own yet."

He lifted me off the chair and pulled me into his arms. After clinging to him for a few moments, I scanned the kitchen. Not seeing a clock, I asked, "What time is it?"

Spader's phone dinged an incoming text. After depositing the

LOIS WINSTON

pizza boxes on the table, he performed a feat of multitasking uncommon to anyone with a Y-chromosome. He answered while reading the text. "Six-forty." He pulled his eyes from his screen and asked, "Why? Got someplace to go, Mrs. Barnes?"

Hard to believe my ordeal had begun only a little more than an hour ago. If I'd had to place a bet, I would have opted for at least twenty-four hours. I shook my head. "I thought I was knocked out for much longer."

Zack adjusted our position, enabling him to scrutinize my face. "What did she do to you?"

I winced. "She tased me."

I felt his entire body tense as he let loose a string of profanity. I didn't blame him, but I was more interested in what had gone down before he and Spader had entered the kitchen. Still in Zack's arms, I twisted my body slightly to address Spader. "Why did it take you so long to get here?" Given the short period of time, by my calculations, Spader and crew should have arrived much sooner.

Zack answered for him. "The tow truck Ira sent got stuck in traffic. When it finally arrived, the driver called Ira to alert him about the smashed window. He failed to mention you were nowhere in sight until Ira asked to speak to you."

"Where did he think I was?"

"He figured you'd hitched a ride home with someone. Luckily, Ira called me, and I immediately called Spader."

Other than the stress and anxiety suffered by Zack, Spader, and Ira, time meant nothing to me by then. Instead, I asked, "What happened to Tonya?"

Spader winked. "One of the team gave her a taste of her own medicine." Then, for the first time, he addressed Gloria. "What

226

about you, Mrs. Sumner? Were you harmed?"

Gloria shot me a quick look before averting her eyes and mumbling, "Not physically."

I reached over and placed a comforting hand on her shoulder to let her know I didn't blame her for anything that had happened. I'd come to realize Gloria was both extremely insecure and too easily influenced by others. I had no doubt Tonya had manipulated her into the half-baked, harebrained scheme she'd concocted. By her own admission, Gloria often acted without thinking, which meant she hadn't considered the ramifications of Tonya's plan before agreeing to it. Or perhaps, she'd been too scared of Tonya not to agree.

Gloria turned to me. "How were you so sure we'd be rescued?"

"I was banking on Tonya grabbing my phone and purse from my car."

"So the cops could track you from your phone?"

"Something like that."

"Don't you think she would've been smart enough to power down the phone?"

"She did," said Zack.

Gloria's head whipped from me to Zack, then back to me. "I don't understand. Then how—?"

"Through an air tag," I said.

"A tracker?"

"I've had so many close calls lately, that Zack insisted I keep one in my purse and another hidden in the car."

"I'm thinking of having them sewn into all her clothes," he added.

Gloria's eyes grew wide. "Seriously?"

He shrugged. "Couldn't hurt."

I knew he was only half-joking, but she looked as if she believed him. I changed the subject. "Did you see where Tonya put my phone and purse?"

"I haven't seen them."

"Which means they're probably still in her car," said Spader. He rose. "I'll get them."

I wasn't sure how Spader knew which of several doors led to the garage, but he guessed on the first try. He'd remained silent during most of the conversation. He hadn't asked Gloria to elaborate on her *not physically* comment, but he'd kept eyeing her in a way that I suspected meant he planned to question her further. I hoped he'd go easy on her. Gloria was just as much a victim of Tonya as I was.

Spader returned a moment later with both my purse and phone and placed them on the table in front of my empty chair. "Check to see if anything's missing."

After Zack helped me to my seat, I took inventory of the items in my purse, mostly concerned with my cash and credit cards. "Nothing's missing."

Spader frowned. "Too bad."

When my head shot up, he offered a shrug, adding, "If she'd removed anything of value, we could've filed some additional charges against her."

I doubted adding petty theft to a kidnapping charge would make any difference in the strength of Spader's case, but what did I know? I'd majored in art, not criminology.

Meanwhile, the scent of pizza that filled the room had triggered my tummy alarm, which emitted a loud grumble. Three sets of eyes turned toward me, but only Zack dared to chuckle. Gloria bit her lower lip to suppress a grin, and Spader covered a chortle with a cough.

I ignored them all, flipping open the top of the pizza box and helping myself to a slice of thin crust. I saw no point in letting a couple of pizzas grow cold when I hadn't eaten in nearly seven hours. The others followed suit.

"You don't have to get back to the station to interrogate Gloria?" I asked Spader.

He spoke around a mouthful of pizza. "She's not going anywhere. I'd first like more details of what happened from both of you."

Gloria nearly choked on a mouthful of pizza. "You're not locking me up again, are you?"

"Not unless you give me a reason to," said Spader. "We can speak here as long as you cooperate."

Gloria silently agreed, but both her hand and lips trembled as she dropped the half-eaten slice back into the box. A quick glance around the table told me I wasn't the only one who'd noticed.

"Let's do this," I said. "I'd like to get home as soon as possible. I need a long soak in a hot tub." I pushed back from the table. With my hands pressed to the tabletop, I gingerly rose to my feet. My legs held firm, no buckling knees.

Zack jumped out of his chair and reached for my arm. "Where are you going?"

"To have a chat with Spader." I raised my hands off the table and took a tentative step. No wobbles. "Looks like I'm back to normal."

Zack hesitated. "You sure?"

"I'm sure."

Zack released my arm. I grabbed Brock's alleged enemies list and took several steps toward the island. "See? Good as new. You

LOIS WINSTON

keep Gloria company." I turned to Spader. "Grab the other pizza box. I'm still hungry."

He barked out a laugh as he saluted me. "Yes, ma'am."

When I shot him an evil eye, he turned questioningly toward Zack. "What did I say?"

"Never call her ma'am. She hates it."

"Noted." Spader pressed a hand over his heart. "My sincerest apologies, Mrs. Barnes."

"Apology accepted, Detective."

We exited the kitchen and walked through the dining room to a small foyer that contained two short staircases, one leading up and the other leading down. Crossing the foyer, we entered the living room. The short tour told me we were in a typical nineteen-sixties split level, one of thousands that dotted the New Jersey suburban landscape. This one looked recently updated to a twenty-first century aesthetic with not a single avocado shag carpet, flocked wallpaper, or crushed velour couch in sight.

After Spader and I settled into two gray herringbone club chairs, I asked, "Where are we?"

"Colonia."

Only a few towns from Westfield. "I heard Tonya tell Gloria that the house belonged to her cousin."

"That text that came in a few minutes ago confirmed Tonya didn't break into this house. The cousin and her husband have been on vacation in Ocean City, Maryland since before either murder. They rented a beach house through Labor Day. Mrs. Benedetto was taking in the mail and watering the garden."

That explained why we were all still in the house, and CSI wasn't currently combing the place as a crime scene. I handed the sheet of paper to Spader. "Tonya claims this is Axel Brock's hit list and proof that he killed both Barry and Rocky. I suspect she was smart enough not to use her own computer. I noticed one on the desk in the office off the kitchen. I'm guessing you'll find the file either on the hard drive or in the computer trashcan."

Spader perused the list. "I'll get a warrant, but back up and start from the beginning."

I spent the next ten minutes filling Spader in on everything I remembered before Tonya zapped me and after I came to. He scribbled notes throughout. I ended by adding, "I hope you'll go easy on Gloria. She had no idea Tonya planned to kidnap me. She's terrified."

"Of what?"

"Of Tonya. Gloria is extremely insecure and easily persuaded. Tonya convinced her that if she didn't go along with her plan, she'd wind up in prison for Barry's murder."

"What was the plan?"

I shrugged. "No clue. Gloria doesn't know, either."

"You believe her?"

"I do. You arrived before Tonya laid out her scheme."

"Any idea what she had in mind?"

"All I know for sure is that she planned to wait until midnight to execute it. I suspect she wanted me to break into Brock's condo to plant that list as evidence."

"We already searched Brock's apartment and did a deep dive into all his electronics. We found plenty to nail him on a host of drug charges that will put him away for decades, but we found no hit list."

"But Tonya doesn't know you searched Brock's condo. By the way, she wasn't wearing gloves when she handed me the list. Her fingerprints are on it."

"As are yours."

"I couldn't exactly slip on a pair of rubber gloves before she handed it to me, could I?"

"Point taken."

"However, I did try to touch it as little as possible without raising her suspicions. I doubt you'll find Axel Brock's fingerprints on that sheet, though."

Spader continued to stare at the list. "Why you? Why wouldn't she plant the evidence herself?"

"At one point, Gloria had bragged to Tonya about my exploits."

"From listening to the podcasts?"

I grimaced. "The gift that keeps on giving. I constantly remind myself that the kids' hearts were in the right place, even if their brains weren't. Anyway, I'm guessing Tonya figured I had the ability to enter the condo without getting caught or leaving any trace of a break-in."

Spader raised both eyebrows. "Do you?"

"Really, Detective? You think I have hidden Houdini-type talents?"

Spader laughed. "Mrs. Barnes, I've learned to underestimate you at my own risk."

When Spader finished questioning me, he escorted me back to the kitchen and told Zack, "You can take your wife home for that hot bath."

"What about me?" asked Gloria.

"I'll drop you off at home after we've had our chat, Mrs. Sumner."

Gloria cast a panic-stricken look in my direction. "Don't worry," I assured her. "I promise you Detective Spader is one of the good guys. He's not out to get you." I turned to Spader. "Right, Detective?"

He zeroed in on Gloria as he spoke, his voice stern. "As long as Mrs. Sumner gives me her full cooperation, she has nothing to worry about."

Would she, though? The more I learned about Gloria, the less inclined I thought her capable of murder. Besides, she genuinely loved her husband, flaws and all. Unless I was the worst judge of character on the planet, Gloria hadn't killed Barry.

However, I was also convinced, she hadn't told me—or Spader—the complete story. Gloria was hiding something. For that reason, I couldn't fault Spader for his attitude toward her. The man had a right to his skepticism.

As for me, I'd completely ruled out Axel Brock as a last-ditch Hail Mary pass, one that Spader would intercept with a minimal amount of detective work. Tonya wasn't bright enough to frame someone without her efforts imploding under interrogation. But in the who, what, where, when, and why, the why still eluded me. Was it as simple as Tonya not trusting the police to expand their investigation beyond Gloria and her?

I got it that some people don't trust the police. Prisons are full of the wrongly accused and convicted. Did Tonya have something in her past that made her fearful of going to prison for a crime she claimed she hadn't committed?

Or had she killed both Barry and Rocky and concocted a plot to frame Axel Brock for the murders? Was she that diabolical? And if so, to what end?

My mind kept coming back to the list of names Tonya had produced. What if the list contained names of Tonya's enemies, not Brock's? If so, what did she have against those men, and did she plan to knock them all off? Had she already eliminated the several other men besides Barry and Rocky whose names were also crossed off?

Still, so many questions and too few answers. I wish I'd had a chance to photograph the list, but even if I'd had my phone, I couldn't do so in front of Tonya. Once Spader had returned my phone, I had no opportunity to snap a picture without him or Zack seeing me do so. I wasn't a good enough liar to come up with a plausible explanation for such an action. I'd have to wait until Spader saw fit to share the names with me, assuming he would.

I placed myself in his shoes and couldn't come up with a single reason why he would. He certainly wouldn't see satisfying my curiosity as counting.

~*~

I expected to toss and turn all night, my mind racing as I tried to match the puzzle pieces of multiple possible suspects to two murders. Zack had other ideas. Between a bubble bath that included a bottle of bubbly and some other tricks he had up his sleeve—not that he wore any sleeves, or anything else, for that matter—my body decided I deserved to ignore my brain and get a good night's sleep.

Before opening my eyes the next morning, I swept my hand across Zack's side of the bed. Both the cold sheets and the blended aromas of coffee and something savory drifting into the bedroom told me he'd arisen some time ago. I quickly showered and dressed. As I made my way toward the kitchen, I caught sight of Detective Spader's unmarked black sedan parked in front of the house. I found one extremely exhausted-looking member of law enforcement seated at the kitchen table with Zack.

After kissing my husband good morning, I addressed the

detective. "I'm guessing you pulled an all-nighter."

He took a gulp of coffee before speaking. "What gave me away?"

"Besides a two-day growth of beard, your bloodshot eyes, the rumpled suit, and the coffee-stained shirt and tie?"

"Your powers of observation never cease to amaze me, Mrs. Barnes. You haven't by any chance solved my case yet, have you?"

"That depends."

Spader perked up. "On what?"

"On what you learned from Tonya and what you found on her cousin's computer."

"For one thing," said Spader. "Tonya Benedetto definitely created that hit list, not Axel Brock."

NINETEEN

I turned from pouring myself a cup of coffee. "You found the file on her cousin's computer?"

"That's not all. We did a search of the other names on the list."

At that moment, the oven timer went off. Zack jumped up, grabbed a couple of oven mitts, and removed a breakfast frittata from the oven. Spader paused until we'd all settled around the table, filled our plates, and tucked into the frittata.

"What about those other names?" I asked.

"Fun fact," said Spader. "None popped in our initial search. They're not reenactors or bowlers. And they're not connected in any way to Axel Brock."

"Not even customers of his?" I asked. "Maybe deadbeats who owe him drug money?"

"They don't show up in any database."

"Then who are they?" asked Zack.

Spader grinned. "You're not going to believe this."

"Try us," I said, getting annoyed with his over-dramatic

delivery.

Spader paused again, then chuckled. "They're romance novel heroes."

Spader didn't strike me as a guy with a secret Harlequin romance addiction. "How do you know that?"

"We ran the names through a search program to find what they all had in common. Then we went back to Benedetto's home and checked her bookshelves. Nothing but romance novels."

"Did she admit to creating the list?" asked Zack.

"Eventually. But she still claims Brock killed both men, and she only wanted to point the police in the right direction."

"Did she offer any proof?" I asked.

"None."

"When you spoke to Gloria, did she admit Tonya made up the story about Barry's memory suddenly returning?"

"She did. Said she was too scared not to go along with it."

"Tonya is pure evil," I said. "She's lied about everything. After my encounter with her last night, I'm convinced she's quite capable of murder." I pointed my fork at Spader. "She's screwing with your investigation because she's got something to hide."

"Yeah, I kind of came to that conclusion on my own, Mrs. Barnes."

"What happens now?" asked Zack.

"That's up to the D.A.," said Spader. "We've got her on kidnapping, assault, and a host of other charges. She's not going anywhere. While she cools her heels in jail, I'm hoping we turn up enough evidence to charge her with the murder of Barry Sumner and Rocky Benedetto."

"You agree with me?" I asked.

"I sure do, but short of a confession, juries want proof. Right now, all I've got is circumstantial evidence."

~*~

After my harrowing encounter with Tonya yesterday, Zack convinced me to work from home instead of going into the office. With our monthly meeting out of the way, I didn't think Naomi would object. She voiced her concern, though.

"Is everything all right, Anastasia? You sound rattled."

Not wanting to go into detail, I gave her a minimal amount of information. "I got a flat driving through Watchung Reservation on my way home last night. It took hours for a tow truck to arrive."

"Why do I get the impression there's more to the story than a flat tire?"

"I was worried about bears. They can rip open a locked car door. I've seen it on the news. I had some awful nightmares last night and didn't get much sleep."

Okay, so some of that was a lie. Not the bear part, though. I had been worried about one or more of them attacking me, and I had once seen a news report that showed a bear getting into a locked car. However, after Zack's ministrations last night, I'd slept like a baby. Naomi didn't need to know that, though.

"I understand," she said. "You must have been terrified."

"More than you can imagine." But as it turned out, it was my encounter with a human that had nearly done me in. She didn't need to know that, either. Before ending the call, I thanked her for her concern and agreeing to allow me to work from home.

Cloris wasn't as easily persuaded. "You're keeping something from me. I know you. Talk to me."

After explaining what had really happened last night, I made her swear not to tell anyone.

"My lips are sealed."

I spent the remainder of the morning bouncing between my computer and the sewing machine in the apartment above the garage. While I worked on some easy memory quilt projects, Zack sat across the room from me and compiled photos for his museum exhibit.

Shortly before noon, my phone rang. "Spader," I said after checking the screen. I answered, putting the call on speaker. "Hello, Detective."

Once again, as was his M.O., he jumped right into the conversation without any pleasantries. "You'll probably get a call from Westfield P.D. at some point, but I thought you'd like to know as soon as possible."

"Know what?" Any information regarding the murders would come from Spader, a county detective, not town law enforcement.

"They found your mother-in-law. Turns out she and her cohorts pooled their Social Security checks and rented a house in Bridgewater."

"All of them?"

"All thirteen crammed into one tiny two-bedroom bungalow. Looks like they've set up a commie commune."

"Was she served with the temporary restraining order?" asked Zack.

"She was, and from what I hear, she's not happy about it."

"Do you know the address?" I asked.

"No, you'd have to get that from Westfield P.D." He paused for a moment, then asked, "Why? You're not planning to pay her a visit, are you? She could use that against you when you go to court."

"Wouldn't dream of it," I said. "But I am considering packing up what remains of her possessions and paying an Uber to deliver them to her. I'd prefer to avoid a confrontation should she show up for them at some point."

"Not a bad idea," said Zack.

"I'll see if I can get the address for you," said Spader.

~*~

The weather gods smiled on us the Sunday of Labor Day weekend, providing a sunny day with a gentle breeze and temperatures in the mid-seventies. No one had declined the invitation to our Labor Day Weekend barbecue. Friends, relatives, neighbors, and coworkers all mingled in small groups in the backyard where Zack and Nick had set up enough rental tables and chairs to accommodate everyone.

Zack manned the grill. Ira arrived with his kids but minus Rowena. I feigned surprise when he mentioned they'd split shortly after he'd introduced us to her.

As soon as Melody, Harmony, and Isaac filled their plates and headed for the den to watch TV, Ira set off in search of any eligible women. He immediately zeroed in on Danica, but so had Tino Martinelli, and from what I observed, Tino had the edge for Danica's attention.

I spent most of the afternoon with a smile pasted on my face as I forced myself to channel Ethel Merman from her role in *Call Me Madam*. However, my efforts fell far short of mastering the *joie de vie* with which she'd imbued the character of Ambassador Sally Adams.

Try as I might, my attempts lacked much of the *joie*. My mother, on the other hand, had not only passed Hostess 101 with flying colors, but she'd also gone on to earn a PhD in it. I watched as she flitted around the backyard, completely in her element. Why hadn't I inherited those genes?

I blamed both my inner wallflower and my continuing obsession over the murders. Spader still hadn't gotten Tonya to confess. Nor had his investigation turned up any concrete evidence proving she'd killed both Barry and Rocky. It's not easy acting the part of "hostess with the mostest" when your mind is on murder.

As I circulated among our guests, refilling drinks, replenishing side dishes, and introducing people from one area of my life to those from other areas, I reminded myself that I'd chosen to step out of my comfort zone to help a homesick new coworker make friends. When I glanced across the yard toward Danica and Tino, I decided the results were well worth a few hours of forced cheerfulness on my part.

About an hour into the party, Gloria arrived with Lance, Billy, and a woman of about my mother's age who I didn't recognize. When I crossed the yard to greet them, Gloria introduced us. "Anastasia, this is Lance's wife Hannah. Hannah, this is Anastasia."

"Welcome," I said. "Please help yourself to some food. Zack is grilling chicken, burgers, hot dogs and an assortment of veggies. Wine, beer, and sodas are in the cooler on the patio. All the side dishes and condiments are on the picnic table near the grill."

Billy scanned the backyard. "Is Nick around?"

I scoped out the yard and found my son buttonholed by Ira. "Over there," I said pointing to the far side of the yard. "I'm sure he'd appreciate you rescuing him from his uncle."

After Billy began to weave his way through the various groups, Lance offered to get drinks for Gloria and Hannah. "I'll have a white wine," said Hannah.

"I'll help you," said Gloria, following Lance.

Once Gloria and Lance were out of earshot, Hannah turned to me. "Gloria hasn't stopped talking about you and your family, how you've gone out of your way to help her."

"You've known her long?"

"Most of her life. Lance and I have been like family, especially after Gloria's father died. Barry's murder has been extremely hard on her and Billy."

"She's lucky to have both of you."

Hannah shook her head and grimaced. "None of us could ever figure out what she saw in that loser."

I played dumb. If Hannah wanted to open up to a total stranger, I was happy to lend both my ears. "Oh?"

She sighed. "As sweet as Gloria is, I'm sure you've noticed she's not the brightest crayon in the Crayola box. Couple that with a stubborn streak as wide as the Grand Canyon, and you can imagine what a handful she was as a teenager."

When I didn't comment, she continued, "Her father tried to break them up. Her mother and I struggled to convince him to stay out of it, that the romance would run its course."

"But it didn't."

She snorted as she stared at her husband's departing back. "It would have. But just like a typical man, he refused to listen to us. He thought he knew better than two women who were once headstrong teenagers. The guy spent the rest of his life blaming himself."

"Gloria seemed devoted to Barry," I said.

Hannah harrumphed. "Her devotion was either her greatest strength or her greatest weakness. I'm not sure which." She then changed the subject slightly. "I understand your son found Barry's body. That must have been quite traumatic, seeing a man with a bayonet sticking out of his chest."

"Luckily, Nick didn't see the weapon from where he stood on the sidewalk. He thought Barry had suffered a stroke or heart attack. My husband discovered the cause of death when he climbed the steps to the porch."

Hannah released a heavy sigh. "At least Gloria and Billy were spared that dreadful sight."

Hannah said nothing more, her attention drawn by something over my right shoulder. I turned to see Lance and Gloria approaching. After Lance handed Hannah her wine, I said, "It was so nice to meet you, Hannah. If you'll excuse me, I need to check to see what foods need replenishing."

Hannah smiled. "It was lovely to meet you as well, Anastasia."

As I walked toward the house, I searched for my son. Not finding him in the yard, I headed toward the house. Before entering, I did a quick scan of the food situation on the picnic table and made a mental note to refill the chip basket.

I found Nick and Billy in Nick's room, once again saving the world from invading space aliens. "Nick, pause the game, please. I need you for a moment."

"Sure, Mom."

I led him from his bedroom into mine and closed the door. His brow creased in worry. "Something wrong, Mom?"

"Did you ever talk to Billy about the details of his father's murder?"

Nick shook his head. "No, you told me not to say anything to anyone, remember?"

"You never mentioned anything about the weapon?"

"No, Mom. I swear. We've only talked about how we both had dads who died. Why?"

"And you never said anything to anyone else?"

"No. What's going on?"

"I'm not sure. Go back to your game."

Nick stared at me for a moment. "You sure everything's okay? What aren't you telling me?"

I placed my hand on his shoulder. "It's probably nothing. We'll talk later, after our guests leave."

"Promise?"

"Promise."

Before heading back outside, I grabbed another bag of chips and refilled the empty basket. Then I casually stopped and chatted with various guests until I sidled up next to Detective Spader. He stood chatting with Tino. Danica practically drooled over Tino and hung onto every word. I guess she'd forgotten all about wanting to get fixed up with Shane.

Spader acknowledged me by saying, "Nice party."

"I'm glad you're enjoying yourself." Then I lowered my voice to a near whisper. "We need to talk. Later. After everyone else leaves."

Spader whispered back. "Does this have anything to do with your new neighbor, her fund manager, and the mystery woman who arrived with them?"

I chuckled. "Can't get anything past you."

Spader laughed. "Good one, Mrs. Barnes."

Danica pulled her attention from Tino. Her eyes darted from Spader to me, then back to Spader. "What's so funny?"

"Mrs. Barnes missed her calling," said Spader.

Tino shot me a side-eye. The guy missed nothing, and for all I knew, he had some miniature high-tech gizmo in his ear, enabling him to pick up every conversation throughout the backyard.

But Danica's eyes had grown wide, and her jaw had dropped. "You mean the amateur detective thing? You're not talking about more dead bodies, are you?"

"Heck, no" Spader barked out another laugh. "Mrs. Barnes should do standup comedy."

Tino winked at me. "Agreed. Mrs. B is one very funny lady."

Was this an inside joke among the various men in my life? I'd certainly heard that suggestion before.

Danica seemed skeptical, though, and who could blame her? I didn't exactly leave my coworkers at *American Woman* rolling in the aisles. I couldn't remember a punch line if my life depended on it.

Then again, maybe they offer Thinking on Your Feet 101 at both cop and special forces school, and both men had employed a bit of misdirection. Before Danica asked me to repeat the nonexistent joke, I excused myself and headed toward another group of guests. I'd leave Spader to pull a joke from his repertoire, assuming he had one, to appease Danica's curiosity. As for Tino, I now expected he'd also hang around after the party ended because he'd obviously figured out something was up and wanted in on the action.

A few minutes later, I noticed Spader and Tino had joined Zack at the grill. I watched as Zack pulled his attention away from them and scanned the yard, a worried expression on his face. When he located me, I smiled and waved. I then saw him nod and expel what I interpreted as a huge sigh of relief.

Did they all think I'd run off on my own to make a citizen's arrest? I shot him an eye roll before he turned his attention back to his grilling duties.

Gloria, Lance, and Hannah didn't stay long. "We just dropped by to say hello," said Gloria. "Lance and Hannah have invited Billy and me to spend a couple of days at their summer home on Long Beach Island before school starts. We're driving down there now."

"How nice," I said. "I hope the weather holds out for you."

Gloria collected Billy, and the four of them departed.

A few hours later, as twilight set in, the party wound down. When Zack and Nick, assisted by Spader and Tino, began folding and stacking chairs and tables, the few remaining stragglers took the hint and soon departed.

Only Mama remained. She made a half-hearted attempt at helping with clean up, all the while complaining about how tired she was. When Tino overheard her and offered to drive her home, she jumped at the chance. As an afterthought, she asked, "You don't mind, do you dear? I'm exhausted."

"No, Mama. Go on home." I kissed her on the cheek, then mouthed, "Thank you" to Tino.

While Mama stopped in the powder room, he turned to me and said, "Don't start without me."

"Wouldn't think of it."

~*~

Thirty minutes later, all the leftovers were stored in the refrigerator, freezer, or pantry, the trash collected, and serving dishes placed in the dishwasher. Zack, Spader, Tino, Nick and I gathered around the dining room table. "Before I begin, I have a question for Detective Spader."

"Ask away," he said.

"At any point was information about the murder weapon used to kill Barry Sumner released or leaked?"

"Released, no," said Spader. "And there's no indication of a leak having occurred."

"Gloria doesn't know about the bayonet?"

Spader shook his head. "We only told her that her husband had been stabbed. She never asked for details."

"Then Tonya Benedetto didn't kill Barry."

"Who did?" asked Nick.

"Lance Melville."

Spader scrubbed at the five o'clock shadow on his jaw. "I'm assuming you have proof, Mrs. Barnes?"

I proceeded to tell them about my conversation with Melville's wife. "Hannah knew Barry was stabbed with a bayonet. How would she know that unless her husband had mentioned it? And how would Melville know unless he was the killer?"

"What about motive?" asked Tino.

I turned to Spader. "I suspect if you subpoena the trust fund records, you may find that Melville has been siphoning off more than he's entitled to as the fund's manager."

Spader raised one of his bushy eyebrows. "Explain."

"I can't. Something about him just doesn't sit well with me, and it's the only explanation that makes sense."

"Why now?" asked Spader. "He's managed the fund for years."

"Maybe he got tired of Gloria insisting he pay off the blackmailers. Get rid of Barry, and the blackmail ends. More money for Melville."

"You think he also killed Rocky?" asked Zack.

I shook my head. "Not unless he was in cahoots with Tonya, which I doubt. I still think Tonya killed her husband. She doctored his dinner, then stabbed him in the back after he passed out from an overdose."

"Why?" asked Nick.

"I don't know the answer to that. What I do know is that

Tonya is crazy. I'm guessing she saw an opportunity to rid herself of her husband, place the blame on Barry's killer, and get away with murder."

Spader rose. "Looks like I have a long night ahead of me, starting with bringing Melville in for questioning."

"You'll find him on Long Beach Island," I said. "At his summer home."

Spader scowled. "That will make for an even longer night. I don't suppose you know where on Long Beach Island, Mrs. Barnes."

"Honestly, Detective, if you expect me to do all your work, I want a consultant fee."

He chuckled. "I'll add it to next year's budget, but don't hold your breath."

EPILOGUE

Sunday and Monday went by without a word from Detective Spader. I wondered if he'd already arrested Lance Melville. Gloria and Billy hadn't returned from Long Beach Island, but school didn't start until Thursday. Would they and Hannah stay down the shore after the arrest?

I found it unlikely. Gloria had depended on Melville for so much. She wouldn't take his betrayal well, nor would Billy. Losing her husband to a killer was bad enough, but to learn that the killer was someone they had both thought of as family, would break their hearts.

As for Hannah, not knowing anything about her relationship with her husband, I couldn't begin to guess how she'd feel when she learned of his heinous crimes. Gloria and Billy weren't the only ones Lance Melville had betrayed.

Tuesday evening, I returned home from work, expecting to find the detective seated in my living room or kitchen, but when I turned the corner onto our street, I found no unmarked car parked in front of my house.

"Should we be worried about Spader?" I asked Zack after I'd entered the house.

"I'm guessing he's busy tying up loose ends. Keep in mind, today is the first day after a three-day weekend. The courts were closed yesterday. We'll hear from him when he has something to tell us." He paused before adding, "Most likely shortly before mealtime."

"He has become something of a fixture around here."

Zack studied me for a moment. "Do you mind?"

"Not in the least. He's much more pleasant company than Lucille. Plus, he often brings dinner and helps with clean up. He's the perfect guest."

With that, the doorbell rang. Zack checked his phone app. "Speak of the devil. Just in time for dinner."

Spader arrived with a large bakery box and two dozen pink roses. "I'm afraid it's not nearly enough for what you deserve for all your help with my case, Mrs. Barnes. I hope you know how grateful I am for your assistance."

I accepted the box and the roses. "I do, Detective." Then I teased, "But maybe next time, how about my very own taser? One would have come in handy the other night."

He laughed. "Look in the box."

My eyes widened. "You really brought me a taser?" I handed Zack the roses, lifted the lid of the box, and burst out laughing. Spader had brought an imposter cake, expertly decorated to look like a taser.

"Black Forest," he said. "I remembered it was a favorite of yours."

"Very thoughtful," said Zack, "and nowhere near as painful."

Nick walked into the living room as I let loose with one more laugh. "What's so funny?"

"Detective Spader brought me a unique gift."

"Cool. What is it?"

"I'll show you later."

After I placed the roses in a vase and the cake in the refrigerator and Nick added another place setting to the table, the four of us took our seats in the dining room. As we ate, Spader caught us up on events since we'd last seen him Sunday night.

"That conversation you had with Mrs. Melville cracked the case for us, Mrs. Barnes."

"I'll bet Mr. Melville regrets bringing her to the party," said Nick.

Spader winked at him. "You better believe it."

"Did he confess?" I asked.

"Not at first. He denied everything. Both Gloria and his wife stood behind him, refusing to believe he had killed Barry or had embezzled from the trust fund."

"What changed their minds?" I asked.

"Proof in black and white," said Spader, talking around a mouthful of spinach quiche. "When we got a warrant for his office and electronics equipment, we found he kept double books. They provided proof he was living off Gloria's trust fund and had been from the beginning. We also discovered a recent online purchase for a bayonet, exactly like the one that was used to kill Sumner."

"What about the saber used on Rocky Benedetto?" asked Zack.

"Melville had nothing to do with Benedetto's death." Spader inclined his head toward me. "Your wife was right about Tonya Benedetto killing her husband. She finally broke and confessed late yesterday afternoon. She'd gotten herself a new lawyer, and they're trying to cut a deal, claiming Benedetto abused her."

"Is there any proof of that?" I asked. "I never noticed bruises or other wounds on Tonya."

"We don't think so. It's kind of hard to prove self-defense when you drug the victim and stab him in the back. But that's in the hands of the D.A. now. Even if they plead down the murder charge, she'll most likely spend the remainder of her life in prison. Max for kidnapping is thirty years, plus fifteen for attempted murder."

"She didn't try to kill me. She wanted me alive to help her."

Spader shook his head. "Doesn't matter. A taser can be a lethal weapon when used on the wrong person. If you'd had a heart condition, you could have died."

"But I don't have a heart condition."

"She didn't know that. The point is, she's going to pay for what she did to you and will never have the chance to harm anyone else."

"What about Gloria and Billy?" I asked.

Spader frowned. "They're in shock. Gloria checked them into a hotel for a few days. She's debating whether to return to the house or sell it and move."

"Where would they go?" asked Zack.

"She mentioned cousins in California. I suggested counseling for her and her son before she made any big decisions."

"Not a bad idea," I said. "She's also going to need a new manager for her trust fund. I don't get the sense she's capable of handling her finances on her own."

Spader nodded. "I took the liberty of telling her about your friend Shane. He might be able to steer her toward someone reputable. She may call you for his contact information."

"That was good of you, Detective." I paused before adding,

"Especially since you once wrongly arrested him for the murder of his ex-wife."

I swore I saw Spader fight against a blush threatening to creep up his neck into his face. He made a show of studying the remaining spinach quiche and tilapia on his plate and muttered, "We all make mistakes, Mrs. Barnes."

Then he raised his chin, and we locked eyes. With nothing but sincerity in his voice, he said, "I'm glad I can rely on you to point out my errors."

I smiled at him. "You're a rare breed, Detective, a man who admits when he's wrong. For that, you get a large slice of Black Forest taser."

"Huh?" With a puzzled expression on his face Nick's head darted between Spader and me. Then he turned to Zack. "What taser? You have any idea what's going on?"

"Sit tight, Nick. You'll see in a minute."

~*~

After we'd feasted on Black Forest taser cake and had cleaned up, Spader said, "Thank you both once again for your hospitality and your help, but I'd better head out. I need a good night's sleep before I tackle the mountain of paperwork awaiting me tomorrow morning."

We accompanied him into the living room where he retrieved the suit jacket that he'd earlier draped over one of the living room chairs. As he started to insert his arm into the sleeve, he stopped. "I almost forgot." He pulled a white business envelope from the inside pocket and handed it to me. "Gloria Forester asked me to give this to you."

I accepted the sealed envelope and saw that my name was printed on it. I looked up at Spader. "Do you know what it is?"

"No clue. Maybe a thank you note for helping solve the case."

I frowned at the envelope. "You told her?"

"I didn't have to. When all the evidence was presented to her, included that we'd never released any information about the murder weapon, she figured it out on her own."

"How?" asked Zack.

"From the very beginning, Melville wanted Gloria to believe that the killer was one of the other reenactors. He mentioned the bayonet to both Gloria and his wife."

"Gloria never asked you about the specific weapon that stabbed her husband?" I asked.

Spader shook his head. "At first, she was in shock. That's normal. Later, she already knew. Or thought she knew from what Melville had said."

I tore open the envelope and removed a folded sheet of paper. Nestled within the folds, I discovered a check made out to me. I gasped. My hands shook as I tried to focus in on the number of zeroes. The amount exceeding by several thousand dollars the balance of my Karl-induced debt.

ANASTASIA'S QUILTED MEMORIES IDEAS

Anastasia chose memory quilts for her January craft feature in *American Woman* because the theme works well for every level of quilter, from beginners to experts, and the amount of time involved can range from a few hours to many weeks or months.

Memory quilts are made with personal items that have special meaning for the recipient of the quilt. They're often made from items of clothing, such as neckties, T-shirts, or dresses, but can also be made from linens, such as napkins and doilies, that have been passed down through generations. Memory quilts have been made from military uniforms, athletic jerseys, scouting uniforms, wedding dresses, ball caps, baby clothes, T-shirts from favorite music groups, concert T-shirts, men's or women's hankies, or any other garment that holds sentimental value.

Although traditional quilts are made from cotton, don't worry about combining different fabrics, fiber contents, prints, and colors for a memory quilt. What counts are the memories these items hold.

If you don't have enough memory fabrics for your project, you can supplement with filler fabrics, perhaps a color that ties all the other fabrics together. Thrift stores are a good place to pick up additional T-shirts and neckties. Antique shops often sell embroidered hankies and napkins as well as scraps of lace that once decorated clothing.

There are many ways to create a memory quilt. They can be intricately pieced using traditional quilt patterns and methods or freeform pieced in the style of Victorian crazy quilts. The quilts can be handsewn and hand quilted or entirely machine stitched. The easiest quilts are made by piecing together 12" x 12" squares. If you're quilting skills are minimal or nonexistent, there are many companies that will turn your squares into a quilt of any size.

Applique, embroidery, buttons, and decorative pins are often used as embellishments. Hand-coloring, using fabric paints, crayons, and markers, can be incorporated when the quilt is a family project where you want to include children.

Tips

Make sure that all your fabrics are washable. Most fabrics, even those that recommend dry cleaning, can be washed on a gentle cycle in cold water. Stay away from any fabric that states dry clean only.

Prewash all fabrics before beginning your project.

For very lightweight fabrics and knits, first apply lightweight iron-on interfacing to the back of the fabrics to stabilize them.

When using garments, you first need to deconstruct them by taking apart the seams. Use a stitch ripper for this. Depending on the project, you may want to keep some of the seamed fabric to incorporate sewn pieces, such as jeans pockets or shirt plackets, into your quilt.

Quilts that Aren't Quilts

Children often get attached to a special shirt or pair of pajamas. However, they usually outgrow their clothes before they wear them out or outgrow their attachment. They get extremely upset when you want to hand the item down to a younger sibling or cousin. To avoid tantrums and meltdowns, think small.

A memory quilt doesn't have to be a throw or a full-size quilt. It doesn't even have to be a quilt. Use the garment to construct a quilted pillow for the child's bed or a stuffed animal. These can be made from one garment or by incorporating several different ones. What child wouldn't want a teddy bear made from different outgrown T-shirts or pajamas?

For adults, pillows are also an option for a small quilt of hankies, napkins, and/or doilies. Or sew them into a quilted table runner or window valance. Framing is another option.

A Quilt for the Grands and Great-Grands

This is a special gift for grandparents or great-grandparents celebrating a milestone birthday or anniversary. You can either use old garments that have special meaning or choose new fabric in their favorite color or colors.

Cut squares of muslin. Using fabric markers, have each member of the family write a personal message on their square. For children, trace their hands on the muslin and have them write their name inside the hand. If you're really ambitious, embroider the words and hand outlines. Sew the squares together or intersperse them with other fabrics for the quilt.

You can also use iron-on transfer sheets and a copy machine to create fabric photos of family members. Fabric transfer sheets are available at most craft and some office supply stores. Use photos of current family members or ancestors. Go a step further by embellishing the photos with fabric markers or embroidery.

Memorial Quilts
Use the clothing of a deceased relative to create memory quilts for the children and/or grandchildren of surviving family members.

Other Ideas for Memory Quilts
School Memories—Use an assortment of clothing from sports teams, Halloween costumes, school plays and other special events in a child's life to create a memory quilt as a gift for a college dorm room.

Baby's First Year—Very few of those cute outfits your baby wore will survive without spit-up and other stains. Cut them into squares for a quilt to celebrate baby's first year.

Bridal Shower Quilt—Friends and relatives of the bride and groom are invited to create quilt squares with their names or initials drawn or embroidered on muslin squares. The squares are then sewn into a quilt presented to the bride at her shower.

Family Record Quilt— Each quilt block represents a milestone, chronicling major events in the family's life. These are often sewn around the center of a larger square that depicts the family's home.

A NOTE FROM THE AUTHOR

Dear Readers,

Years ago, when my husband and I purchased a home in a New Jersey suburb, the house across the street stood out for all the wrong reasons. It was a dilapidated mess in need of major repairs. We suspected the residents were elderly with a limited income. Much to our surprise, we discovered the owners were a couple in their late thirties or early forties and had two school-aged children.

The parents didn't seem to have jobs. They'd camp out on the top step of their small concrete landing for hours at a time, either together or individually. Just sitting and smoking and often drinking beer, but never conversing with each other. I dubbed them the Stoop Sitters.

Often the husband would remove his shirt and lie back on the landing, his massive stomach pointing heavenward. He'd remain that way for hours, apparently napping.

When Mr. Stoop Sitter wasn't sprawled bare-chested on the landing, he'd spend hours mowing his lawn, an extremely small, barren patch of packed dirt and weeds. He'd walk behind his mower, trimming the nonexistent grass, until the mower ran out of gas. The next day, after refilling the mower, the scene would repeat. It continued each day throughout the year, except during rain and snowstorms.

One day, my concentration was broken by a cat fight between two women. I looked up from my computer screen to find Mrs. Stoop

Sitter standing on the sidewalk, accusing another woman of trying to steal her husband. The scene was right out of *Real Housewives of New Jersey*, minus the camera crew. Eventually, Mrs. Stoop Sitter hurled one last warning, stormed up the steps, and entered her house, slamming the door behind her. The other woman turned and walked down the street. I never saw her again.

Now, Mr. Stoop Sitter was no one's idea of a catch, but the scene I'd witnessed proved otherwise. Obviously, there's someone for everyone. At least in Mrs. Stoop Sitter's mind.

I've always had a weird fascination with unusual personalities and often put them in my books. For example, Anastasia's communist mother-in-law is based on my own communist mother-in-law, minus the French bulldog.

My former neighbors have been parked in a recess of my brain for two-and-a-half decades, itching to spring forth as characters in a book, but I wondered if readers would think they were too over-the-top. When I related the story to my newsletter subscribers and asked if they thought the Stoop Sitters should become characters in my next book, everyone who responded loved the idea.

Thus, was born *Seams Like the Perfect Crime*. I hope you've enjoyed reading it as much as I've enjoyed writing it. If so, please consider leaving a review wherever you post book reviews.

Happy reading!
Lois Winston

ABOUT THE AUTHOR

USA Today and Amazon bestselling author Lois Winston began her award-winning writing career with *Talk Gertie to Me*, a humorous fish-out-of-water novel about a small-town girl going off to the big city and the mother who had other ideas. That was followed by the romantic suspense *Love, Lies and a Double Shot of Deception*.

Then Lois's writing segued unexpectedly into the world of humorous amateur sleuth mysteries, thanks to a conversation her agent had with an editor looking for craft-themed mysteries. In her day job, Lois was an award-winning craft and needlework designer, and although she'd never written a mystery—or had even thought about writing a mystery—her agent decided she was the perfect person to pen a series for this editor.

Thus, was born the Anastasia Pollack Crafting Mysteries, which *Kirkus Reviews* dubbed "North Jersey's more mature answer to Stephanie Plum." The series now includes fourteen novels and three novellas. Lois also writes the Empty Nest Mysteries and has written several standalone novellas. Other publishing credits include romance, chick lit, and romantic suspense novels, a series of romance short stories, a children's chapter book, and a nonfiction book on writing, inspired by her twelve years working as an associate at a literary agency.

Learn more about Lois and her books at www.loiswinston.com. Sign up for her newsletter to receive a free Anastasia Pollack Crafting Mini-Mystery.

Made in United States
Orlando, FL
10 December 2024

54753656R00169